Leaving Poppy

Kate Cann

SCHOLASTIC
PRESS

To Jill, Jim, Clare and Josephine, with love

Scholastic Children's Books,
Euston House, 24 Eversholt Street,
London, NW1 1DB, UK
a division of Scholastic Ltd
London ~ New York ~ Toronto ~ Sydney ~ Auckland
Mexico City ~ New Delhi ~ Hong Kong

First published in the UK by Scholastic Ltd, 2006

10 digit ISBN 0 439 96871 2
13 digit ISBN 978 0439 96871 3

Typeset by M Rules
Printed by Nørhaven Paperback A/S, Denmark

10 9 8 7 6 5 4 3 2 1

Part 1

Chapter  One

The path up to the front door was thick with leaves fallen early from the plane tree by the gate. Amber put down her huge suitcase and rummaged in her bag for the key, miming to the cab driver that she was OK, everything was OK.

But he still didn't drive off. "You gonna be all right, luv?" he called.

"I'm fine!" she cried.

"Want me to wait, make sure it's the right house?"

Amber made herself turn back, forced a smile at him. "It's OK! This is definitely it!"

He shrugged, in a some-people-won't-let-themselves-be-helped way, started the car up again, and accelerated off.

Amber was alone.

If it's the wrong place, she told herself, I'll hide my suitcase in the bushes, and go and find a call box, and phone. . . Who will I phone? It'll be the right place. It has to be.

She was trembling with a mixture of fear and intense

relief at the cab driver going. Throughout the ride he'd managed to convey to her how flaky she was, how not up to it, how destined to fail. It had been a nightmare, like the long train journey before it, which she'd spent huddled in her seat, sheer terror at what she'd done, what she was *doing*, growing with every mile that sped by. She'd come without food or drink and hadn't found the will to stand up and work her way down to the buffet car. She'd grown hazy-headed with thirst and hunger.

When the train pulled into the Cornwall station she'd been overtaken by panic and a kind of desperate determination. She'd lugged her case as fast as she could to the taxi rank and claimed the first car in line, even though an old lady arrived at the same time as her. The cab driver was short with her because of the old lady, and said he'd never heard of the address she gave him: 17 Merral Road. He'd made a phone call to his depot and no one there knew of it either, but they'd suggested he try Merral Park Avenue on the outskirts of town. And they'd gone there and driven round and round, searching, and he'd got more and more irritated, and she'd felt more and more faint with hunger and nerves, and when he'd asked her what she was doing here, was she on a late holiday, she'd blurred her answer so much she'd sounded retarded.

In the end he'd parked in a thin little cul-de-sac with no street sign. It ended in wooded wasteland and its houses were tall and thin, most of them broken up into shabby-looking flats. He'd told Amber to get out and knock on one of the front doors to ask, but she froze, she acted like she hadn't heard him, so he got out, swearing, and just then a man came out of the woods with a dog, and the cabby shouted to him and the man said he was pretty sure it was Merral Road, or maybe Merral Way, Merral something anyway. Then the cabby had found number seventeen, and now Amber was alone.

She picked up her dead-weight case, and plodded up to the porch. Carved in a brick above the lintel was a date – 1887. Nasturtium tendrils snaked across the path, right up to the front door, fat round leaves hiding yellow and orange flowers. Dead leaves, twigs and bits of moss were banked up in the corners of the porch. The whole place had an air of no one going through its door for a long time, which was weird, because this was meant to be a student house. . . She picked up the knocker and, somehow knowing it wouldn't be answered, banged it down.

Silence, just the echo of the knock. She banged again. Then she gripped the key, and pushed it into the keyhole. Amber was bad with keys, she always had been. She panicked and tried to force them round, she hadn't the knack. . .

But this key was turning.

It was just a key, going into a lock, turning slowly, stiffly, but turning round, grating round. It was just a door creaking open, swinging wide on to a dusty hall. But it made Amber feel faint. It seemed like the floor of the hall, old red and black tiles, was swinging up to meet her.

She heaved her suitcase over the threshold. Sunlight was coming through a half-open door at the end of the long corridor.

Leaving her case where it was, she walked down to meet it.

Chapter Two

Hi Amber! said the note propped up against the mug with a picture of a comic dinosaur on it. *Welcome to our shit-hole – sorry we're not here. Mama Kaz has left a sarnie in the fridge for you. Your room's upstairs first right. Hope it's OK! Back at 6/7. My turn to cook – lucky you!!! Ben XX*

Amber picked up the note and held it for a moment, then she laid it back on the little pine table and looked around. She was in a medium-sized, friendly-looking kitchen. It had battered pine cupboards round the walls, an old-fashioned deep sink in front of a window, and a wide glass door that led on to a leafy garden and let in the sun.

She went over to the sink, filled the kettle, switched it on. She opened the fridge door (covered with magnets – a cartoon cat, a dolphin, fruit, and the words *wash up Rory u dckhed* in red and green letters) and took out a bottle of milk and a large white-bread sandwich on a plate covered in cling film. Then she went back to the kettle, and made a cup of tea in the dinosaur mug.

She suddenly felt euphoric. Faint with nerves and hunger, but euphoric. *I got away*, she thought, *I did it. I'm here!*

She sat at the table, and took a sip of the hot sweet tea which shot into her veins like a drug. Then she unwrapped the sandwich and bit into it, chewed and swallowed, and her stomach seized on it like life coming back in, like finding out you were going to live after all. Thank you, Mama Kaz, she thought, fervently. The sandwich was ham and cheese and lettuce, it was wonderful.

She finished the sandwich, then on an impulse jumped up and went over to the glass door, mug in hand. A key lay on the counter near it; she grabbed it, turned it in the lock, and stepped outside.

It was good out here in the low, early-autumn sun. She stood, sipping her tea, looking around her. The garden was seriously overgrown, screened by trees heavy with yellowing leaves. More nasturtiums flourished here, snaking everywhere with their pretty, stalked flowers. If they cleared it up a bit, she thought, it would be great when summer came round again. . . "Amber, you're here," she breathed, walking along the cracked concrete path. "Here!"

She thought back to her nightmarish journey, and everything that had gone before. The summer had been hideous. It should've been great, because she'd finished her A levels and wanted to celebrate, but it had been hideous. She'd arranged to go on holiday with three girls she'd met at her sixth-form college, to an apartment in the Seychelles for two weeks. It was the first time she'd done anything on her own like that; it was going to be amazing. But ten days before she was due to go, Poppy got ill again.

Poppy was her half-sister, fourteen months younger than she was. Poppy was "fragile", prone to wild fears and periods of depression. Their mother couldn't be expected to cope on her own, not without the routine of school, not with Poppy refusing to get dressed or eat properly and crying, *crying* all the time. . .

Amber couldn't abandon them. She couldn't be that selfish.

She stood on the cracked path and took another mouthful of tea and remembered the pure, good, empty feeling she'd had when she'd cancelled her holiday. She'd lost loads of money through it, her new friends were really upset with her and probably wouldn't stay her friends now, but her mother had been tearful with gratitude and she knew she was doing the right thing. . .

And then Poppy had recovered, remarkably quickly. Amber had been expected to rejoice in this, but somehow, she hadn't. Instead she'd felt something like rage growing in her, resentful, confused rage, growing and building. Not even the arrival of her good A level results cheered her up.

"I'm so sorry about your holiday, darling," her mother had said. "But there'll be other chances for you, won't there? You're the lucky one. Not like poor Poppy. When's she ever going to get a holiday. . .?"

Amber had shut herself away in her room for hours, browsing the Internet, looking at gap year travel routes to Mexico, India, Cambodia, all of them terrifying and deeply alluring and out of the question because soon she'd be off to the university in the next town. It was only a forty-minute bus ride away, which meant she could still live at home, safe from trouble, supporting and helping like always. . .

Then one afternoon she'd stumbled on flat share websites. She was amazed at the choice, there were rooms going all over the country. She entered into correspondence with several; Scotland, Cornwall, Leicester. She reinvented herself as she wrote, loving the chance to escape from her life. She told them she'd had gap year travel planned but it had fallen through (she hinted at a broken relationship) and now she just wanted to get away for a bit, work for a bit, get her head together . . . it seemed OK as she tapped it out, an OK story to have happened to anyone. The replies she got told her it was OK, too.

The house in Cornwall was particularly keen for her to join them. They were all at college there, about to start their second year, someone had left them in the lurch, they couldn't afford an empty room, could she come as soon as possible? They told her she'd love it, it was a great scene, and there'd be jobs going, because workers left after the summer season. . .

It started to be real, the idea of going, as if the act of writing about it and having other people engage with it made it real. It began to be possible that she could actually go.

Without talking to her mother or half-sister, she contacted her university and found it surprisingly easy to defer entrance for a year. Then, with the people in Cornwall, she agreed rent, and a date to move in.

It was only when she paid for her train ticket that she knew she wasn't playing any more, that she was really going to go. She drew up lists of what she needed to take with her. She bought some new clothes, a duvet set (they'd told her it was a single bed, but a large one) and towels, which she hid under her bed.

She felt like she was split into two. There was the half that was doing all this secret planning, and the half that continued to function in her cramped and isolated family, helping her mother in the house and spending a lot of time with Poppy to stop her getting depressed again.

And the second half was rigid with guilt about what was being planned by the first half.

Three days before she was due to go, Amber took all her courage in her hands and told her mother and Poppy she'd been invited down to stay with a friend in Cornwall for a couple of weeks, before university started. Her mother looked stricken, because now she'd have to deal alone with Poppy starting new at sixth-form college, but she still felt bad about Amber missing out on her Seychelles holiday, so she tried to be positive. She even shushed Poppy when she moaned that she'd like to go too, that it wasn't fair, that she'd never had a proper holiday in her life and now Amber was going away all on her own. . .

Amber had no offers of help for her trip; it had simply not occurred to her mother or to Poppy to make any. Amber was the strong one; they were doing enough just letting her go.

Amber left for the station at six a.m., weak with panic, not waking them as agreed, having said her goodbyes and lying "see you soons!" the night before.

And now she was here, standing in this overgrown garden, about to go in and look at her new room. The knowledge that she'd have to phone her mother some time soon and tell her she wasn't coming back to go to university, she was staying on in Cornwall for months, the whole year maybe, was like a vast unspeakable burden of guilt at the edge of her mind.

She walked back into the kitchen.

Chapter Three

"Who the hell are *you*?"

The boy standing at the fridge was so out of Amber's league it was a joke he was talking to her. And his question seemed fair enough. Who the hell *was* she?

Then he grinned lavishly and said, "*Shit* – sorry! Our new housemate, right? Should've registered the bag in the hall – didn't expect you to come in out of the garden."

"Sorry," mumbled Amber, looking down at the floor, then making herself look at him again. He was tall, skinny-elegant, with longish dark hair, and his face blazed at her.

"No problem. So – I'm Rory. And you're. . ."

"Amber."

"Amber, Amber, right, Kaz told me. Well – welcome to Merral Road! D'you like your room?"

"I was . . . I was just going up to look at it."

"You haven't *seen* it yet? Come on. I'll give you a hand up with your case."

He ambled out of the kitchen, Amber following. "When did you arrive?" he demanded.

"Only just then," she answered, hastily. "I was starving, so I—"

"Went out into the garden to forage for berries." He turned, wide mouth jeering. "*Joke!* Come on." He picked up her case and hefted it towards the staircase. "Jesus, what've you got in here? Rocks?"

She laughed nervously, and took hold of the back of the case where the useless little wheels were. Together they heaved it up the wide, steep flight of stairs towards a huge, gilt-edged, ornate mirror at the top. Rory's face was bent towards hers as he backed up step by step, but she couldn't look at it. She could smell smoke on his breath, though, and some kind of musky male cologne, and hear him breathing. . . . "I gotta give up the fags," he said. "This is doing me in. Hey – stop ogling my arse in that mirror."

Amber squeaked "I wasn't!" and forced another laugh, wondering what it must be like to be so utterly sure of yourself you could throw off remarks like he did, *be* like him. Desperate to change the subject, she said, "It must be worth a fortune."

"My arse?"

"The mirror! It's gorgeous."

"Yeah, but it's kind of plastered into the wall. Otherwise I'd sell it. Come on, push. . .!" They both heaved, and landed the case on the landing. Rory stood up straight and grinned at her, and she tried to smile back. "That mirror's not the only bit of class here," he said, conversationally. "There's wardrobes, chairs, tables – all antiques. The landlord says some of it's been here since the house was new."

"Wow. Why doesn't he sell it?"

"Dunno. Some of it's pretty battered . . . I s'pose he just never got round to it." He picked up her case again, stomped across the landing, and said, "Here's your room."

Opening the door to it, Amber's first thought was how practical it was. She wasn't going to be in love with it, she thought, not like her bedroom at home which was her refuge, her haven – no, this room was going to be a base, a base to lead her new life from. It was a good size, square, with a window filled with a view of the trees in the garden. There was the wide single bed she'd been promised, a chest of drawers with an old mirror stand on top of it, and a generous oak wardrobe. All you needed to lead a life from.

"Pretty dreary, eh?" Rory said. "Foul curtains."

"Yeah," said Amber, thinking she liked them – they were 1970s style, sandy coloured with palm leaves printed on them – thinking how she was going to change the room, make it hers.

"Shove a few posters up, it'll be OK," Rory said. Then he yawned, and backed out of the door. "That's the bathroom," he said pointing, "and that's Ben's room, and that's the airing cupboard, and Chrissie's room is down there – Kaz and I sleep downstairs. *Not* together, I hasten to add."

On the other side of Ben's door, tucked behind the airing cupboard (which was built on to the wall at the top of the stairs, the one with the huge mirror on it) was another flight of stairs. A strange, somehow gloomy light fell on them, and they were much more narrow and steep than the main stairs.

"There's another floor?" asked Amber.

"Yeah, the attics."

"What are they used for?"

"Dumping rooms for junk."

"Can't they be rented out too?"

Rory shrugged. "There's only one bathroom for the whole house – that and the *apology* for a shower room on the ground floor. There's health and safety stuff to do with bathrooms and numbers, isn't there."

"Yes, but if the landlord turned one of the attics into a bathroom. . ."

"They're pretty crap. Low ceilings, tiny skylights. Plus I guess the landlord can't be arsed to do up the place – not many people want to live round here – only students and nutters like you." He grinned again, and for a moment Amber thought he was going to ask her what she was doing here, but he didn't, he just said, "I gotta get some coffee down me, I got an essay to finish that I should've done last term. See you at dinner, yeah?" Then he jogged off downstairs.

So that was Rory, she thought. She hadn't had any dealings with him, only Kaz and Ben by email and phone. They were the two organizers in the house, that was clear. Then there was Chrissie . . . and now her. Amber, the fifth housemate.

She opened the door to the bathroom and found it, like her room, a good size, useable, practical. When she came out she glanced towards the attic stairs, thinking she'd like to investigate the attics, too. A pale streak of sun ran down from a small skylight at the top of the stairs, and dust was moving in it, making a long, thin shape. There was something weird about it that Amber couldn't put her finger on, then she realized that dust motes usually sparkled in sunlight, but these didn't, they looked dark, they didn't glitter at all. . . She felt suddenly very weary, standing there, weary and sad. What she'd done, the break she'd made, the betrayal . . . it threatened to overwhelm her. She decided to start unpacking, keep her mind busy. It was quarter to six, and Ben had said he'd be back soon to cook. . .

Chapter Four

"Hey Amber! Amber! You up there? You gonna join us?"

Amber came to with a start. She was lying on her new bed, with the duvet in its wonderful brand-new purple cover wrapped round her, and the light had almost gone from the room.

"Coming!" she shouted, scrambling to her feet, heading to the mirror to brush her hair. Panic rose in her as she thought of meeting the rest of her house mates – suppose they were all as incredibly glamorous as Rory? – and she tamped it down, hard. "It's fine," she mouthed at herself as she slicked on some lipgloss, wishing like always that she looked better, less . . . *nothingy*. "It's all going to be fine. Just get on with what's in front of you."

Before she'd fallen asleep she'd hung up her jeans, shirts and skirts and her one dress in the wardrobe, and folded her tops and jumpers and put them in the chest of drawers with her underwear at the top. Everything fitted. She even found the perfect place for her jewellery – in the little drawer in the mirror stand. There was something not right about the room, though . . . she felt on edge, anxious. . . It'll be OK when I've settled in, she told herself, and she'd pulled out the new duvet set, overcome with wanting to make up her bed, make it up for tonight when she could rest at last, and she'd only lain down on it for a minute or two, just to see how it felt. . .

"Oh, sod it," she muttered, as she hurried downstairs, "I've been up since four thirty this morning – what d'you expect me to feel?" And she kind of threw herself into the kitchen like you would the deep end of a swimming pool, not giving herself time to think.

Three strange faces, two female, one male, turned to face her, smiling, saying "Hi, Amber!" "You OK?" "Welcome!"

"Hi!" she croaked back, registering that Rory wasn't there, and the three strangers kind of folded her into the steamy kitchen, which smelt deliciously of frying meat and garlic. "I hope you like pasta!" The boy at the stove grinned. He was sandy-haired, stocky, and ordinary-looking, but his smile was warm.

"I love it," said Amber.

"Well, that's good," said one of the girls, "it's all he can cook! Amber, that's Ben, that's Chrissie – I'm Kaz. Welcome, honestly." Chrissie had layered blond hair and looked a bit sporty. Kaz was voluptuous, with beautiful dark eyes, and rich wavy black hair flowing on to her shoulders. She was dressed in a turquoise shirt and white baggy trousers and

Amber thought she looked gorgeous. "We're so glad you took the room," she added, smiling.

"Or we'd've been seriously out of pocket," said Chrissie. "We had to find the extra rent."

"That's not the only reason we're glad!" Kaz laughed and laid a hand on Amber's arm, like touching was just a part of how she communicated with people.

Chrissie poured out a glass of red wine, and put it into Amber's hand, asking "D'you like the house?"

"It's great," Amber said, "my room's great too. Oh, and thank you for the sandwich, Kaz. That was so kind of you."

Kaz beamed, and Ben at the stove said, "OK, it's done – is the table ready?"

"Yes," said Kaz, even though the little pine table in the middle of the kitchen was covered in cooking stuff. She handed Amber a basket of sliced baguette, picked up the wine bottle and a pile of plates, and said, "Follow me!"

Like a procession, each carrying something, the four of them crossed the hall and went into a large and extraordinary room. Richly-coloured hangings were tacked to the walls; rugs blanketed the wooden floor, and glowing shawls were draped across the chairs and sofa. A painted screen at the end of the room half-shielded a wide bed, covered in red and silver silky cloth. Cushions tumbled everywhere. In the centre of the bay window was a huge old mahogany table where Rory was standing, bad-temperedly chucking down knives and forks more or less at random.

"What a fantastic room!" said Amber.

"If you like Moroccan brothels," said Rory.

"They don't have brothels in Morocco, Rory," said Kaz.

"Bet they do," said Rory.

Amber was still taking in all the details. On one side of the bay window a large potted palm flourished, on the other stood a white-painted, twiggy tree-branch, festooned in glittery chains and bangles. Candles glittered across the surface of the table; more shone on the mantelpiece, and in the fireplace. "It's lovely," she said. "Really lovely."

"Thank you," said Kaz, smiling at the expression on Amber's face. "It's my room. We often eat in here."

"Don't you mind?" asked Amber.

"Mind?" Rory snorted. "She bloody insists on it! You just try eating in the kitchen!"

"Oh, shut up!" said Kaz, happily. "We eat in here because I've got by far the biggest room—"

". . .and she hardly pays any extra rent for it," chipped in Ben.

"—and I *like* it being a dining room too! We've had a couple of brilliant parties in here – hey, we'll have to have another, won't we? Now Amber's here?"

"Give me strength," groaned Rory.

Kaz picked up a ladle and smacked Rory on the shoulder with it. Ben took it from her, started dishing out the pasta, and said, "Come on, everyone, sit down."

Amber tucked into the mound of spaghetti bolognese in front of her with gusto, amazed at how hungry she felt.

"Don't let Kaz scare you," said Chrissie, passing Amber some bread. "We don't do this all the time. We're not some kind of over-organized, happy-family set up—"

"Could've fooled me," said Rory.

"—it's just – we take it in turns to cook. Or, if you're Rory, buy takeaway. Nothing regimented, and Kaz does more cooking than the lot of us put together, but . . . well. It kind of works out."

"It sounds great," said Amber. "I like to cook." At home, it had been a way of escaping when things were bad without upsetting her mother and sister by leaving the flat.

"*Really?*" Kaz beamed. "That's brilliant! It seems to work out for Wednesday nights, maybe Sundays too . . . you just announce you're up for doing a meal, and split the shopping cost between whoever wants to eat—"

"Two pounds eighty tonight, that OK?" put in Ben.

"—Chrissie's boyfriend often comes, that's fine. We don't have a rota – we don't seem to need one."

"That's 'cos you're such a bossy cow you do instead of one," said Rory.

Kaz laughed, and shied a bit of bread across the table at him, and Chrissie rolled her eyes at Ben. Amber, watching all this, thought: *Kaz really fancies Rory.* She was blown away by the thought of becoming part of this, this house with its chat and friendships and talk and intrigues and *normality*. . . She was still nervous, anxious that they'd like her, but she was beginning to relax into the evening. It helped that two bottles of cheap red wine circulated –

included, Ben said, in the price of the meal. To her relief, the four of them did most of the talking. They told her what their college was like and which courses they were doing, and how great life was in Cornwall if you knew where to go and what to do. Which, they said, they did – and they promised to show her. Then, just as Rory was going into overdrive describing a new club he'd discovered, Amber suddenly put down her knife and fork and muttered "Oh, *shit*."

"What's up?" asked Kaz.

Amber looked stricken. "I forgot to phone. Home. They'll be so worried . . . they . . . oh, *God*."

"Phone now," Rory shrugged.

"Is there a . . . is there a . . . phone in the house?"

Everyone was looking at her, because she seemed so devastated. "No," said Ben, "we've all got mobiles."

"Haven't you?" asked Chrissie.

"Out of credit," lied Amber. She'd never owned a mobile, there'd been no need. "Is there a call box near here. . .?"

Kaz leapt to her feet, fetched a silver-cased mobile from the mantelpiece. "Use mine," she said. "Go on."

Amber made herself smile her thanks, and fled out to the hall. She wasn't entirely sure how to use a mobile, but with a few false starts she worked it out, and then her mother was on the other end, voice shrill and hysterical, "Hello? *Hello?*"

"Mum? It's me. I'm fine, Mum – I'm fine."

"Oh, *God!* Oh, we've been so *worried*! We were

expecting you to phone hours ago – Poppy's been hysterical. . ." Then her voice went distant, saying, "Yes, yes, it's her, darling, it's Amber, she's OK, she's fine. . ."

"*Mum!* Look – I had to borrow a mobile, I can't talk long—"

"But Amber – what happened?"

"The train was delayed," she lied, "and I couldn't find the place, and all the call boxes were out of order, and there isn't a phone in the house, it's been awful, but. . ."

"There isn't a *phone*? But how can I contact you, how—"

"Mum – I'll phone *you*. Every day."

"Tomorrow? You promise?"

"Yes. I'll find a call box. I've got to go, Mum."

"All right, Amber. Oh, Poppy's shouting something, I can't hear her – *I'm coming, darling!* Talk to you tomorrow, then. Don't let us down."

Amber flicked the phone off, breathing fast, thinking: I can't believe I forgot to phone. Then: Mum didn't ask one question about what it's like here. Then she went back into the room.

"Got through?" Kaz beamed.

"Yes, thanks. I owe you for the call –"

"No you don't. Part of the welcome package. Anyway, you were dead fast. Everything OK?"

"Yes . . . well, Mum was pretty upset. . ."

"Don't worry. You phoned her, didn't you?" said Ben.

"I forgot to phone for two weeks once, when I was travelling," said Rory.

"Yeah, but you're an insensitive git," said Chrissie.

"I can't believe I forgot to phone," muttered Amber, sitting down again. Over her bowed head, Chrissie and Ben exchanged raised-eyebrow glances, and Kaz reached out and squeezed her arm. "Hey," she said, "stop beating yourself up about it. Have some more wine. Here." She topped up Amber's glass. "Now. You said you needed work. What kind are you looking for?"

"Er . . . restaurant or bar work?" said Amber.

Amber had only ever had one job before, a Saturday job in a shoe shop. She'd saved just about every penny from it for the Seychelles holiday that she'd dropped out of – she was able to save because she didn't go out much. It was just so hard to leave Poppy behind – tears and pleadings from Poppy, her mother trying to see her side of it but always ending up saying "Just this time dear? Surely it won't make that much difference if Poppy comes along. . ." In the end, it was better just to stay at home. It was always awful if Poppy came along.

"Got references?" demanded Rory.

"Er . . . only one."

"Make 'em up. I'll write 'em for you if you like. Actually, they're gonna give you a trial if they like the look of you, sod the references. So many people have left now summer's over. . ."

"I'm going into town tomorrow," announced Chrissie. "Want to walk down with me?"

"Oh, yes please," said Amber. "If that's OK."

"There's a notice up in Tate's – we can start off there."

"Yes – thank you. Look –" Amber got a bit unsteadily to her feet – "can I make a start on the washing up? Only I need to get to bed, I was up at four thirty this morning. . . ."

"Get to bed," said Kaz. "No washing up. Go on."

"Oh, thank you. It was a lovely meal, thanks. I –" She took in a deep breath, made herself say it, "I know I'm going to really like it here." Her eyes were fixed down on the table, she didn't see them smiling at her. "Er – what time are you going into town, Chrissie?"

Chrissie shrugged. "When I'm up. Ten-ish? No rush."

"Great. Goodnight." And she walked out of the room, swaying a little. She wasn't used to wine.

She pulled the door to and stood there, silently. Listening outside doors was a survival skill she'd learnt at home. "Wet or *what*?" she heard Rory say, and Kaz going, "Shhhh!" and Ben saying "Give her a chance, she's only just got here." Then Chrissie said something about her overreaction to forgetting to phone her mum, and Kaz murmured how tired she'd looked, and Rory growled, "She's neurotic as hell," and Kaz ssshed him again and said how stupid it was to judge on the first night.

Amber didn't mind any of this, because it was the old Amber they were talking about, and she knew she was going to change. She also didn't mind because she felt she'd deserved it, she'd tricked them with her reinvention of herself, her stories about gap year travel falling through and hints about a broken relationship. If they knew the truth about her life – how sad and small and anxious it was, how *weird* – they probably wouldn't have let her in over the threshold.

She turned silently, and made her way upstairs.

Something made her glance towards the attic stairs as she headed for her bedroom, and she found herself looking for the strange, dark dust shape again. But light from the bathroom was splashing through its frosted glass door and on to the landing, and there looked to be nothing there at all.

Chapter Five

Amber lay in her new bed, sliding into sleep, letting her mind drift. Guiltily, she thought about Poppy lying awake at home, in the little box room next to her room, and told herself that now she'd moved out, Poppy could have her room. . . She drifted on into the strange half-world between sleep and awake, remembering Kaz's wonderful room and how she'd said they had parties there, how she'd said they ought to have one for her, Amber, how amazing, that she'd said that . . . she was back at her first big birthday party, when she was ten, the only party she'd ever had. . .

Poppy was very upset, one of her friends had been mean to her, and Mum was carrying her out of the room as she sobbed and kicked. . . "She's a pain, isn't she?" someone said. "Just 'cos Marie wouldn't let her try her bracelet on. . ." Then, from upstairs, the sound of Poppy shrieking. Horrible, mad shrieks like a creature being killed. All the girls fell silent and looked at Amber, relishing the awfulness. "Is your mum spanking her?" Katy asked, eyes huge. "For spoiling your birthday?"

Amber shook her head, ashamed. "Mum never hits Poppy," she whispered, and someone had scoffed, "Maybe she should."

Then Mum came downstairs again. She was carrying Poppy on one hip, cuddling her tightly, and she announced in a shrill, tight voice that tea was ready in the kitchen. Everyone went through, and Mum sat Poppy down in a chair next to Amber. Amber wanted to slap Poppy, slap her hard for spoiling everything, but she didn't, she passed her sandwiches and babied her and fussed over her, while the other girls nudged each other and rolled their eyes.

Then suddenly Poppy stood up, on her chair . . . she stood up, and picked up a china plate, and threw it as hard as she could at Marie. It hit Marie on the forehead; Marie screamed and Poppy burst into tears again. Mum rushed to pick her up, and when Amber and the other girls tried to tell her what Poppy had done it was as if she hadn't heard them, she just hugged Poppy and bore her out of the room and they heard her running upstairs with her. "She didn't even look at your face!" said someone, and someone else said, "There's a really red mark, Marie, maybe you should go to the hospital," and Marie sobbed, "I'm going to phone my mum, I want to go home!" and someone else said, "I'm not staying either," and suddenly everyone was scrambling down from the table, and Amber couldn't look at any of them. She ran upstairs. Poppy and her mum were huddled up in Mum's big bed together. "Mum, come down!" she wailed. "Everyone's going!"

"Let them!" hissed her mum. "They're horrible girls!"

"Mum, they're *not* – it was *Poppy*—"

"Oh, Amber, *don't*! Don't say that! Look how upset she is!"

"*Please* come down . . . they're phoning their mums!"

"I can't face them. Tell them Poppy's ill – tell them I've got a bad headache." Mum groaned, then she pulled the duvet right over her and Poppy's heads.

When Amber got downstairs again, she found her friends closed in ranks of normality against her. Josie was comforting Marie, and the rest of them sat on chairs at the edge of the room, faces prim and disapproving, waiting to go home. Katy was on the phone. "I know, but it's over *now*," she was saying, dramatically. "And Amber's mum isn't here!" The mothers, when they came, said vague things as Amber tried to explain about her mum being ill but they didn't really look at her so in the end she gave up trying to explain and everyone left very quickly.

In the quiet flat, Amber stood still and looked about her. The paper from pass-the-parcel was still on the floor; the party bags that Amber had begged for and laboured over, choosing sweets and a pretty hair slide for each, lay untouched on the sideboard. She went into the kitchen, made Mum a cup of tea, and took it upstairs.

"Have they gone?" Mum asked. Poppy was curled up asleep beside her. Amber nodded, and handed her the tea.

"I don't know what I'd do without you, Amber," Mum whispered and Amber felt full of love, and pride; she thought she'd stay and look after Mum and Poppy for ever. "Get into bed with us," Mum said. "*Darling* girl." It was warm and safe in bed, no one criticizing or sneering, and the three of them had slept for a long time. When they'd woken up, it was dark, and Mum said, "Come on, we're going to have a midnight feast!" and they went down to the kitchen and ate up the sausage rolls and egg sandwiches, then Mum brought in a lovely yellow cake with a face like the sun, and they lit the ten candles and sang "Happy Birthday" and Mum said, "All for us, a whole cake just for us three, this is better, isn't it!"

"Tate's is pretty cool," Chrissie said the next morning, as she and Amber walked down the steep hill towards the little Cornish coastal town and the huge sea. "It's dead stylish, and I know the owner's nice, he always shares the tips out OK..."

"Sounds great!" said Amber, as breezily as she could, although she felt sick with anxiety. Her nerves were still taut and stretched after yesterday, and now she had job-hunting to face. She'd slept badly; she'd lain awake wound up with guilt about leaving home, then when at last she'd dropped off, the window had rattled, jerking her awake again. She'd got up to try and wedge it with paper, but it hadn't worked – it had woken her twice more that night.

Amber, though, had had a lot of practice at hiding how

awful she felt inside. She walked on next to Chrissie, chatting, until they drew up in front of Tate's.

It was shiny and minimalist, a restaurant designed to cash in on the increasingly affluent people coming to Cornwall in the warmer months of the year. But the cold-call interview didn't go well. The owner couldn't hide his disappointment when he discovered it was Amber and not Chrissie looking for a job, which made Amber shrink into herself and stumble over her words. He told her very little about the place, just asked her to leave her mobile number so he "could get back to her". She had no number to leave, of course, so Chrissie had to leave hers. It was like the final seal on her inadequacy.

Outside, Amber muttered, "That was hopeless."

"Well, you need to *sell* yourself more!" erupted Chrissie. "You hung back too much!"

"I could tell he didn't want me."

"Look – if you have that defeatist attitude you won't get a job anywhere! And what was that with the mobile? I thought you'd just run out of credit?"

"It was stolen," said Amber. "I just didn't . . . I just didn't feel like going into it last night."

"What's to 'go into'? Everyone gets stuff nicked."

Both girls fell silent, then Chrissie moved off and Amber followed her along the street. *She hates me,* Amber thought, *she thinks I'm a real loser.*

Chrissie turned, face set. "There's a new bar opened up along here, they might need someone. . ." she announced, and set off again before Amber could reply. The bar looked like the restaurant – seriously stylish, aiming high. Amber felt terrified just standing outside its door. "Are you going in?" demanded Chrissie.

Driven by panic, Amber said, "I will, but I *so* need a pee first."

"There's some bogs down on the seafront. Straight ahead. I'll show you."

"Chrissie – you've done enough. Seriously. I can't take up your morning."

"It's OK."

"*Honestly.* I think I'm better on my own. The thing is, when they see you – they want you, not me."

Chrissie smiled at the compliment, said, "Nonsense." But she'd thawed a bit.

"The loos are straight ahead, yeah?" Amber rattled on. "I'll try in the bar – then have a wander round."

"D'you know your way back to the house?"

"Yes. Straight up the hill, isn't it. I'll be fine."

"OK, if you're sure," said Chrissie, relieved. "See you back at the house, then!" And she strode off.

Chapter Six

Locked inside a peeling lavatory cubicle, Amber tried to calm her panic by breathing deeply and slowly. *You've got to do this,* she told herself. *You've got to get a job.* It wasn't just the need for cash – although what money she had would barely see her up to November – she needed a job to give her life a pattern, and stability. She needed roots – new roots. She hadn't prepared for job-hunting, though. That first huge hurdle of escaping, getting the train, finding the house . . . it had been so momentous she hadn't thought beyond it. She sat on the closed lid of the lavatory pan and rocked herself, feeling like she was at a crossroads. One way pointed back home, the other way pointed forward, to the unknown. It was so hard to take the path to the unknown with Mum and Poppy always saying how difficult things were, how terrible life was, always creeping back home and calling her with them. . .

One summer, when the girls had been nine and eleven, they'd had to move to a smaller, cheaper flat twenty miles away. On the morning the September term had started at their new school, the three of them had got as far as the main entrance to the flats, then Poppy had got hysterical and refused to go any further. The three of them had gone back in, and Mum had cried and cuddled Poppy and said they'd try again tomorrow, and Amber had looked at the two of them, clinging together and crying, and a fear far worse than her fear of the new school had got hold of her. She'd run out of the door, and gone to school all on her own.

Thinking of that, Amber stood up, and unlatched the door to the cubicle. "This is only the second hurdle," she told herself, walking out on to the esplanade again. "After this, you've got the third hurdle: telling Mum and Poppy you're staying on in Cornwall. So you'd better get on with it, hadn't you?"

She went straight back to the new, stylish bar, and peered in at the window. A glass tube of lilies stood on a table by the window; a thin girl in a white apron sneered behind the bar. Chilled, Amber turned away. "There must be other places," she thought. She prowled through the narrow little streets, seagulls swooping and screaming above her on the rooftops. A tea room called Cath's Kettle caught her eye, and she made herself push the door open and ask if there were any jobs going. "I put a card in the window if I need anyone, and as you can see, there's no card," she was told, briskly. She went into a cinema, another tea shop, two pubs, and a fish and chip shop. The cinema and one of the pubs took her name and address but all the others told her she had no hope, because the season was over. So much, she thought, for Rory's assurance that she'd get work easily because so many workers had left now summer's over. . . She wondered if he had to work. She thought he probably didn't. He had *indulged* written all over him.

She was starting to go back along the same streets now, past the same places, and she was exhausted with tension and the effort of making herself walk into strange places and ask for a job. She told herself she'd go back to the house, and try again tomorrow, but hearing her mother's words inside her head made her quicken her pace again. "If there's a job going here, I'll find it today," she told herself. Grimly, she started to make her way back to the new bar, but she took a wrong turning and ended up back on the seafront again. All along it, cafes and bars were closed or closing up for the winter. Two men were stacking chairs, and dragging outdoor tables into beachside lock-ups; a bright sign outside a small restaurant said *See you in May!* Hopelessness settled on her. She walked on to the beach, and scuffed along the sand. The sea washed in and washed out again, desolate, grey and cold. It seemed to go on for ever, fading into the sky at a pale horizon. A few metres ahead of her, wide wooden planks had been laid on the sand to form a ramshackle boardwalk running out to the water. At the top were a couple of kiosks, for ice cream and maybe beach toys, both shuttered and bolted for the months ahead. Further down, nearer the sea, was a long, low wooden hut painted terracotta and blue. Amber walked towards it. A sign on its side said *The Albatross*. Another sign said *Breakfast, Lunch, Tea*. The windows were steamy, and the door slightly ajar. Amber took in a shaky breath, and pushed it open.

Inside, it was warm, and there was a wonderful light. It looked far larger than it had from the outside. Two wide windows looked straight out to sea; between them a blackboard listed the brief menu for the day. The wooden walls – two blue, two terracotta – were covered by startling and vibrant paintings, all by the same artist, with price tags on. About ten tables – all different sizes, but all bare, worn wood – were arranged about the floor, with people – all different sorts of people – sitting at most of them. There was a loud group of kids, probably students, right in the middle by a pot-bellied stove with its chimney running up through the roof. Two lots of workmen had their newspapers open, and two arty-looking middle-aged women were chatting animatedly on a sofa against the far wall. There were two lovers, hands clasped across the table, and people on their own – an old man, a young woman, a man in a suit. In a far corner, there was a pile of beautiful driftwood, like a sculpture. Stones and shells lay on the low table in front of the sofa where the arty women sat.

Amber decided she loved the feeling of the place. Absolutely loved it.

Swing doors at the side banged suddenly open, and a tall, weathered-looking man came through, carrying two mugs. He had thick greying hair and he was wearing a butcher's apron. "Just you is it, luv?" he demanded.

"Er, yes," said Amber. "Er – actually – I was wondering if you were closing for the winter?"

"Does it look like it?" the man asked, putting the mugs down on one of the workmen's tables. "My regulars'd starve!"

"In that case," she took a step towards him, and lowered her voice, "I was wondering if there might be a job going here?"

"What – waitressing? 'Fraid not, luv."

"Ah," said Amber, then took in a breath and blurted out, "Only you're busy, aren't you?" And she nodded towards two nearby tables, with people waiting and no plates in front of them.

The man frowned. "This isn't McDonald's," he said, needled. "They're waiting for their food to get cooked. *Real* food. Talking of which, I'd better get back before Marty burns those steaks. . ." He bulled his way through the swing doors again.

Everything in Amber told her to give up and go away, go back to the chilly, elegant bar and beg for a job, but somehow, she stayed standing there. The doors swung open and a tall, broad-shouldered boy about her age charged through with a plate of steak and chips; he flashed her a wonderful grin, put the plate down in front of the man in a suit, and went back to the kitchen.

Amber stayed standing there. When the doors swung back for a third time, it was the man in the apron again. "You still here?" he demanded. "I told you – we don't need waitresses."

"D'you cook everything from scratch here?" asked Amber.

"Yes. I don't buy in anything ready made, I make it fresh. Call me an idiot but that's how I do it. *Marty!* Check the soup, will you?"

"Why don't you get someone in to help you cook?" she asked.

"*Cook?* D'you know how much that would cost? Now – I gotta get on, luv. I've got a box of lovely Bramleys that'll end up rotten if I don't make them into apple crumble sometime soon. *Marty!*"

Amber took in a deep breath. "I can make apple crumble," she said.

Chapter Seven

The man in the apron looked at Amber, hard. "You're persistent, I'll say that for you," he said.

"I really need a job," Amber said. "And you need help. Let me make the crumble – call it a trial." She could hardly believe these bold words were coming out of her mouth, but they were.

"I told you – I can't afford a cook's wages."

"So pay me waiter's wages. I can help wait too."

"*Jesus!*" barked the man, and he raised his hands like he wanted to shove her out of the door. Instead, he landed them on his head, scrunched up his hair, and said, "Right. Sod it. Follow me." He punched his way through the swinging doors, and Amber followed in his slipstream, into a kitchen that was clean but a riot of disorder, with dirty plates piled by the sink and half-prepared food lined up on the surfaces. "There's the apples," he said. "Get peeling."

"Well, I'll make the crumble first," said Amber. "Or the apple'll go brown."

"You do know what you're doing, don't you?" He bent to a cupboard and pulled out a large deep-sided metal tray. "Here. Fill this. All you need is in that tall cupboard over there, and the fridge. Use that small oven. OK?"

"Mixing bowl?"

"Here." A large plastic bowl was slammed down in front of her, then the man headed for the stove, grabbed the spoon from Marty, tasted the soup, swore, and added more salt.

Amber knew she couldn't ask any more questions, or expect any more help.

Full of triumph and determination, she turned the oven on, washed her hands, and fetched a large sack of flour and some sugar from the tall cupboard. She'd only ever made tiny crumbles before, just enough for three, but crumbles just needed twice as much flour as fat and sugar, so she couldn't go wrong, could she? She weighed out two kilograms of flour on a battered old pair of scales, and decided it looked enough. Then she fetched butter and marg from the fridge and weighed out a half kilo of each of that. It was a huge amount to rub in, but she chopped the fat and got stuck into it, lifting the mix with both hands, circling fingers and thumbs together.

She felt strangely peaceful as she worked, suspended in time. You couldn't hurry it; you just had to keep at it. The café owner was working flat-out frying steak and chips and mixing up salad, and Marty was ladling out soup and slicing up French bread and both of them kept hurrying out with full plates and bursting in again with dirty ones, but Amber didn't look at them. She worked on till her hands were stiff, then she weighed out a kilo of sugar, and rubbed that in until it looked like breadcrumbs, just as it should. The apples were past their best, but they'd be tasty. Amber peeled and sliced at top speed, then shot over to the cupboard. She wanted this crumble to be special. She found a small sack of sultanas and, in among the tubs of spices and herbs, cinnamon and cloves. She added generous amounts to the apple, then smoothed over the topping. She opened the oven door, slammed the tray in, and checked her watch. It should be ready in about an hour.

Amber was on a roll now, full of energy. She headed for the huge sink, and washed up all the saucepans and cooking trays filling it. A green light flashed on the huge dishwasher to the side of it, so she pulled it open and unstacked it. Three long shelves on the wall held piles of identical plates and bowls; it was easy to see where everything went. Then she filled the dishwasher with all the mounds of dirty plates and cutlery that had been dumped on the counters, and set it to run again.

The smell of the apples and spices was filling the kitchen deliciously, but the café owner didn't comment on it, nor on the neatness of the kitchen. Amber picked up a cloth and spray-cleaner, and started furiously wiping the counters.

She checked her watch – the hour was up. She found a skewer, opened the oven, and pushed it into the crumble. The apples were soft, perfect; the topping golden brown.

Oven gloves on, she pulled out the tray and stood there for a minute, just holding it. She was alone in the kitchen; her heart was racing with what had come into her mind. Then she carried the tray out through the swing doors and into the café. Except for the arty women on the sofa, the people at the tables had changed, but nearly every table was taken still. "Pudding anyone?" she called out. "This apple crumble has just come out of the oven and though I say it myself it's *perfect.*"

Laughter followed; a workman grinned at her, said, "Wish I had the time, love." One of the arty women cried, "Oh, that smells divine!" and the other one said, "Oh, Ida, shall we? Just one more cup of tea and some of that?"

A grumpy-looking old man by the window had turned round. "How much?" he demanded.

"Three pounds fifty," said the café owner, smartly. "With vanilla ice cream."

"Ain't you got no custard?"

"No."

"Go on then," said the old man, begrudgingly.

"Ice cream's in the freezer, OK?" the café owner said at Amber.

"And one for us, dear," called one of the women. "Two spoons!"

Amber headed back into the kitchen, put the tray on the hob, fetched two dishes, and found the ice cream. She reckoned there were twenty-four portions in the tray. She scooped out two, added ice cream, and was about to take them through when Marty came in, beaming. "I'll take those," he said. "You got two more orders!"

When Amber took the second lot of crumble through, the lunch time rush had started in earnest. Three people were waiting, and the arty ladies were budging up on the sofa to make room, exclaiming over all the time they'd wasted just chatting and enjoying themselves.

And someone had chalked "*Spicy Apple Crumble and Vanilla Ice cream – £3.50*" on the bottom of the blackboard between the two windows that looked straight out to sea.

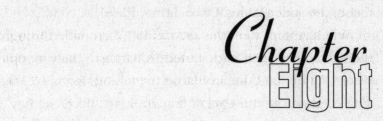

Chapter Eight

It was ten to four and Amber's furious energy had ebbed almost completely away. She'd worked non-stop for nearly four hours without any lunch, just a bit of French bread she'd grabbed on the run. She'd dished out the whole tray of apple crumble, cooked cheese on toast for some latecomers who'd missed lunch, made endless pots of tea, laid out scones and sliced banana-bread, and cleared and washed up. There were only three people left in the café now.

"He's going to say *Thanks, but no thanks*," she said to herself, "and kick me out without pay. I've been an *idiot*." But she carried on wiping the counters and washing the last of the pots in the sink. Marty came through and she asked, "When's closing up time?"

"When everyone's gone," he shrugged.

Then, from outside in the café, she heard the sound of windows being shut and the door being bolted, and Marty collected a huge broom from the corner and said, "Gonna help clear up out there?"

She went out with her cloth, and wiped down all the scrubbed wooden tables. Once, Marty made eye contact and grinned; she kept her eyes down after that. When they'd finished they trooped back into the kitchen; the café owner was sitting by the door, counting the takings from the till. "Made eighty-four quid out of that apple crumble," he said. "Not that it's all profit, of course. Got to take off the ingredients, and ice cream, and the gas for cooking . . . and if I got to pay you as well, I'm not going to have much profit left at all, am I?"

Amber felt like she was going to explode, or burst into tears, or both. "Yes you are!" she cried. "You could pay me six pounds an hour and still have loads of profit! And anyway, that crumble's not all I did, is it? I washed up, and loaded the dishwasher, and cleaned, and made cheese on toast and tea and. . ." She stopped, because the man was laughing at her.

"Bert, shut up!" said Marty, although he was laughing a bit, too. "Or she'll walk out and not come back again!"

"What's your name?" said Bert.

"Amber," said Amber, heart thumping.

"Well, Amber, you are an extraordinary young lady. You're just about the first person I've come across under the age of thirty who can do any sort of decent cooking at all."

"*I* cook!" said Marty.

"Marty – you wash food, and chop it up. Under my relentless supervision, or you make a complete bog-up of it. Where d'you learn, Amber?"

"At home," she said. "I used to cook a lot for my mum, she . . . she used to get migraines and stuff. I enjoyed it."

"Any good with fish? Ever gutted it?"

Marty groaned, and Amber said, "No. But I can learn."

"Well, you've got a job if you want it—"

"Oh *fantastic*!" Amber squealed.

"—although why anyone would want to work here beats me when there's trendy places like Tate's in town."

"I hated Tate's!" said Amber, beaming.

"She'll fit in here," Marty grinned, and for the first time Amber looked at him, properly, and smiled back.

"OK," said Bert. "Well, my café stays open all year 'cos I cater for people who live here, not just bloody tourists. Six quid an hour, start at eight-ish, finish around four. I shut Sundays and Mondays – I'm not into this bloody twenty-four-seven society, or whatever it's called. Free food. Share of tips. OK?"

"Yes," breathed Amber.

"It's hard work – but you saw that today. And if you work out, I s'pose I'll have to do it all proper, like with Sonny Jim here, and pay National Insurance and all that, but for now it's casual, OK?"

"OK."

"Good. Start tomorrow?"

"Thank you. I – *thank* you. *Brilliant*."

"Oh *fantastic*!" crowed Marty. "I've been on at that tight old git to take someone else on for ages, but he wouldn't."

"I wouldn't because I needed a cook, and they *cost*, and

then they won't muck in, and Amber here – she just did what was needed. You realize I'm exploiting you, Amber, only paying you six quid an hour."

"Evil capitalist!" said Marty.

"I don't care." Amber laughed. "I'd sooner cook than wash up all the time . . . I like doing a bit of everything."

"Well, that's great," said Bert. "You better watch your back, boy, or you'll be out of a job."

"Oh, *no*—" began Amber, but Marty said, "He's joking. He needs me. He needs both of us. You saw how crowded it was today – this place is on the up. And now you can make some of those dishes you were on about, Bert, can't you, you can expand your talents a bit beyond fish and chips and steak and chips and every sodding thing and chips, yeah?"

"We'll see," growled Bert, but his face was bright. "Right. What we got in the fridge? You two must be *starving*."

An hour later, Amber was dancing her way back up the steep hill to 17 Merral Road. Her stomach was full of a wonderful Spanish omelette that Bert had made them, her bag bulged with a large margarine tub of home-made coleslaw he said needed eating up, and her purse was heavier by twenty-seven pounds and thirty pence. Bert had paid her for four hours and given her half the afternoon's tips. Tips, he said, were just for her and Marty.

Halfway up the hill, she deviated off to a small parade of shops. She got some provisions – bread, milk, ham, apples –

at a little supermarket and looked through the window of a mobile phone shop, checking out which one she'd buy when she'd earned a bit more. Then on an impulse she went into a sharp-looking boutique and tried on a lilac-coloured top that was pegged out in the window under a shower of exotic beads. It was tighter than she normally wore, and it looked terrific. It was also nearly thirty pounds.

"That," said the shop assistant, "will wash and wash. I've got one, in a really cool pink. It's brilliant quality."

"Thirty pounds – less than a day's wages," Amber thought. She paid for it, and danced on, thinking about Marty, the long-legged lopey way he moved and how his grin had transformed his face. "He's bound to have a girlfriend," she thought, "he's so sweet. Anyway, it's not a good idea to get involved with someone you're working with." Then she laughed out loud on the street. It was fantastic just to be thinking that way. But the red phone booth at the end of the line of shops brought her up with a jolt. She looked at it, and the fizzing excitement from the job and Marty and the new top evaporated. She had to phone home – she'd promised. She put her hand in her pocket, and palmed the two pound coins she found there. She'd tell them the holiday was going well, then listen to their worries and complaints for two pounds' amount of time, and no more.

Chapter
Nine

"Hey – *Amber*!" said Rory, backing elegantly out of the fridge, "we were wondering what had happened to you!"

"You've been *hours*," said Chrissie, accusingly. "I'd've phoned you if you'd got a phone."

"Sorry," said Amber, putting her bags down on the kitchen table. "I've been—"

"You got lost, didn't you?" interrupted Rory. "Chrissie abandoned you, on your first day here, and naturally enough – due to her *criminal* negligence – you got lost?"

"Shut up, Rory," snapped Chrissie.

Amber smiled. Just to be in this kitchen again made her feel better. She'd had a dismal phone conversation with her mum and Poppy. They were gloomy and anxious, and Poppy had talked about how scared she was of starting at the sixth-form college and she'd snivelled without holding the phone away from her mouth. Amber had been filled with guilt and repulsion and confused, choking anger.

But now, those feelings were ebbing away. "I didn't get lost," she said, "I've been working. I got a job!"

"*Yeah?* Great!" said Rory.

"Where?" demanded Chrissie.

"The Albatross."

"Oh my God, that café down on the beach? I didn't think of trying *there*."

"Why not?" asked Amber, stung.

"Well – it'll be a bit dead in the winter, won't it? Did you ask in that new bar?"

"Yes," lied Amber. "No joy."

"I don't know The Albatross," said Rory.

"Yeah, you do," said Chrissie. "We went there a couple of months ago. Painted blue and orange, kind of scruffy –"

"Oh, *yeah* – great chips."

"And brilliant fish, straight off the boat. But it's not exactly a commercial enterprise – it's run by this old drop-out."

"Bert," said Amber. "My new boss. I really like him. Anyone want some coleslaw?"

Two hours later, Amber was wearing her new lilac top and sitting on a bench between Rory and a mate of his, Max, in one of the local pubs. Chrissie and her boyfriend Ellis were across the table from them, with another couple from the college they were all at. The conversation was loud and relaxed, and Amber was drinking icy white wine and trying to hide how excited she was just to be there.

Rory spent quite a bit of the time talking to Max across her, but she didn't care. She was joining in the general conversation and she liked him leaning in close to her. She kept giving his model-boy profile sideways glances. Girls would come in the pub and ogle him, assume she was with him and look at her enviously. Amber had never been envied before. Even though it was a mistake it felt good.

"So – your new job!" Rory said suddenly, as though he'd had a pang of conscience about ignoring her.

"Yeah?"

"Won't it get a bit boring? Just chopping and mixing and cooking and stuff?"

Amber smiled. "I don't think cooking's boring."

"Yeah, but doing it all *day*. . .?"

"Maybe. But I got so stressed out with my A levels, I quite fancy doing something . . . well, a bit more *practical* for a while."

"You ought to go travelling," said Max. "It's the best. India was just . . . mind-blowing."

"I want to," said Amber, and it suddenly seemed possible.

"I worked for six months," said Max, "saved as much as I could, and travelled for six months. Brilliant."

"You're not gonna save much here, are you?" said Rory. "Paying rent and everything."

"No. Maybe not."

"So why didn't you stay at home and save?"

"Rory – leave the girl alone!" cried Max, campily. "She has dark and awful secrets she doesn't want to share!"

"Oh, yeah," said Rory, "weren't you running away from some . . . some psychotic possessive boyfriend?"

They both laughed, and Amber, embarrassed and a bit overwhelmed, got to her feet, saying, "It's my round, yeah?" just as Kaz sailed up to their table and dumped a lovely, squashy, turquoise bag right down in the centre of it.

"Mama Kaz!" crooned Rory. "You got my text."

"Yep."

"And you *came*. Just in time for Amber's round."

"Amber, sit down," ordered Kaz. "You're not buying drinks on your second night here. *My* round. You get them, Max, you know what everyone's drinking." She rummaged in the squashy bag, drew out twenty pounds, and handed it to him. Obediently, he headed for the bar, and Kaz plonked herself down next to Rory. She leaned across him to Amber, and said, "That's a great top. That colour really suits you."

"Thank you!" said Amber.

"And it's great news about your job. Chrissie told me. They paying you OK?"

"Yeah, enough. And I think the tips will be good."

"What about the hours?"

"Eight till four."

"*Eight?*" squawked Rory. "That means you'll have to get up at seven! No one gets up at seven!"

"Yeah, they do, Rors," said Kaz. "You might even have to one day. But you'll be knackered by night time, Amber." She grabbed her bag from the table, pulled out a lipstick, and applied it without aid of a mirror. "I know! You're gonna have to have a siesta! Just for an hour or so, when you get back from work. Then you'll be racing for the evening. You gotta be on top form to come out with us!"

Amber smiled back at her. She loved her confidence, and her bossy generosity – the way she was folding her into the life of the house. "A siesta's not a bad idea," she said.

"It's a *great* idea," retorted Kaz. "Spanish people swear by it – it's like having two days instead of just one. Hey – we'll have to have a house outing to The Albatross soon, yeah, Rors? Taste Amber's cooking."

"God, Kaz, stop *organizing*," Rory groaned, then he slung his arm round her shoulders and squeezed.

"You should come," said Amber. "The people there – the clientele – they're great, honestly. Mostly locals, Bert said, and really interesting sorts."

"Amber – *local* and *interesting*, as applied to this place," said Rory, "is a contradiction in terms. You'll learn."

And they all laughed, together.

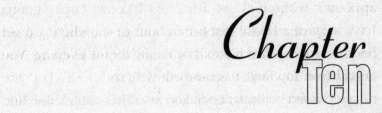

Chapter Ten

Amber slept deeply that night, partly due to the three glasses of wine she'd drunk. She was woken once, by the window frame rattling, but when she got out of bed to try and fix it, it suddenly stopped. She peered out at the dark garden; the trees were perfectly still. She told herself the wind had dropped, that was all, but it spooked her. She went back to bed and pulled the duvet up round her ears. When at last she fell asleep she didn't wake again until her little alarm clock went off at quarter to seven.

She showered and dressed simply in jeans and white T-shirt, and as she went downstairs, she turned to examine her reflection in the huge ornate mirror, swivelling to examine her side view, then her back. . . She'd never been thin, "big-boned" her mother called it, but she knew she had shape, and looked healthy. . . But her reflection in this mirror depressed her. As she twisted in front of it, for a moment she looked truly grotesque . . . awful. Then back to just not special enough. Not enough to draw Marty, anyway.

She left the house without breakfast, shutting the front door quietly behind her. No one had stirred in the house. On the fast, downhill walk to the beach, she cheered up; the sea air cleared her head and filled her lungs, nourishing her. She timed the walk so she'd know exactly when to leave the house tomorrow – it took just under thirty minutes.

When she got there, The Albatross was deserted, its door shut and windows shuttered. She turned her jacket collar up round her ears, and sat down on the boardwalk to wait. The sea looked more positive today, with the early sun sparkling on it. Gulls wheeled about, calling. She had nothing to do but wait and watch the waves coming in and going out. She made her mind clear, watching the waves.

It was eight fifteen before a little blue truck came bowling across the sand and came to a stop in front of her. "How long've you been here?" Bert shouted, from behind the wheel.

"Not long," Amber called back, although she'd been waiting for at least half an hour.

"Well, sorry, love. . ." He climbed out, and hefted a large box of courgettes, another of aubergines, and several trays of eggs from the back of the truck. Amber hurried over to help him. "Thing is, when I say eight o'clock to Marty, he takes it to mean eight thirty or so."

"It's OK, I was fine waiting," she said. "I could watch the sea for ever."

"Me too." Bert laughed. "Why d'you think I rent this café? Come on, let's get the coffee on."

Bert fried bacon and made fresh, creamy coffee that he was pouring out just as Marty arrived. "He smells it," Bert said. The three of them had barely finished eating their bacon rolls before the first customers arrived, and they were in business.

It was hard work, but the day had a good rhythm to it. As the breakfast rush dwindled, they started to prepare for lunch. Marty and Amber stood side by side chopping onions, courgettes, aubergines and tomatoes to make ratatouille to serve with baked cod. Amber kept sliding her eyes sideways, to look at him. He didn't talk much; he kept checking his mobile, and sending texts. He was vague when Amber asked him how long he'd worked at The Albatross, and how long he'd lived in Cornwall. When she asked when they got a lunch break, though, he laughed. "We don't. That is – there's no set time. Take a break when you can, and when it's not too busy just tell Bert you're going out for a breather, and go."

"Really? That's great."

"Yeah, it's the way the café runs. No rules, no timetables. Lunch is ready when it's ready – if you're too early for it, you get offered breakfast. It's kind of . . . organic, you know? It's why I like it here. You want another coffee?"

"Love one."

Marty loped over to put the kettle on the stove. "When

Bert says you get free food on the job, by the way, he means it. I eat breakfast, lunch and dinner here. I hardly ever buy food."

"But what about at home?"

"Well, I mainly live on the leftovers Bert gives me. And I've got a good trade going with that, with my house mates. Never underestimate what someone with the munchies will pay you for a slice of old apple pie."

Amber laughed. "Do you really *sell* it?"

"Well – only when I'm seriously skint. But it's a great trade-off, believe me. I get my room cleaned, I never wash up and I smoke all the weed I could want."

Amber was longing to ask him about the house he shared, but he suddenly pulled his mobile from his pocket again, so she didn't.

When Bert shut the door on the last customer, at ten to four, Amber was exhausted. It was a good kind of exhaustion, though, purely physical, not the anxious, strained exhaustion she used to feel at home. She knew the day had gone better with her help; no one had had to wait for their meal, and the kitchen had never once descended into the chaos of yesterday. She'd made the ratatouille her way, draining off the liquid and simmering it to intensify the flavour, then pouring it back, all thick and glossy. Bert had relayed several compliments about it to her.

He came into the kitchen now, beaming. "OK, kids, pay time!" he announced. "And Amber – welcome aboard. We served . . . oh, about twelve extra people, today, I reckon. Just by getting the grub out quicker. Which means, of course, more tips – just in case Marty's got a beef about sharing 'em."

Amber pocketed her money, and a cling-filmed ham sandwich that Bert insisted on making her even though she said she was still full from her late lunch, and left.

The steep, cobbled road ahead of her looked daunting. It was fine, she thought, bowling down in the early morning, but dragging up at the end of a long hard day was something else. But she set off determinedly, and as she climbed, her heart pumped, and the tiredness from the day started to evaporate, and she was suddenly filled with triumph. It was like the feeling she'd had when she'd first let herself into 17 Merral Road, but better, deeper, because this was based on her new life taking shape – her new life *lasting*. A sense of freedom was flowing into her, energizing and intoxicating her. The sweet fact that she was in charge of everything, absolutely everything in her life, was taking shape in her.

"I'm going to get properly fit," she thought. "For starters I'm going to walk up this hill every day – I'm not even going to find out about buses." At home, she'd tried to exercise but she could never keep to any kind of routine. Some drama or problem would happen to stop her going out, or Poppy would want to come along too and end up spoiling it . . . it was easier just to hide away in her room. And *food* – food had been a major source of suffering. Mum and Poppy had gone on and on about diets and being thin – the three of them had lived on a neurotic mixture of starvation salads and junk-food binges. Amber had always felt tired and somehow unwell.

But now, Amber told herself, now it was different. She could eat well and healthily at The Albatross (which would also save her serious amounts of money) and every day she could climb this hill, and maybe when she'd built up some stamina, she could think about swimming, or a dance class. . .

Time, so cramped and anxious before, spread out in front of her, full of possibilities. Even Marty was a possibility, for all his texting. At least to be a friend. And when she got back she'd see what her house mates were up to tonight and maybe go out with them. . . She quickened her pace again. The walk took her forty minutes; she was panting with a sense of real achievement as she turned into Merral Road.

An old woman was coming out of the woods at the end. She had on a long, shapeless bottle-green coat and a basket over her arm, and there was something about the witch-like way she came through the trees that made Amber uneasy. She quickened her pace, thinking she'd make it to her gate and inside before their paths crossed. But the old woman sped up too, and she was fast, despite her crooked appearance. She drew up in front of Amber just before number seventeen. "Hello, dear," she said. "You've just moved in here, haven't you?"

Chapter
Eleven

The old woman was gaunt and lined. She was smiling, but her eyes were narrowed, scanning Amber's face.

"Yes, that's right," said Amber stiffly. "I moved in a couple of days ago."

"How nice. A whole houseful of young people. They've been there for a year now, haven't they?"

"I think so, yes."

"It was empty, all boarded up, for a long time, you know, dear. They just couldn't seem to sell it. The Wilsons . . . they were here in the Fifties, then the Marshalls in the Seventies . . . none of them seemed to stay for long. . . Then someone bought it to rent out to students, and when that happened, I said to myself, maybe that'll do it, maybe. . ." She trailed off, then announced, "I live just up the road, at number eleven. I've lived here all my life."

Amber felt obliged to say, "Really?"

"Yes, dear. I never married. My father died when he was only sixty-three, and I kept my mother company, and then cared for her when she was elderly, and she left me the house. . ."

"You must have seen a lot of changes here."

"Not really, not on this road. The trees at the end have grown, of course, and some of the houses are flats now, but. . ." She suddenly took a step closer to Amber and hissed, "Do you like the house?"

Involuntarily, Amber stepped back, away from her. "Yes," she said, "it's OK."

"What room have you got? One on the top floor?"

"No – the attics aren't used –"

"Oh, I didn't mean the *attics*!" the old woman said, and giggled, weirdly. "I mean the floor underneath the attics?"

Amber looked down at the pavement, thinking, *She's going gaga*. Then said, "Yes, I'm on the top floor."

"Oh. Oh, I thought you would be."

"Well, I'd better get in – lots to do."

"Of course dear. Still settling in, aren't you. Would you like a blackberry?"

She thrust her basket at Amber, who glanced at the dark, oozing berries and wanted to say "no", but took one, and ate it, muttering "Thank you."

"Aren't they sweet? They've had all the summer to get sweet. I've just been gathering the last of them, at the back of the wood. There's a lovely sunny patch there. You should go there."

There was a pause, Amber shuffling her feet, then the

old woman said, "Well, I must let you get on. Why did the last girl leave, do you know?"

"What last girl?"

"The one before you?"

"I've no idea. Just found somewhere else, I guess. I've really got to go."

"Of course. Be *positive*, dear. Be *positive* and I'm sure it'll be all right. . ."

Nutter, thought Amber, as she smiled stiffly and said, "Bye!" Her neck prickled as she hurried up the path to the house. Without turning round, she knew the old woman was still standing there, watching her until she disappeared inside and shut the door behind her.

Amber went straight into the kitchen, hoping someone would be there, but no one was. She put the electric kettle on and pulled Bert's sandwich out of her bag. She had meant to eat it, then go upstairs and have a siesta, just like Kaz had suggested, but she felt far too wide awake. She didn't admit it to herself, but the gaunt old woman had really spooked her. She wanted to tell someone about it, have them laugh and say, "What, the old granny from number eleven? She's a bit of a pain but she's harmless." She wanted to find out why the girl before her had left, too.

She went out into the hall, and called, "Hello? Anyone there?" longing for Kaz's door to fly open and for Kaz to come out and join her in a cup of tea. But the house remained silent, the sort of silence that tells you no one's there but you.

Amber went back into the kitchen, drank her tea and ate the sandwich, then she headed upstairs. She opened the door to her bedroom, reluctantly. It still didn't feel like home. "This is ridiculous," she thought. "I'm not going to sleep." She put down her bag, and went out on to the landing again. Late afternoon sun was streaming through the skylight at the top of the attic stairs, lighting them invitingly. For a second, Amber thought she saw the long, thin dust shape again, then it vanished in the light.

She walked over to the stairs, and started to climb.

Chapter Twelve

At the top of the attic stairs Amber turned on to a narrow corridor, with three doors leading off it. The two nearest doors were open, and the third – the one to the room above her bedroom – was shut. She walked through the first door. The room was like a cosy little box, with its sloped ceiling and skylight and tiny iron fireplace, but it was almost entirely filled with junk. She stood among the broken chairs and carpet cut-offs and imagined what it would have been like to be a maid living here, back in 1887, when the house was built. "It must've been a bloody awful life," she thought, "up at dawn, to bed exhausted, very little time off. . . It'd make my eight till four shift look like a doddle."

She moved on to the next attic. Someone had dumped some lengths of wood inside, wedging the door open, and it too was jam-packed with junk, but this lot looked older and more interesting. There was a box of battered toys, some garden tools, several glass lamp shades and two Bakelite radios, all piled higgledy-piggledy on the floor. Amber thought she'd have a root round in here, and discover something to make her room more interesting. One of the lamp shades, for example . . . or that Eastern-looking rug. . .

But first, she'd check out the third room. She walked further along the thin corridor. The sun from the skylight at the top of the stairs didn't reach this far, and it was very dim. On the tobacco-coloured walls, she could just make out three pale rectangular shapes, where pictures had been taken down. She reached the third door and took hold of its handle, and as she turned it, her neck prickled, just as it had done when the weird old woman had stood watching her go up the path. "Stupid," she muttered, and pushed the door open. This was the largest room, and easily the best. The skylight was wider, the sloped ceiling less cramping. Junk was piled everywhere, of course, and this lot looked to be the oldest and most interesting yet. There were two old-fashioned telephones with dials, boxes of old plates and ornaments, piles of books, and pictures stacked against the walls. A mountain of faded carrier bags stuffed with old clothes nearly covered a brass bedstead on the far side of the room. There was an old oak rocking chair, too, and a chest of drawers, half hidden under yet more junk.

Amber was heading for the carrier bags on the bed when something happened.

Last winter, she'd made it to a friend's party without having Poppy in tow, and she'd set out to have a really good time. She'd drunk too much and, at the end when people had sat on the floor and joints had started circulating, she'd taken a few deep puffs. The joints had really had an effect. People were giggling, saying what strong stuff it was – Amber, feeling weird, had stumbled out into the garden for some fresh air and when she'd looked up at the trees, they'd changed into towering archangels. She shut her eyes and shook her head and they were trees again . . . then the archangels came back, tall, swaying, branch-arms, wings leaf-feathered, and it was as though the trees and the angels were both as real as one another, overlying one another, both somehow there at the same time. . .

It was like that now.

The light from the skylight had gone; it showed purple, as if a storm was outside. In the gloom the carrier bags on the bed faded, dwindled into shadows, but the bed stood out sharp and strong, with black rails and four shiny brass knobs. She shook her head and shut her eyes and when she looked again it was all back to normal . . . but then, as she stared, the clutter on the floor half-dissolved, showing bare boards and a skimpy rug . . . the chest of drawers was clear beneath the piles of things on top of it, and the rocking chair too, the *rocking chair*. . .

Amber slammed her hands over her eyes, breathed deeply. But she still heard the chair tipping back and forwards, rocking slowly on the wooden floor. A wretched feeling engulfed her, half fear, half misery, and she rubbed furiously at her eyes, made herself look again. The chair was still again, covered in clutter, its rockers jammed on to piles of books, any movement impossible. She stared at the bed – the carrier bags were back, solid and real, spilling clothes. But as she looked they seemed to falter, fade, and the bed shone out again . . . the stuff piled round the walls seemed to hover, shake, like a mirage, unreal. . . Amber stumbled backwards to the door. Then she fled down the corridor, down the narrow steps to the landing, and down the main stairs into the warm kitchen again.

Chapter Thirteen

Amber sat at the kitchen table with a second cup of tea, telling herself she was still all wound up with the stress of the last few days, she'd overdone it powering up the hill, she was tired and she'd just been seeing things. But thinking that her mind could play that kind of freakish trick didn't make her feel much better. Then the front door banged shut, and Ben came cheerfully into the kitchen and dumped a pile of folders and books on the table. "That's me done for the day," he announced. "Three hours in the library, a lecture *and* a seminar – what a hero! D'you know if anyone's cooking tonight?"

"No. I dunno," she mumbled.

"Hey – what's up?"

"Nothing. Just knackered."

"Works you hard, does he, your new boss? I'll make some more tea."

While Ben had his back to her, filling the kettle at the sink, she asked, "Who had my room before me?"

"Katie Robinson. Sociology student."

"Why did she leave?"

Ben shrugged, "Just wanted a change, I think." It seemed to Amber that his voice had changed, gone kind of closed off, but she couldn't be sure. "We didn't fall out or anything," he went on, "if that's what you're worried about. It's OK, this house. It's a great mix and we all get on OK."

He clattered about, making the tea, and when he bought two mugs over to the table and sat opposite her, all companionable, she blurted out, "Ben? D'you think old places can have a . . . I dunno, an *atmosphere* about them? Something you can pick up on?"

Ben stirred his tea and left too long a gap before asking, "What d'you mean?"

I can't tell him what I saw, Amber thought. *He'll think I'm a nutter*. And she mumbled, "Oh, you know. Old ruins and castles and stuff – having a feeling in them that's beyond just the creepy way they look . . . it was just something I was . . . reading."

"Well, as it happens, I do," said Ben, his face brightening. "Especially if something really nasty happened there. In Year Nine we went on a school trip to a castle, and we went into this dungeon that felt really sick, really hideous. Then we went round a corner and there were all these implements of torture on the walls. . ."

"*Urrrgh*. Horrible."

"It'd been where Roman Catholics had been interrogated, back in the sixteenth century. Over these

70

plots to put a Catholic on the throne, you know, like Guy Fawkes. . ."

"But you felt the atmosphere before you saw the torture stuff."

"Yes. That was the thing. We had this drama teacher with us and she was going on about how the walls had just *absorbed* all the evil that had gone on in the past, and was throwing it out again . . . she made us write about it when we got back."

"But no one actually . . . saw anything."

"What, like the ghost of someone on the rack? Er . . . *no*! But we got ourselves really spooked, it was great."

Then Ben changed the subject back to the tough day he'd had at college, and Amber drank her tea, and decided she was right not to say anything about her experience in the attic, or ask anything else about why Katie Robinson had left, or mention the weird old woman. "I don't want them thinking I'm more screwed up than they probably already do," she thought.

She went to bed early that night, claiming job-adjustment exhaustion, and as she lay there she remembered with a guilty jolt that she'd forgotten to phone home. She buried, groaning, under the duvet. Poppy and Mum would be anxious, resentful, asking her *how* she could forget them when they thought of her all the *time*. . . Slowly, the attic above her head filled her mind. She saw again the way the room seemed to break through the clutter and junk overlying it . . . as though how *it had been* was breaking through everything, all the time that had passed, all the changes that had happened since. . .

Crazy, crazy, she thought. *Don't go crazy*. She turned over in bed, desperate for sleep, but into her thoughts came the old woman's face, cross-hatched with lines, eyes narrowed as she stared at Amber's face, searching, searching. . .

Finally, Amber drowsed off, but it was a fitful, shallow sleep. She came to in a panic with a sense that someone was outside her door. "Kaz?" she called. "Kaz, is that you?" A car started up on the road outside and underneath the noise of it she thought she heard muttering, then the sound of a key turning in a lock. Heart pounding, telling herself it was nothing, she lay frozen for several long minutes, then she shot from her bed and went to her bedroom door. As she'd known it would be, the door was unlocked, its key on the inside, and the landing, when she peered outside, was empty. "You, girl," she told herself, "have got to get a grip. Stop *imagining* things."

Back in bed, she at last fell deep asleep, and dreamt one of her guilt-dreams. She had them often; they were all about running away from Poppy, leaving her abandoned somewhere she didn't know the way back from, and just running, running, deaf to her screaming . . . sometimes they were violent, desperate, where she pushed Poppy down steep stairs, or over a railing into space. . . They always ended the same, with her mother's sad, sweet face weeping. They always made her feel weak with guilt and confusion the next day.

*

Amber woke just before her alarm went off, got straight out of bed, showered, and ran downstairs. She knew she'd arrive at the café far too early but she was longing to get away from the house and down to the sea. She grabbed her coat, opened the front door – and jerked back, an ancient, animal part of her reacting in fear, almost before her brain registered that something had been left on the middle of the step.

She steadied her breathing. It looked ominous, left with intent to harm, to curse: a small, grey cardboard box, torn on one side, and something was seeping through it, staining the side and bottom dark black-red. . . *Who left it there?*

She took a step forward, made herself look into it.

And half-wanted to laugh out loud. She'd been imagining severed fingers, a liver, a dead mutilated rat . . . it was blackberries. Ripe, oozing blackberries, with their juice seeping through the cardboard. That weird old woman had offered her one the other day, hadn't she? They must be from her.

Anger surged in her at how scared she'd been. What was the old cow doing, leaving them on the step like that? She kicked the box under the overgrown bush beside the path.

Let them rot, she thought.

When Bert turned up at The Albatross, Amber pretended she'd only been waiting a few moments, although she'd been pacing the beach for over twenty minutes. Under the huge sky, in front of the sea endlessly flowing, she'd begun to feel better.

Breakfast at the café was very busy, then there was a lull before lunch time when Amber and Marty stood side by side, peeling and chopping vegetables for soup. Amber shut down on everything but the vegetables in front of her, and Marty beside her. She told herself she'd phone home that night, then banished it from her mind along with the weird old woman, her freak-out in the attic, and the eerie night she'd spent. Marty seemed different today, happier, more open; he was joking and laughing with her, and his mobile stayed in his pocket. They worked well together, sharing the chores and the kitchen space. She knew she was starting to really like him. It lifted her spirits just to be with him; as he ranged about the kitchen, all relaxed and easy, she couldn't keep her eyes off him.

Around three o'clock, Bert butted his way into the kitchen, looked around at the general tidiness, and said, "How did we manage without you, Amber? Now get out into the café, will you? Work your miracles there."

Warmed by the compliment, she went, and cleared up, enjoying being out in the big, bright room, with its windows and pictures. People chatted with her, ordering extra cups of tea or egg on toast; one old man she recognized from the day before left her a huge tip and told her not to share it with Marty. When Bert started pulling the shutters over and asking the last few customers if they didn't have homes to go to, it almost felt too early.

*

As she'd resolved to, Amber marched as fast as she could up the steep hill but she felt a drag on her feet as she got near the top that had nothing to do with tiredness. She was dreading meeting the old woman again, hearing something weird that might wriggle into her mind, and she was dreading the house being empty. But to her relief, Merral Road was empty and, inside number seventeen, the kitchen was full to bursting. Kaz and Ben were sitting at the table, with two of Ben's mates and a girl called Rachel who had long auburn hair and a wonderful, loud laugh. Amber got drawn in as they all loudly discussed a band they wanted to see the week after next in a nearby town.

"The tickets are *exorbitant*," said Kaz. "At least twenty quid, maybe twenty-five."

"I know, but me, Alec and Sam are definitely going," said Ben. "I'll get the tickets – maybe I'll get a group discount too if people could stop pissing around and decide if they're up for it or not."

"I'd like to come," said Amber. "They sound great."

"Fantastic! Kaz?"

"Not sure."

"Rachel?"

"Yeah, put me down. I'll get the money even if I eat nothing but bread and chips for a week."

"Good for you. That's all I eat anyway. No one seems to cook here any more."

"Oh, for God's sake, Ben!" said Kaz. "Untrue! Just 'cos you cooked last – I did it *twice* before that!"

"I'll do a meal," Amber heard herself announcing. "When's a good night?"

Kaz turned to smile at her. "You're cooking all day at the café," she said, "you don't want to have to do more in the evening!"

"It's fine, honestly. Maybe I can get stuff from the café. Leftovers and stuff."

"Amber," said Ben, "that would be great. And any night's good – just let us know, OK?"

"Anyone know if Rory's going to the concert?" asked Kaz. "Maybe I'll text him."

Amber slipped up to her room, got out her notepad and calculator and curled up on the bed. All very well agreeing to go to the concert, she thought, all very well buying lovely lilac tops, but it was time to do her maths and find out just how much of everything she could afford each week. She worked out she was earning two hundred and forty pounds a week – and tips came to at least twenty-five pounds more. On the minus side, rent was sixty-two pounds a week, and bills and the basics kitty, Kaz had said, was around a tenner on top of that. She punched in the numbers. That left her a hundred and ninety-three pounds. If she continued to feed herself almost totally from the café she'd have one hundred and ninety-three pounds a week for everything else.

She smiled. That was *loads*. For clothes, the concert, a mobile, going to the pub – it was loads. She might even start to save some, for travel later.

"I'm independent," she thought. "However small time,

I'm doing it for myself, and I'm *fine*." It felt terrific. She ran back downstairs to the kitchen again. Two more people had turned up at the house, one of them a good-looking Asian boy. "Marty's not the only fish in the sea," Amber thought, and she was filled again with a gleeful sense of life opening out in front of her, and she suddenly felt really good, more than able to hold her own with all the people there. One of Ben's mates was gathering a kitty together to go out for some beer and chips, and she gave him five pounds. Rory came in soon after, and flirted with Kaz, and the nine of them had a great evening together in the loud, warm, crowded kitchen.

It was eleven thirty before Amber remembered she'd forgotten to phone home again.

Chapter Fourteen

The next day, Amber waited for the breakfast rush to die down, then told Bert she had to go out for half an hour or so. He smiled at her over the pile of squid tentacles he was chopping and said, "No problem." She dashed along the seafront to the phone booth that stood next to the toilets. Her heart hammered as she punched in her home number, dreading what was waiting for her.

Mrs Thornley was full of hysterical relief when she heard her daughter's voice. She wailed at Amber that she'd phoned the local Cornish police late last night to ask them to call at 17 Merral Road and check she was still alive. "They were awful to me," she said, in a strangled voice, "just awful ... they *laughed* – told me two nights' silence was nothing for a young girl on holiday ... think how that made me *feel*, when they laughed!"

"I'm sorry, Mum. I meant to phone, it just got so late I . . ."

"I felt sure something awful had happened because

Poppy started college on Wednesday. We were so sure you were going to phone to wish her luck. . ."

"I was, I'm sorry. . ."

"Poppy was so brave, she went, even though she was sick with worry about you. . . She had a dreadful time, though . . . the people there sound *awful* –"

"They're not, Mum – they were OK when I was there."

"– and she didn't make it back today . . . she hasn't even got out of bed, poor thing, she's really low. . ."

"Oh, I'm sorry. . ."

When at last Amber was able to ring off, after she'd promised to phone again tomorrow, she felt she'd said sorry so many times that the word had lost all meaning.

And then it was Saturday night, and the start of Amber's first two days off work. She was nervous of the unfilled time that lay ahead of her, and – although she hardly liked to admit it to herself – nervous about being in the house on her own.

About ten of them went out together to the new club Rory had discovered, and Amber drank a lot and danced and fell into bed exhausted and happy. On Sunday everyone at the house was nursing a hangover, and ended up going out for a sprawling pub lunch with some other friends. Then they lazed about in Kaz's room, talking, Kaz and Ben claiming they were working, until it got dark, and Ben lit a smoky fire in the grate. She slept well that night, barely disturbed by dreams.

But then Monday arrived. Amber told herself she

deserved a lie-in but she found herself lying in bed wide awake listening as, one after the other, everyone left to go to college. When the front door slammed for the fourth time, the house seemed to close in on her, vacant and threatening. Then she jumped in fear as the window suddenly rattled. "I'm being ridiculous," she told herself. "I'm going to beat this." She leapt out of bed, and jammed another folded-over square of paper into the window frame, fixing it tight. Then she showered and dressed, marched down to the kitchen with her laundry, and crammed it in the machine. She ate some cereal, stomped up to her bedroom again, and set about rearranging the furniture, dragging her bed from its central position to under the window, and shifting the chest of drawers with its old mirror unit on top to stand next to the wardrobe on the opposite wall. Now the room looked far bigger, and she was on a roll, driven by determination to make the room hers. She flew out on to the landing, and took the narrow attic stairs at a run. In the middle attic she crashed about, dragging the Eastern-looking rug she'd spotted out from under a pile of junk. She also noisily salvaged an amber glass lamp shade, a huge white vase, and a Bakelite radio. "I'll be back," she said, into the dusty air. "Soon as I've got all this arranged in my room, I'm turning over the end attic!"

The exotic rug covered her dingy carpet perfectly, and fitted well with the palm leaves on the curtains. Her hundred-watt light bulb was transformed by the mellow glass shade; the vase looked striking standing in the corner, just needing some tall grasses to stand inside. But the best thing of all was that, placed on her chest of drawers and plugged in, the radio not only worked, but gave out a really good sound. As Amber tuned it to the sharpest-sounding local radio station she could find, she realized that it was picking up sound waves created three quarters of a century after it had been made.

She looked around herself in satisfaction. The room was so much better now. There was still something about it that wasn't quite right, but she couldn't put her finger on it . . . maybe she just needed to live there for a bit longer. She shrugged, and went down to the kitchen to make coffee. The washing cycle was finished; the sun was out. She hung her washing out in the garden, made two cheese sandwiches, and left the house to head for the seashore.

Chapter Fifteen

Amber nestled further into the warm, shielding tussocks of long grass, and looked out at the cold, crashing sea. She'd climbed right to the top of the cliff at the far side of the bay, the sun was still out, but the wind had got up. She pulled the packet of sandwiches out of her pocket, and the carton of apple juice she'd bought on the way through town, and realized she felt perfectly happy.

It's just – simple, isn't it? she thought. It's simple to look after yourself, and it's simple to be happy. Just here, in the warm grass, sheltering from the cold wind, looking at the sea, biting into this good brown bread and cheese. Mum would buy hopeless books about how to fix your life and sort yourself out and they'd end up making her more anxious and miserable than before because she couldn't follow their advice because basically she was incapable of just . . . keeping it simple.

Forget the grand master plan, the solution that will solve everything, the "one day we'll be happy" . . . because it was now. It was now.

She stared out at the horizon, heart thumping, and knew she could never go back home, back to living all cramped and fearful. And yet the thought of a complete break from her family terrified her. How could she manage, on her own?

Leave it, shelve it, she thought. Don't think about it now.

It wasn't until she was back at the house putting her key into the door, with a fistful of stunning grasses that she'd picked at the cliff base for her new vase, that she remembered she hadn't got round to ransacking the end attic. But there was noise and laughter coming from the kitchen – it was too late now.

Over the next week, Amber got into the habit of going to the phone box on the beach at the end of the day's work. She'd shut herself inside, breathe hard for a few minutes to psyche herself up, then phone home. The regularity of this seemed to set it apart, so that she could forget about home for the rest of the time. As soon as she left the phone box she'd power up the hill, sloughing off the claustrophobia of the call. She was walking faster and faster; she could feel herself growing fitter. Something stopped her examining herself in the huge, ornate mirror at the top of the stairs, but if she balanced on the edge of the bath she could see almost all of herself in the mirror above the sink, see that her waist, legs and arms were slimming down and toning up.

In the mornings, she got down to the beach early so she could walk along the seashore, too. She felt she'd never had such energy before. It surged through her, a high-octane pulse of physical drive and enjoyment. At the café, she was a whirlwind; Marty kept telling her to slow down, and stop making him look bad. She threw herself into the life of the house, joining in on anything and everything. She saw the old woman a couple more times, on Merral Road, but just waved and hurried on. And at night she slept like a log; no dreams now, no waking to the window rattling.

Ben got her a little silver-blue mobile, cheap – one of his mates was ditching it for an upgrade. She loved it from the start, and put all her house mates' numbers in, and life took another leap onward as she got texts telling her to meet them at the pub or asking her if she fancied a film or a club that night. She put Marty's number in, too. He still had an erratic relationship with his mobile; texting non-stop, then turning it off. When it was off he spoke to her more; they got on really well when it was off. There was an exciting kind of tension between them, a waiting to move on.

She still used the phone box on the beach to call home, though, partly so the pips could limit their talk, but mostly because it would ruin everything if Poppy and Mum found out she had a mobile and could contact her any time. Her freedom would be gone.

She opened a bank account so she could manage her money and make sure she paid in at least what she needed for rent and bills each week. She had her nondescript hair cut, a wonderful layered style that lifted her whole face. Kaz, admiring it, offered to shape her eyebrows for her and this was such a success that she went on to put heavy bronze shadow on her eyes, both of them in fits of laughter at the Cleopatra effect she produced. After that, Amber bought tweezers and mascara, an eye pencil and a bright gloss lipstick. She bought another new top, and a silky sea-green skirt from a charity shop that she wore with a belt borrowed from Kaz.

When Bert asked Marty what Amber had done to herself, she was looking so much better, he agreed, but couldn't put his finger on anything. "Maybe she just likes working here," said Bert, "it's that's what's done it," and they laughed, and said how great it was to have her on the staff.

Amber was doing what she wanted. She was having fun, throwing herself into life. And being so busy stopped her remembering that the end of her fake holiday was drawing closer all the time and she still hadn't broken the news to Mum and Poppy that she wasn't coming home. She thought she was like a cartoon she used to watch when she was little, the one where Wily Coyote ran off the cliff and just kept running on air, until he looked down, and then he fell.

"I can't wait for you to come back, darling," Mum kept saying. "I'm counting the hours." Poppy was having a dreadful time at college. She'd only actually managed two full days there, so far, and she was depressed and weepy the whole time, longing for Amber to come home too.

It was OK if you just kept running. It was OK if you didn't look down.

Towards the end of Amber's second week in Cornwall, Bert brought a great box of sea trout that had been a "proper bargain" into the café. He showed Amber how to gut them, then, between them, they worked out the perfect stuffing of rice, orange flesh, pine nuts and coriander. Business was good and the baked trout was very popular, but there were still quite a few fish left at the end of the day. "I knew I wouldn't get through all of them," said Bert. "I'll take two – for me and the cat tonight – the rest I'll dump on the shore for the gulls."

"Can I have them?" asked Amber.

"Sure. Marty – you want some?"

"What – raw fish?" Marty grimaced. "No ta."

"There you go, Amber. All yours."

"Really?" said Amber. "That's terrific." She headed for the box of fish, started counting. "There's . . . nine left, after you've taken your two. Brilliant. Can I take that leftover stuffing too?"

"Go ahead." Bert shrugged. "What you up to? Dinner party?"

"Sort of. I'm going to cook a house meal. I've been promising to for ages."

"Well, they're lucky bastards, getting that," said Marty. "It's ace, that stuffing you did." Amber turned half away then blurted out, "You can come if you want. There'll be loads."

"Really?"

"Sure. Come round. Eight-ish."

Marty smiled at her. "I'd like to. Thanks." There was a pause, while Amber held her breath waiting for him to say "Can I bring my girlfriend?" He'd spent another day texting furiously.

But he didn't. He just said, "Want me to bring some plonk?"

"No!" Amber laughed, "not plonk, something good!" She gave him the address.

Amber extravagantly took a cab back that night, carrying the fish and stuffing and an extra bag of rice and onions she'd scrounged, with some French beans and red peppers that she'd told Bert were on their way out. He'd disagreed about the peppers but let her take them anyway.

She'd texted her house mates and got grateful acceptances from everyone except Ben, who was playing footie and going straight on to the pub after. He did however wonder if a portion could be heated up in the microwave when he got back. Chrissie's boyfriend Ellis was coming too, and when Rory asked if his mate Max could come if he brought serious quantities of alcohol Amber said yes. Kaz said she'd be back in time to clear the table in her room, and bring in extra chairs. It was turning into quite a party.

Keep running. Don't look down.

Back in the kitchen of 17 Merral Road, Amber worked

flat out. She had no worries about being in the house on her own now; she was too busy working out how to fit all nine fish into the odd assortment of lasagne dishes and baking trays the kitchen cupboards offered up, and then how to fit all these into the little oven. There wasn't quite enough of the wonderful stuffing to go round, but the large pot of rice mixed with peppers and onions she planned to make would compensate for this. This was going to be a spectacular meal – a party thrown by her, Amber, to celebrate the end of her fake holiday – to mark the night she *really* joined the house.

Everything was ready. The baking fish were beginning to fill the kitchen with a savoury smell; there was at least half an hour before she had to put the rice on. Amber took in a deep breath, ran out from the kitchen, and left the house, slamming the front door behind her.

Chapter Sixteen

"Mum?"

"Amber! Oh, darling, I was beginning to wonder if you'd forgotten us again! It's so late. . ."

"It's not even seven yet."

"No, but you usually phone before five, don't you? And I so wanted to talk to you tonight."

"Well, here I am."

"Yes, and you'll be home soon, won't you? Only two days to go, thank God!"

In the sour-smelling phone booth halfway down the hill, Amber grimaced. "It's a *holiday*, Mum. Why would I wish it away?"

"Oh, you know what I mean. We miss you!"

"Well, Mum . . . actually . . . that's why I'm phoning."

"When you arrive, get a taxi from the station, Amber. I'll pay."

"Mum—"

"Poppy's going to do you a special meal – she's been

talking about it. I was so pleased when she suggested it, she's been so depressed recently she—"

"*Mum!*"

"Amber? What is it?"

"I'm trying to tell you something! I . . . I've been asked to stay on longer!"

"Oh, no! For how long? Do you *want* to?"

"I. . ." It was so hard to say yes, so hard to say she wanted anything other than to be at home, with them.

"It's very awkward," Mrs Thornley went on. "What about your ticket – you won't be able to change it, will you?" Her voice was resentful, tight. "How many more days do they want you for?"

Don't bottle it, Amber railed at herself. She felt faint, leaning up against the cold metal wall of the phone booth, faint and hollow. "It's not a few days. . ." she croaked.

"But you've got university to prepare for!" Her mother's voice was rising with anxiety. "You'll be cutting it fine, if you stay down there much longer. . ."

"Mum, I've been doing a lot of thinking, while I've been in Cornwall. I really do want to have a gap year, Mum."

"Oh, Amber, we've been through all this! Just the thought of you trekking off to some strange country makes me *ill*, it—"

"I wouldn't be going off. I'd be here, down here. I've been offered a job here. And somewhere to live. I really like the people here."

90

"What? I don't understand. I don't understand what you're telling me."

"I'm saying. . ." Amber took in a deep breath. "I want to stay on here, Mum. Have a gap year, here."

"But it's too late to defer entry, surely." Her mother's voice was suddenly icy. It meant she was hurt, so hurt she'd shut off inside herself where she couldn't be reached. When she was a little girl, Amber would have done anything, said anything, to thaw the ice out of that voice, to reach her again.

"No, it's not too late. I've contacted the admissions people, at uni. It's . . . it's easily done."

"I see. So you've already done it."

"Yes. I've done it. And I've started the job. I'm staying on, Mum."

There was a howling silence down the phone. Amber felt as if she'd stopped running at last, and looked down, and now like Wily Coyote she was falling, falling. . .

"So you're doing this . . . you've made this decision . . . without talking it over with us?" said Mrs Thornley, at last. "I can't believe this, Amber."

Amber, eight years old again, forced out the words. "Look – I knew what you'd say. I knew you wouldn't want me to."

"You *know* how Poppy's been, at college. She *hates* it there! She doesn't like any of the other students, and she misses you so much. . ." There was a pause. Amber could tell her mum was fighting not to cry. "You're just *abandoning* us," she sobbed, "you don't care about anyone but yourself. . ."

"Mum – it's *my life!*"

There was a click. Amber's mother had put the phone down.

She walked out of the phone booth feeling more alone than she'd ever felt in her life. She was sick with fear, sick with needing to go back, phone her mother again, put things right. But there was exhilaration pulsing there, too, a wild excitement. She let the phone booth door glide shut behind her, and headed back to the house.

Chapter Seventeen

"Hey, Amber! That smells wonderful!" Kaz, in the process of putting a bottle of white wine in the tiny overcrowded fridge, straightened up again. "You all right? You look a bit odd."

"Oh – just had a row. On the phone, with my mum."

"Oh, *that.*" Kaz looked dismissive and understanding, both at the same time. She waved the bottle of wine at Amber. "Want to open this now? It's cold enough."

"I'd love to."

Kaz pulled two glasses out of a cupboard, and started searching for the corkscrew in the cutlery drawer. "What was it about, this row?"

"Oh . . . Mum wants me to come home."

"Don't you dare!"

"Don't worry, I love it here!" Amber blurted out, and they smiled at each other, almost shy, then Kaz started rummaging in the drawer again.

"So," she said, "why does your mum want you to come home?"

"My sister . . . well, half-sister . . . she's having a tough time at college, and Mum thinks I can help. . ." Amber felt like she was trying to translate what had happened into a foreign language, a language Kaz could understand. It all sounded so normal, so not a big deal, the way she was talking about it now.

"Bloody parents," Kaz groaned, uncorking the bottle at last. "I've got two little brothers, and the parents are always on at me to have them for the weekend or whatever so they can have a bit of freedom before they get past it. Here." She handed Amber a large glass of wine. "My advice is, do the minimum you can get away with without causing outright war. I mean – why should we prop up *their* lives?" She clinked her glass against Amber's, as though to put a seal on their agreement.

Amber took a sip, longing to keep talking, longing to unburden herself to Kaz. It would be like rolling a great weight off her back, a great secret weight, to talk about where she'd come from, who she *was*. But past experience had taught her to be careful. Before she'd had to pull out of the Seychelles holiday because of Poppy, she'd excitedly told her new friends that it was just about the first real holiday she'd ever had. When they'd asked, incredulous, *why,* she'd explained a bit about her mum and Poppy, how anxious they got, how difficult things could be. "So they're anxious," Mel had said, dismissively. "Why does that stop you going away, on your own?"

"It's not that easy," Amber had muttered. "Poppy gets so upset –"

"Oh, *Poppy*," Ruth had snapped, "Jesus, if that was my sister, ruining everything all the time, I'd wring her neck."

Amber had fallen silent. Her mother and sister's anxiety, their fear, was infectious, and their endless *need* sapped your strength. She lived marinated in this, day after day – it was impossible not to be brought down by it.

Made like them.

But she couldn't explain that to her friends.

"You OK?" demanded Kaz, and just then the door crashed open, and Rory and Max came loudly and glamorously into the kitchen, with two more bottles of wine and a six-pack of beer.

"You *alkies*!" said Rory. "Look – they've started in on the booze already!"

"This," said Kaz, "is called the cook's perks. Now get out of here and leave Amber to it. You can come and help me clear off my table, OK?"

They left the room and Amber focused everything in her on cooking. She put the rice on to boil, fried the onions and peppers, and basted the fish, which was beginning to flake tenderly from its bones. At eight o'clock on the dot, Marty arrived, ushered jovially into the kitchen by Kaz. He seemed completely at ease in the strange house, with people he'd never met before. He set to work as if he was in the café, draining the beans, carrying plates and dishes through to Kaz's room, tasting the fish and telling Amber she was brilliant.

The dinner was a triumph. The stuffed fish was perfect,

and everybody made a big deal about how great it was to have a real cook in the house. Kaz, as usual, presided; Rory and Max were loud and funny; Marty fitted in fine. But as the meal drew to an end, Amber looked at everyone through the wavering candlelight, and tried and failed to feel good. She couldn't finish the food that was on her plate. Inside her head, her mother's words replayed; she kept hearing the final click of the phone going down. Her throat was tight and dry, her head felt as though it was floating. "I'm getting ill," she thought, "don't let me get ill." She got up from the table, and went back to the kitchen to fetch a glass of water.

Standing over the sink, she couldn't move. Even lifting the glass to her mouth seemed too much to do. She stared at her face in the black window, and it stared back at her, gaunt and bleak.

And then an arm came round her shoulders, tentative, and warm, and Marty said, "Amber? What's up?"

Chapter
Eighteen

"Aren't you feeling well?" asked Marty.

"No," whispered Amber.

"Too much to drink, eh? Have this water."

Amber took a sip, and croaked, "My throat's all sore."

"Getting a cold?"

"Maybe."

Marty dropped his arm from her shoulder, but stayed standing close. Then Amber blurted out, "I've done something awful."

"Blimey," said Marty, "what've you done?"

Amber felt that inner check again, the check that had stopped her unburdening herself to Kaz. But this time her need to talk was so strong that she took in a breath and said, "I've run out on my mum, and my little sister, and they need me."

"They *need* you – what for?"

"Just – you know – support. My little sister . . . well, she's my half-sister, really – she's . . . she's had a really tough time."

"In what way?"

"Her dad – Tony – he left when she was six, and there were all these problems, Mum and him fighting over custody and access rights . . . it was a horrible time, dreadful. It affected her." Side by side with Marty, talking at her face in the window, the words flowed out of her. "She never seemed to settle at playgroup, or school – she couldn't make friends . . . she's so *anxious,* you see – over-sensitive. She needs me."

"She's still got you. You're in touch, aren't you?"

"Yes, but it's not the same as being there."

"How old is she?"

"Sixteen."

"*Sixteen?* Jesus, Amber, the way you were talking – I thought she was about ten or something! If she's sixteen it's about time she started getting over it all, getting a life on her own, isn't it?"

"She tries to – but she can't. The last school she went to was awful. She got bullied – she had loads of time off. She managed to get five GCSEs and she's gone to the local sixth-form college but that's not working out, she hates it. Mum was on the phone to me last night, *and* the night before, telling me how awful it was, and tonight I . . . *tonight* I. . ."

Marty's arm, warm and kind, came round her shoulders again. "Hey, it's all right," he said. "It's all right."

Amber was crying. She tried to force it back, choke it back into her throat, but she couldn't stop them, the tears came. It felt so good just to let them come. "Oh, I'm sorry," she gasped. "God, I'm sorry!"

"It's OK. Blub away. Here – have my snot-rag. It was clean last week." He handed her a red spotted handkerchief, and she blew her nose. Then he asked, "OK, what did you do tonight?"

"I told them I was staying on here. I told them I was taking a gap year, and staying on here, to work. They thought I was just down for a holiday."

There was a long silence. Then Marty said, "You never planned it as a holiday, did you? I mean – moving into a student house and everything."

"No. I just said that to Mum, so I could get away. But right from the start, I meant to stay." It was the first time she'd told anyone the truth; it felt reckless, freeing. "Don't tell the others, will you?" she muttered. "Kaz and everyone? I don't want them thinking I'm a weirdo. I mean – what's the big deal? Coming down to Cornwall to work for a bit – why should you have to lie about it?"

"I won't tell them, of course I won't. But you shouldn't worry – loads of people have mad families they lie to. My dad drinks, and I lie to him that I care about what happens to him."

Amber sort-of laughed, then she blurted out, "I just feel so *guilty*. I thought I could do it, but I can't . . . . I'm going to have to go back. I'm going to *have* to."

"Have you talked to your mum about it? Maybe she wouldn't want you to go back."

"*What?*" His words made no sense to Amber. "Of course she would. It's so much easier when I'm there."

"Yeah, but if your sister's too dependent on you, maybe the last thing your mum wants is for you to go back just as she's learning to manage on her own. . ."

"I don't think she thinks like that," Amber muttered, and at last she turned away from the black window, and faced him. "D'you want a coffee?" she said. "I'm so sorry I've . . . *collapsed* on you like this. . ."

"Shut up. S'OK. I'll put the kettle on."

As he filled the kettle, and she got the mugs out, he said, "Tell me about your dad."

"What?"

"Your *dad*. You did have a dad, didn't you?"

"Yes – course I did. But I don't remember him. They split up before I was born, and Mum always got so upset when I asked about him, I just gave up in the end."

"Weren't you curious? To find him?"

"Not really. I couldn't do that to Mum. She must hate him – she's never even shown me a photo."

They made the coffee and then leant side by side against the counter with their mugs, because all the kitchen chairs had been carried through into Kaz's room. "So let me get this straight," Marty said. "There's Poppy, six years old, going through a horrible time 'cos her dad and mum are splitting up. And what's Amber – eight years old?"

"Yes."

"What's she doing while this is going on?"

100

"What d'you mean?"

"Well – did Tony treat you like his kid?"

Amber shrugged. "I don't remember. I *think* so. I liked him – he was fun, it was awful when he left. . ."

"So it upset you, too . . . and the rows and fuss . . . it must all have upset you?"

"I don't remember. I just remember Poppy. Wailing, and screaming – it was awful. We'd do anything to get her to stop. And I remember Mum saying – 'You're the strong one, Amber. You're so lucky.'"

Marty scuffed at the worn flooring in front of him. "Doesn't sound like you were very lucky to me," he said.

Chapter
Nineteen

Kaz and Rory came laughing through the kitchen door, carrying piles of dirty plates and making jokes about what Marty and Amber were getting up to all on their own out here.

"What a great meal that was!" Kaz beamed. "Brilliant food! What do we owe you, Amber?"

"Nothing. Honestly. It was all leftovers from the café."

"Well, that's brilliant. I felt we were dropping off a bit, with house meals, and your gorgeous fish really ... I dunno ... it's *inspired* me!"

"Oh, *God*," Rory mock-groaned.

"Shut up, Rors! It's about time you bloody made a meal! Anyway – I'll cook next. I'll cook *soon*."

"Not sodding chicken casserole again."

"You love my chicken casserole!" Kaz purred, into his face. He grinned, eyes downcast, and turned away.

Amber watched them, sad for Kaz. She knew what Kaz was up to, planning another meal so soon – she was homing in on Rory. She was obsessed by him – anyone could see that. And he knew this and played along with it, he exploited it. It was just in his nature to use the fact that Kaz loved him, like he would any resource.

And Poppy, she thought, *is the way she behaves just in her nature?*

Ben came back from the pub, demanding his meal to microwave, and Max came into the kitchen carrying empty bottles, and in all the noise Marty turned to Amber and said he'd better be off.

She saw him to the door, and it was almost as though nothing had passed between them, they were back to being practical workmates again. He thanked her once more, told her he'd see her tomorrow, and went, pulling the front door shut behind him.

Amber stood in the dark hall, feeling tired and empty. Her throat was throbbing with pain; she couldn't face going back into the noisy crowded kitchen. "They'll understand," she told herself. "They won't expect me to clear up, if I cooked." She turned to the wide stairs, and started climbing.

The steps seemed much steeper than they normally did, and the glass of the great ornate mirror at the top was blank and black, reflecting nothing. She only saw herself when she was right in front of it, and then she looked wispy, vague, half there. Her head was swimming, drowning. The landing was pitch black; her eyes couldn't focus; the darkness seemed to curdle, thicken, and as she peered a gleam of moonlight on the attic stairs was blotted out. "Don't get ill," she whimpered, as she stumbled into the bathroom. "*Please* don't get ill. Not now."

She washed her face quickly and brushed her teeth. She didn't dare open her mouth wide in front of the mirror and look at her throat; she was terrified of seeing the ominous white patches that meant she had tonsillitis starting. Ever since she was a child she'd gone down with tonsillitis, once or twice a year. Her mother hadn't taken her to the doctor – she said doctors didn't know anything. She'd given her TCP to gargle with, and let her have days and days off school. . . "Mind over matter," she thought, searching for the bottle of TCP she'd brought with her. She diluted some in a mug, and gargled with it determinedly.

As she took hold of the door handle of the bathroom, a thin shape passed behind the frosted glass, and she waited because she didn't want to bump into Chrissie. It could only be Chrissie, being that thin. All she wanted was to get to bed and sleep away the illness that was circling her, trying to find its way in.

The darkness of the landing crowded in on her as she crossed it.

As Amber lay in bed, the enormity of what she'd done overwhelmed her. She kept hearing her mother sobbing that she was abandoning them, hearing again and again the click as she put the phone down. Fear and loneliness lapped at her, and she remembered the good times they'd had at home, times that would never come again, like when she was ill and they'd look after her, just the three of them safe in the flat. . .

She fell asleep, but strange dreams haunted her. Half asleep, she thought she heard someone talking, saying *your fault, your fault*. She was woken twice by the window frame rattling by her head. The extra bit of paper hadn't fixed it at all. Then, just before dawn, she jerked awake in panic, feeling she was suffocating, as if something was pressing on her, pressing down. Her throat was tight and aching. She got up and went into the bathroom, gargled with more TCP, and took a drink of water back to bed with her. She lay there unable to get back to sleep, listening to the birds starting to sing in the trees outside, watching the light grow on her bedroom walls, going over and over the conversation in the phone booth, telling herself she wasn't going to get ill.

Chapter Twenty

"Hello, young lady," said Bert. "Let's put the coffee on."

"I'll do it," croaked Amber. She'd dosed herself on paracetamol to get here, and her throat felt like sandpaper.

"I'm tossing up between a mushroom-and-cream or tomato-and-pepper pasta bake today, with chicken . . . or maybe we could do both?"

As Bert rambled on, Amber watched the door, longing for Marty to arrive. If she could only talk to him, talk like they'd talked last night, she might get the strength to stay on here, to phone her mother back and be firm. . .

The door crashed open. Marty walked in, face set and angry. He nodded hello, poured out a large mug of coffee, and went over to sit alone by the café kitchen window, mobile already palmed in his hand. "God, I wish he'd get it over with and dump her," Bert muttered.

"Her?" Amber muttered back, and her heart thudded.

"Well, I'm assuming that's who he's texting. The girl he was with all summer."

"So . . . she's not here now?"

Bert shrugged. "Gone back to college. He keeps trying to get her to come down at the weekends . . . she says yes one minute, no the next."

Amber swallowed, then said, "What's she like?" and tried to ignore the sideways smile Bert gave her.

"Pretty enough, but a bit of a cow," he grunted. "Putting him through the wringer, anyway."

Amber clamped down on her disappointment. Deep down, she'd known it had to be a girl Marty was texting in such an extreme way – she'd just hoped that maybe it was her hassling him and not the other way round. . .

"Women, eh?" Bert was saying. "Present company excepted of course. Now – you want to start getting the breakfast stuff out? I'm thinking scrambled eggs, for a change. . ."

Amber lost herself in hard work that day. She drove herself on, ignoring her sore throat, so that she wasn't sure if it had got better or if she'd just got used to it. Marty hardly spoke to her. The café was extra busy and they worked side by side in silence, neither of them taking a break. Bert couldn't shut up till nearly five, and he was delighted by the takings. He gave them each a ten-pound bonus as well as the tips.

On the way out, Marty seemed to focus on her for the first time. "You OK?" he asked.

"Yes," she said, all closed off from him. "I'm fine."

She'd been wrong, she thought, to tell him all that stuff last night.

"Called your mum back yet?" he asked.

"No."

"She'll come round. They give you a hard time at first, then they come round."

Amber smiled, stiffly. She couldn't imagine her mum ever "coming round", not to this, not to the way she'd run out on them. . .

"Bit too much drink, last night, eh?" Marty went on.

"Yes," she said, dully, "that was it."

She made herself walk home, although her body was telling her to take a cab. Disappointment about Marty was surging round her, and she didn't want to stand still because that would let it in. Her throat was prickling again, too, and she felt if she drove herself on, she'd drive it out, force it out. . . Then she planned to sleep straight away when she got back, sleep from exhaustion with no time for her thoughts to plague her. She was faint and dizzy when she reached the house and, somehow, not surprised to see the gaunt old woman again, standing by the gate as if she was waiting for her.

"Hello, dear!"

"Hello," said Amber.

"I walked by your house last night, dear, and you all seemed to be having such a good time in the front room. . ."

"Just a meal."

"Oh, that's lovely. All together, round the table . . . it's what the house needs, that is, people happy and laughing. . ."

Amber half-smiled and put her hand out to push the gate open, but the old woman reached out her own gnarled claw and stopped her. "You look peaky, dear. Aren't you well?"

"Bit of a sore throat."

The old woman moved closer, face brimming with concern. "Oh, you must keep *well,* dear! What about some nice fresh air, why don't you go down to the sea. . ."

"I've just come up from the sea."

"Or that lovely sunny clearing I told you about, in the woods here where the blackberries grow. . ."

"I'm going to go to bed," said Amber.

Panic flitted across the old woman's face. "Sometimes that's not the best thing, bed, that bedroom, sometimes—"

"I need to sleep," insisted Amber, and she pushed past and marched up to the front door.

Ben was in the kitchen, making a sandwich. "Can you take a look at my window?" she demanded. "I've tried to wedge it but it keeps rattling. It's ridiculous."

"Sure," said Ben, not turning round. "And hello to you too."

"Sorry. Hello."

"Been one of those days, has it?"

"Yes. Look – if you can't fix it, I'll contact the landlord," she said, tartly, and marched off upstairs.

She gargled again with TCP, stripped down to her underwear, subsided full of relief into bed, and fell asleep almost immediately.

When she woke, it was dark; her little travel clock told her it was ten past ten – she'd been deep asleep for about four hours. Stretched out under the duvet, her legs felt like lead, like she'd never get them to move again. She thought her throat felt a bit better but she didn't want to test it out by getting up – anyway, there was no point now. She unhooked her bra and dropped it on the floor, then took a sip of water, and settled down again, meaning to sleep right through till morning.

But this time she drifted in and out of sleep, hazy, half there. The window was rattling again, and her dreams were full of Poppy, Poppy running away, lost, frightened, and she was running after her, searching for her, full of grief and terror, calling out, "Sorry, I'm sorry. . ."

Then, half-awake, she was sure Poppy was in the bedroom with her. There was a pressure at the end of her bed, as though Poppy was sitting there, just the way she'd sit when she came into her room sometimes at night, when she was afraid or anxious . . . Amber peered through the darkness, saw a shape there, a thin shape. She felt a chill of fear. "Poppy?" she whispered. "Poppy? What are you doing here?" There was no answer. She peered closer; the shape had gone. Her throat was beating with pain now, her head swimming. She huddled back down, then drifted back to sleep . . . she heard a voice, faint and shrill, complaining, complaining . . . it made her feel guilty the way her mother and Poppy did, but it wasn't them, it wasn't the right voice. . .

Then she was awake, fully awake. She heard a key turn in a lock, so close it had to be her door, even though her key was on the inside. Silence, then someone muttering *it's your fault, your fault*. . . and then, directly above her head, there was a noise, rhythmic, repetitive, wood on wood.

The rocking chair.

Chapter
Twenty-one

Amber stayed awake then till dawn. Above her head, the sound of the rocking chair faded, and stopped, and when it did, her heart stopped pounding. She needed to pee, but she didn't dare get out of bed, not till the room was filled with early light.

"I was asleep," she told herself, gargling furiously in the bathroom. "It was a dream, like thinking Poppy was there was a dream. It seemed real because I got delirious because of this bloody tonsillitis, coming and going."

She raced down the hill to the café, but her stomach wouldn't unclench from its knot. She was filled with sheer fear – about what would happen if she got really ill, about the break with her family, about the eeriness in the house . . . about going mad. At the café, she worked like a slave, chopping and cooking, smiling and chatting to the regulars, but she couldn't block out the fear. Her throat ached ominously. The coming night pressed in on her, terrifyingly.

"Just get through till Sunday," she told herself. "Don't think, just get through till then. Then you can sleep, and work out what to do. . ."

At around four o'clock, she got a text from Kaz – *I'm cooking 2nite?* She texted back *Yes please!*

Poor Kaz. She didn't have a chance with Rory, any more than Amber did with Marty. She'd get drunk at the dinner, she decided, she'd buy a bottle of wine and drink all of it herself, then she'd sleep through anything that night, she'd sleep away her madness and delirium and panic and guilt, she'd sleep away all of it.

Ben met her in the hall as she let herself into the house. "I had a look at your window," he said.

"Thank you. Did you fix it?"

"Well, I replaced those bits of paper you'd shoved in the frame with some wood, but I don't see that it'll make much difference. You'd got it wedged tight as a drum – I can't see how it rattled. Sure you weren't imagining it?"

She smiled wanly at him, and made her way upstairs. Her reflection wavered bleakly in the huge mirror at the top. The dust-shape was there again, on the attic stairs – thin, only just visible, but she knew it was there, there or in her head.

Everyone gathered in Kaz's room soon after seven; she'd cooked chicken casserole as promised. It wasn't a great success, not like Amber's fish dinner had been. They all seemed a little subdued, as though they were hurrying through it to get to the real Friday night. As soon as he'd cleared his plate, Rory pushed back his chair, got to his feet, and ambled towards the door. "Hey – where d'you think you're going?" Kaz squawked, indignantly.

"I *told* you, darlin' – I'm meeting some mates in town. I'm already late."

"So phone them. Call them and say dinner was delayed and you're not the kind of arsehole to just walk off and leave everyone else to do the clearing up!"

"But I am that kind of arsehole, aren't I? Come on, Kaz – give us a break. I gotta go."

Kaz yanked up the cushion she was sitting on and hurled it at his head. In one slick movement, he caught it, and lobbed it back, hitting her on the chest.

"You *shit*!" she exploded, and flew at him, cushion in hand, and started bashing him with it. He laughed, folding his arms up over his head for protection, trying to snatch it back at the same time. Everyone was waiting for the moment Kaz wanted, when he'd grab her to stop her pummelling him, but he got the cushion first. There was a short tug-of-war, then a ripping sound, and then Kaz squawked "*Ergh!* Oh, my God. *Eeeeeergh!*" and threw the cushion from her to the floor.

Kaz stood there, face frozen. All the fun, the mock-anger and the desire, had suddenly gone, sucked from her.

"What the hell?" muttered Rory, peering down at the cushion. Then he too changed. He stepped back and said, "Eugh. What is it? *Euugh,* that's nasty."

The three at the table hurriedly got to their feet and crowded round, staring at the cushion. Its outer cover, shiny green and gold stripes, had split wide open, revealing a much older cover inside. This was a dull red brocade and it too had torn, and now a slump of grey-white feathers was spilling out on to the floor.

Three finger-sized objects poked from the feathers.

"What the hell are they?" Chrissie quavered.

Ben stirred the feathers with his foot, and the objects fell clear. There was something indescribably malevolent about them. No one wanted to pick them up.

"Jesus, it's *hair*," said Rory, crouching down and staring. "Put the light on, the overhead light . . . yes, it's hair."

"Then what's that red stuff?" Kaz breathed.

"It's some kind of thread, twisted round the hair . . . and there's something else in there. . ."

There was a silence. Then Kaz fetched her big scissors from her desk and, using them as tongs, picked one of the finger-shapes up and laid it on the table right under the light where, illuminated, it looked even more sinister.

"Cut into it," said Chrissie. "See what's in there."

Kaz didn't move, then she croaked, "I feel weird about doing that."

"What," scoffed Rory, "you saying it's got a curse on it, or something?"

"Well, what does it look like to you?"

"I dunno. Just hair, tied up. With – that looks like metal?"

"Children's hair. Look how soft it is."

"OK, children's hair . . . the Victorians were big on locks of hair weren't they? Lovers' hair in lockets. . ."

"Hair of people who'd died made into mourning rings," put in Amber.

"That's sick," said Ben. "Hairy mourning rings? That's sick."

"Oh, for Christ's sake," said Rory, and he took the scissors off Kaz and stabbed down into the finger-shape, severing the red thread, slicing into it.

It opened like a sickly flower, folds separating. "What are they . . . *needles*?" gasped Chrissie. In among the hanks of hair, all knotted and tied up with red thread, were short thin lengths of some kind of metal, blackened in places, and twisted.

"It's been burnt," gasped Kaz. "Look – the hair . . . it's burnt too, and the needles have melted on to it. . ."

"Why the hell would someone do this?" Ben said. "It's vile."

"Playing witches," grunted Rory. He stirred at the last of the hanks, and jumped back. Kaz screamed.

At the centre of the bundle were three tiny milk teeth, discoloured with age.

Chapter
Twenty-two

"Look, *calm down,* will you?" Ben was insisting, over the shouts and squawks of fear, disgust, horror. "It can't *hurt* you, it's got no *power* – someone had a sick mind, that's all!"

"A *really* sick mind," exploded Kaz. "This wasn't kids playing witches, an adult did that – it's done so well, the way it's all woven in together, and the needles have been twisted in a fire – and they sewed up the cushion properly. . ."

"OK, an *adult* with a sick mind."

"*Who used to live in this house!*"

"Oh, *Kaz*! I thought you were over all that!"

"Over what?" faltered Amber.

There was a silence. Her four house mates turned to look at her, as though she'd been suddenly hurt in some way and they were checking to see she was all right. Then Ben sighed and said, "Kaz makes out she has this room 'cos she doesn't mind it being a dining room too. Well, that's only partly true. Last year, she had my room, but. . ."

"But what?" whispered Amber. Though the answer was already in her mind somewhere.

"I got jumpy," mumbled Kaz. "I thought I heard noises. In the attic."

"She thought there was a *ghost* in the house," said Ben, scathingly.

"So why stay on?" said Amber.

"Why stay –?! 'Cos there isn't a flaming ghost in the house, that's why, and it's a great house, and Kaz just has an overactive imagination!"

Kaz turned to Amber, and smiled apologetically. "It's true, I'm crazy," she said, "I used to think I could see something, this thin shape, on the stairs to the attic."

Amber suddenly felt faint, like everyone's voices were a long way away from her, like her head was full of drumming.

"Are you OK?" asked Chrissie. "You look awful." She put her arm round Amber's shoulders, and helped her to a chair.

"Sorry," Amber gasped. "Sorry, I've been feeling rough all day. . ."

"It's not this stupid cushion set you off, is it?" demanded Rory.

"It's my throat . . . I get tonsillitis. . ."

"She's burning," announced Chrissie, with her hand on Amber's forehead. "You're going down with it bad, kid!"

Kaz was at Amber's side, looking anxiously into her face. "You should be in bed," she said. "Come on, let's get you to bed, I'll fetch you some paracetamol and a cup of tea. . ."

"I'm OK," said Amber. "I don't . . . I don't want to go upstairs. . .!"

"She's spooked," said Rory.

Kaz pulled a chair over close, sat next to her, took her hand and said, "Now look, Amber – *please* don't get all twitchy about this. I went through a bit of a weird time when we first moved in, that's all. I'd just split up with my boyfriend at home, and I was really wobbly about everything, and I met this old woman down the road who said some weird stuff. . ."

"The woman from number eleven?" whispered Amber.

There was a shift in the room. "Yes," said Kaz, evenly. "Have you met her too?"

"Not really. Just . . . what stuff?"

"Oh, she told me she was glad some lively young people were moving in, she said the house needed some happiness, that's all. . ."

"She said something like that to me," croaked Amber. "And she asked me about the girl who had my room before me. She asked me why she'd left."

"Oh, *what*?" said Rory. "She just – *left*, that's all!"

"Yeah – it was no big deal," said Ben. "It was ages after *madam* here got it into her head that there'd been a *murder* or something, and got herself in a froth about noises in the attic. . ."

"It was so stupid," said Kaz. "We worked it out later, heating the house after it'd been shut up for so long dried everything out, and the wood creaked and stuff. . ."

"And a bird must've got into the attic once," said Chrissie, "and knocked stuff over. . ."

"Did you find the bird?" asked Amber.

"It must've got out again."

"Really, Amber," went on Kaz, "I was pathetic . . . you expect noises in an old house, don't you?"

Amber wanted to say *But you still moved down to the ground floor, didn't you?* but her mouth wouldn't move.

And then Ben scoffed out a laugh and said, "Kaz made me wedge the rocking chair with books. She thought it moved at night."

Amber wanted to cry out, she wanted to tell them she'd heard it too, but everything in her head was shifting and surging, and then it went dark.

Part 2

Chapter Twenty-three

Amber came to amid whiteness and light, and her first thought was that she was dead because her throat had been cut. It seared with pain, pain so hot and strong it had its own separate existence and didn't seem to be part of her body at all. She was terrified. She didn't try to move or open her eyes. There was something evil near her, she could sense it, something twisted and evil. . . It hated her, it was waiting to do her more harm, it was near her. . . As she slid back into blackness, the voices started. *Bring her round. . . It's important she comes round now. . . Morbid fear of hospitals. . . It seems the mother refused. . . Morbid fear. . . Morbid fear. . .*

"Darling! Darling, wake up!" Amber swam back into consciousness. Her mother's face was hovering near, eyes wide in alarm, mouth tight and anxious, saying "Wake up, wake up!"

"I've had a nightmare," Amber thought, "I've been

screaming and woken Poppy . . . oh, God, Poppy will be terrified, Mum should go to her. . ." She tried to say sorry but her mouth was rubber, hard and set like rubber . . . it was so good to drift off again, so good to sink down to the dark and silence. . .

Later again, she surfaced again. She wanted to stay in the blackness but she couldn't. She squinted across the white sheets at her hand, which was up in the air. It was being held by the wrist by a sturdy-looking nurse, who was looking at her watch, saying, "You're telling me, they're a right pair. Took them ten minutes to make up their minds to go and get a cup of coffee. I could've slapped the mother, quite honestly, the way she carried on when she got here."

Then another voice said, "You know the family doctor pressed for a tonsillectomy when Amber was twelve?" and the nurse went, "*No!*" and the voice said, "Yes. And every time after that when she went down with tonsillitis. It's on her record." Then the nurse said, "*Hey!* Are we awake at last?" Her kind round face bent down towards Amber, breathing peppermint into her face. "Amber? Amber? You OK, sweetheart?"

Amber tried to speak but her throat felt seared; sealed up with swelling pain. She was longing for water, although just the thought of swallowing was horrific. Then, as if she understood, the nurse was lifting her head, holding a glass of water to her mouth. "Just wet your lips, pet, that's right. How's the pain?"

Amber frowned, and two tears squeezed their way out from the corners of her eyes. The nurse gently adjusted something in her arm, and Amber felt herself drifting off again, escaping again, it felt so good just to slide off. . .

"Hey, come on . . . don't go back to sleep," said the nurse, brightly. "Don't you want to know how you ended up in here? You gave us a right scare, you did! Good job you've got some good friends, young lady – they called the ambulance, and came with you . . . you were in a *state*. Acute tonsillitis, that's what you had – you were delirious with it, saying all kinds of crazy things! The doctors don't like to operate when the tonsils are infected but they decided to get yours out as quick as possible – they were *nasty*!" She laughed, she was squeezing Amber's hand as she talked, keeping her awake. "And I've got some good news for you. . . Mum's here! And your little sister. They just went off to get some coffee, I don't know what's taking them so long, but they'll be here in a minute . . . hey, come *on* . . . Amber? Stay awake so you can say hello to your mum. . ."

Mum's here. . . Mum's here . . . and your little sister. . .
And your little sister.

Chapter
Twenty-four

"Oh, Amber, you're awake! She's awake, Poppy! Oh, Amber, thank *God* you're all right!"

Amber focused on her mother's tearful, smiling face, then on Poppy's little heart-shaped one. They were leaning over her, tension crackling from them like static. "We're here, darling . . . we're here . . . you're going to be all right . . . d'you want anything? Some water?"

Blearily, Amber nodded. Relief flooded into her. The sight of her mother's face made tears come into her eyes.

"Here, Poppy, hold the glass . . . that's it . . . let me pour in a bit more . . . that's it, darling, well done, you hold it to her mouth. . ."

Poppy's hand was shaking as she pushed the glass against Amber's lips, and quite a lot of water spilled over her chin. When Amber felt her lips grow wet, she pushed the glass away and focused on her mother; her mouth formed the word *sorry*.

"It's all right, it's all right, darling, the worst is over.

You'll be out of here soon and Poppy and I will take care of you. Oh, it's such a relief to see you with your eyes open, such a *relief* . . . oh, it's been so *awful*, Amber! You were in the operating theatre already when we arrived . . . no one would tell us anything, they wouldn't let us see you. . ."

"We've been sitting up all night," said Poppy. Her voice was even higher pitched than usual. "Just in a corridor, on chairs."

"Poppy put her head on my lap and slept for a bit. . ."

"I didn't. I just pretended to."

"And then they let us see you, first thing this morning. But you were *out,* unconscious, it was terrible. . ."

"You looked dead."

"Oh, don't say that, Poppy! But you did look dreadful, Amber, it was terrifying . . . the whole thing's been such an ordeal!" Mrs Thornley's voice broke, and she jabbed her knuckles in her mouth. "From the moment your friend phoned us – Kaz, is that her name? – and told us you'd been admitted, we've been in shock, haven't we, Poppy? We didn't know what to do, it was so *late* when she phoned, we thought we really couldn't set out then, so we got up early the next morning, yesterday – only yesterday! It seems like *days* ago, doesn't it, Poppy?"

"Weeks," said Poppy.

"And came down . . . *what* a journey!"

"It was horrible," said Poppy. "We were so scared."

"And so worried about you, darling. But you're all right

now. Aren't you? Oh, I can't wait to get you away from this dreadful place. . ."

Amber closed her eyes. She wanted to ask her mum to be quiet, just to hold her hand and be quiet. . . Their fear was like a swamp she was being sucked into . . . she was drowning in fear and guilt, guilt that they had to be here, that she'd put them through all this. . .

Her mother's voice came again. "Amber, look. Can you hear me, darling?"

Reluctantly, Amber opened her eyes.

"You mustn't worry. About what you said to me on the phone. About not coming home again. I know you wouldn't have . . . *been* like that if you hadn't . . . if you hadn't been getting ill. We'll talk about it when you're better, all right? And we're *here*. We're here to take care of you."

There was a long silence. Amber shut her eyes again. Tears oozed from under her closed lids; against them she could feel her mother's and sister's eyes burning, burning. . .

"Lunch up!" carolled the sturdy nurse, trotting up with a tray which she plonked on Amber's legs. "Now I *know* you don't feel like it, but you're going to try for me, aren't you?"

"Surely not!" squeaked Mrs Thornley. "Surely you don't expect her to *eat*. . ."

"Oh, indeed we do. Don't we, Amber? Just some nice soup and soft bread to start off with, then we're going to get her on to cornflakes, eh? Scrape that throat out so it can heal nice and cleanly!" She pulled Amber up to a sitting position, plumped up the cushions behind her, then perched beside her on the bed. "Now," she said, "d'you want me to spoon-feed you?"

Amber smiled at her, shaking her head, and picked up the spoon. She sucked a little of the thick, tepid soup into her mouth, pushed it against the roof of her mouth with her tongue. Then, with a huge effort of will, she made herself swallow.

"There!" said the nurse. "Not so bad, eh?"

"No," croaked Amber, although she felt like she'd swallowed half her throat with the soup. It was the first word she'd spoken since the night she'd collapsed.

"Come on, another spoonful."

"Don't overdo it, Amber," said Mrs Thornley.

"She's not *overdoing* it!" said the nurse. "She's helping herself get better!"

Amber spooned in some more soup, and swallowed.

"I think we'd better go now," said Mrs Thornley, quietly. She was deeply offended with the nurse, Amber could tell. "I'll try and be in first thing tomorrow morning, darling, but to be honest I think I'm just going to get back and collapse. Now I know you're all right."

When Amber woke the next morning, she felt so much better it was almost unreal. She announced this to the nurse who brought her breakfast, and the nurse beamed and said, "That's what we want to hear! The anaesthetic's out of your system, and you've got rid of those foul tonsils, so you should be feeling lots better. You'll be off the painkillers next.

You youngsters mend really quickly." She plonked the tray down, adding, "Aren't you going to ask when we're letting you out of here? That's what patients usually want to know."

"Oh . . . yes," mumbled Amber. "When?"

"A couple more days. You've been really ill, sweetheart. We'll let you out when you're eating well and we're happy it's all healing up fine. So come on . . . tuck in!"

Amber started to eat her boiled egg. She sucked the bread before swallowing it, and drank lots of the sweet, lukewarm tea, and every mouthful scraped its way down her throat like barbed wire. She was hungry, though, and it felt good to have something in her stomach. Afterwards, she lay back down again. The thought of leaving the hospital dismayed her. It was horrible to want to stay in hospital, but where else could she go? Her family had come to fetch her back home. They meant to sweep all she'd said about staying on in Cornwall aside and take her back with them so everything could carry on just as before. Relief that they seemed to have forgiven her was mingled with dread of going home again.

And sheer fear filled her when she thought of returning to 17 Merral Road.

The last minutes before she'd passed out spooled into her mind. "I was delirious," she comforted herself. "I over-reacted to things Kaz said, what Rory said. . ." But she knew delirium hadn't invented the torn cushion with the slump of dirty-white feathers spilling out of the split, and the obscene, finger-like . . . *things*. . .

Don't think about them, don't think about them. Amber looked towards the door of the ward. Visitors were starting to arrive, drawing up chairs to bedsides; the chatter of conversation grew louder. She looked for her mother, half dreading to see her, half longing for her to come in and be there for her again, take care of her like she'd done when she was tiny. . . The ward was filling up. Only one other bed besides Amber's didn't have a visitor. Amber tried not to stare at the wide ward doors, but she couldn't help it. And then suddenly there was Kaz strolling in, Kaz in a brilliant blue jumper with her mass of black hair half-tied back, holding a bunch of white daisies in one hand and waving furiously with the other.

She hurried over to the side of Amber's bed, crying, "How are you, babe? They wouldn't let me visit before! Then today when I phoned they said you're a lot better – you're certainly *looking* better!"

"I'm *feeling* better. Oh, Kaz – it's so good to see you!" Kaz stooped down to hug and kiss her and she sobbed *Thank you* into Kaz's hair, which smelled of passion-fruit. "Kaz, I know what you did, and I can't thank you enough, I—"

"Oh, and like it was a big deal? We just called the ambulance and did what was needed."

"All the same, you did it!"

"Anyone would've done it! *God,* Amber, I'm so glad you're OK! We thought you were going to croak on us, we seriously did!" Then she kissed her again, and put the flowers in water, and told Amber how she'd gone with her in the ambulance.

Amber told her what it was like waking up, and they shared the relief that it was all behind them now.

Kaz leaned forward; her hand with its three silver rings looked brown and alive against the white sheets. "The doctor asked us what you'd been doing," she murmured. "Just before you collapsed. If anything . . . *unusual* had happened. If you'd had a shock."

"Oh." A chill slid down Amber's spine. "What did you say?"

"We just . . . we said nothing had. I don't know why, it just all seemed so weird, and stupid . . . none of us wanted to explain. Rory told him we'd just been having a meal, and none of us contradicted him. I hope that wasn't wrong."

"It was fine. I mean – *I'm* fine, forget it."

Kaz leaned in a bit more. "Look – I know we *said* that, but . . . look. I'm not going to pretend it didn't happen. That cushion – those *things* – they were real."

"Yes," breathed Amber. "What've you done with them?"

"Ben chucked them out. He took them down to the local tip, and binned them. They're gone."

There was a pause. Then Amber muttered, "I don't know if I can face coming back, Kaz."

Kaz was stroking the sheet as if she wanted to comfort it. "Look," she said, at last, "OK. Maybe something awful *did* happen in the house. Certainly whoever made those shitty little talismans had a screw or two loose. But – I don't know and I don't *want* to know. I bet horrible things have happened in an awful lot of old houses. My gran . . . she used to live somewhere where a maid hung herself from the banisters over the stairs. Gran only found out about it when she'd lived there for ten years and it was only *then* that she swore she felt an icy draft in the hall!"

"Yes, but . . . that's it, isn't it. It was when your gran knew about the maid she felt something. You *don't* know, and you heard stuff – you saw that shape on the stairs. . ."

Kaz exhaled. "Just a shadow," she murmured.

Amber sighed. "I've seen it too," she said. "It's not . . . it's not a shadow."

Kaz sat back. "Oh, come on, Amber. The light from the attic skylight makes this shape on the stairs, that's all."

Amber was silent. She thought about saying she'd seen it even in the dark, it was darker than the dark, and she'd seen the far attic room go back to how it was maybe eighty years ago, and she'd heard the chair rocking too, above her head, but she knew Kaz was set solid against hearing it. "It just . . . I dunno," she mumbled. "It feels weird sometimes, in the house. Creepy."

"I know," Kaz said warmly, "darling, I know it does. I felt it too, when I first came." She leaned towards the bed again, all confidential. "Look – maybe we did pick up on something. First me, then you. Maybe the house does have nasty vibes somewhere. And you and me – we're just more sensitive than the others, yeah? More emotional."

"Maybe," whispered Amber.

"I felt that when I met you – we're two of a kind."

Amber smiled. It meant so much, Kaz saying that.

"I was all screwed up when I moved in," Kaz went on, "you know, being dumped and everything . . . God, I was in a state. And you . . . you seemed on edge at first, and – well, tell me to butt out if you want – but from some of the things your mum's said – she didn't want you to come, did she? Didn't want you to have a gap year."

Amber shook her head, agreeing.

"So we were both in a bit of a raw state when we moved into the house . . . shitty boyfriend, family row . . . and we both picked up on things. But no one else has seen or heard *anything* – and for months *I* hadn't, either. I'd quite literally forgotten all about it till Rory ripped that stupid cushion open, I really had. So maybe it's just something . . . that people like you and me, emotional people, going through a bad time . . . we pick up on, when we first move in. Yeah?"

Amber, powerless, nodded. She was full of wanting to believe Kaz.

"So now I feel. . ." Kaz went on, "I'm not gonna let some weird vibes spoil things. Maybe someone sick lived there once but now it's a great house with great people, and I'm not going to let some stupid spooky feeling that I don't even *feel* any more spoil things, OK?"

"OK," croaked Amber, and Kaz seized her hand and squeezed it, and Amber thought: The main reason she wants to stay in the house is Rory. And he must be *mad*. I don't understand why he doesn't absolutely fall for Kaz. She's wonderful, she's like a fire – not, not as wild as a fire, a stove, a lovely polished warm stove that you can crouch next to and get warmth and strength from and she doesn't even know she's helping you. . .

"And anyway," Kaz went on, breezily, "your little sister's moving into the end attic. She's clearing it all out as we speak. That'll lay any ghosts that're up there, won't it?"

Chapter
Twenty-five

Amber felt sick, stunned, like she'd been struck hard in the stomach. A nurse came up to her bed and said, "I hope you're not talking too much, young lady. I hope you're not wearing yourself out."

"Oh, I'm doing all the talking, trust me," beamed Kaz, and the nurse smiled back saying, "OK, five more minutes. Then she should sleep."

"What do you mean," croaked Amber, as soon as the nurse had gone, "what do you mean my little sister's *moving into the attic?*"

"Well, it was pretty crowded, your mum and her sharing your bed last night. I say night, but they went to bed soon as they got back, about three in the afternoon . . . still, I guess they were exhausted, poor things."

"So . . . they're staying at the house? At Merral Road?"

"Yes. Didn't they tell you? I suggested it, actually . . . they didn't wanna fork out for a B and B, did they?"

"No," muttered Amber, although she'd assumed they

had. The thought that her mother and Poppy were in her house, *her* house . . . she hated it, it repelled her.

"Anyway, as I said, it must've got pretty crowded, and they had some kind of a row this morning, I dunno, tension I suppose – I heard both of them crying. Then Poppy just took herself on up to the attics. I made them both a cup of tea – your mum was still in bed, she went on and on about the window rattling and said she'd hardly slept a wink. Then when I took Poppy's tea up to the attic, there she was, wrapped up in an old eiderdown, lying on that old iron bed."

Amber shuddered.

"*She* doesn't seem to feel the bad vibes!" Kaz laughed. "Or mind the spiders!"

"I'm sorry," Amber mumbled. "I'm so sorry they've been . . . you know . . . awkward. . ."

"Hey, come *on*! They're bound to be wobbly with you in here, aren't they? Anyway, Poppy asked me if it would be OK if she slept up there tonight, and I said of course it would. I could hear her clearing stuff out as I got ready to come and see you."

"But . . . what's the point of her going to all that effort?"

Kaz shrugged. "It gives her something to do."

Amber's throat was throbbing with pain, she knew she should stop talking, but she had to keep on, she had to find out what was happening. "In a couple of days," she grated out, "I'll be out of hospital, and they'll be going back. . ."

"Not yet, your mum said. You'll still be pretty weak, you'll need caring for."

"She said that?"

"Yes! Amber, you might've rowed, but she's still your mum!"

Amber stared down at her hands, lying on the white sheet. Then she whispered, "Did she say anything about me going back with them?"

"No, nothing," said Kaz. "Hey – don't look so worried! She'll see it your way, parents always do in the end. She'll wait till you're better, then she'll go back. She's gonna have my bed when you get out of hospital. . ."

"Oh Kaz, you can't give up your bed!"

"It's fine! I'll sleep on the couch, it's only for a few nights till she sees you're fit enough to be left." There was a pause. Amber was shaking with conflicting emotions. So Mum was planning to stay on, just to take care of her . . . *her*, not Poppy. . .

Kaz cleared her throat. "You weren't exactly honest with her, were you?" she said.

"What?"

"She thought you were having a holiday to start off with, didn't she?"

"Oh, God – did you tell her the truth?"

"No. I fudged it. She asked me if I was the *friend* who'd invited you down, and asked me if it was me who'd persuaded you to stay on after the *holiday*. She was pretty pissed off at me."

"Oh, God, I'm *sorry* . . . what did you say?"

"I just avoided all the facts and blithered on about it being your choice, no one could make you do what you didn't want to do, blah blah. Queen of fudge, that's me."

"What about the others?"

"I've told 'em to keep schtum. It's OK, Amber – it's worked out."

The nurse was looking at them from the other side of the ward; she was starting to walk towards them purposefully, tapping her watch. "Poppy's pretty, isn't she?" said Kaz, ruefully, getting to her feet. "Really sexy mouth. And so *thin*, the bitch! Rory was letching over her last night, the *shit*. I told him – she's sixteen! She's barely legal!"

It wasn't till early evening that Mrs Thornley and Poppy came in to visit Amber again, but they were smiling and sweet as they walked up to her bed, and full of apologies for it being so late. Mrs Thornley had bought her chocolates; Poppy some satsumas. They focused on her, warm and caring, asking her how she was, telling her how good it was to see her looking so much better. Amber felt almost tearful with it all.

"Your friend Kaz is a really nice girl, isn't she?" Mum said. "And *so* considerate. She went down to the café you've started working in, Amber – she told them what had happened."

Amber held her breath, waiting for some kind of recrimination about her having a job at all, but there was none, so she asked, "What did they say?"

"That it was fine, I think – they're keeping the job open for you."

"Oh, that's . . . that's *great*."

There was a pause, Amber still waiting for them to accuse her of treachery, of abandoning them, waiting for them to demand that she come back home with them. But nothing was said. Instead, Mrs Thornley carolled, "Ben's lovely too – the boy with fair hair, sort of reddish fair hair? He's cooking us a meal tonight. Isn't he, Poppy? Really sweet of him."

Something deep in Amber hated the thought of her mother and half-sister being in the house, mixing with her new friends, but she wouldn't acknowledge it. She pushed it down, crushed it down – told herself not to be so mean-spirited when they were being so loving. "Ben does great pasta," she croaked, "but I think it's all he can cook."

"I like him," said Poppy. "He's funny. *And* Rory. I like him too."

"They've all made us so welcome," said Mrs Thornley, and smiled, beautifully.

It was then that Amber knew that they weren't going to talk about what had happened. That was how the three of them lived. If the truth hurt, they'd silently agree to avoid it.

Well, maybe it didn't matter. Maybe this was going to work out. Maybe she could stay on in Cornwall, and they'd understand and support her, and not hate her for it after all. And now her mum was saying how much clearer Amber's voice had got, how she hardly rasped at all any more, and asking if she'd reduced her painkiller intake. She seemed so full of concern, of *love*.

Maybe it would just be . . . *OK*, Amber thought.

Two more days went by, with everyone from the house, even Rory, coming in to see her at least once. Kaz told her all about Bert wishing her a speedy recovery and keeping the job open for her. Then, the next evening, Bert and Marty turned up together.

Amber's heart thumped when she saw Marty walking through the ward doors. He handed her a bunch of beautiful rust-coloured chrysanthemums, and she thanked him but found it hard to meet his eyes. She was dying to know what was going on with the girl who'd left, the girl he kept texting, but there was no way she could ask him, of course. Bert filled in the awkward silence by giving her some home-made fudge that he said he'd cooked up extra soft "so it would just slip down" and demanding to know when she was coming back.

"Kaz told me you'd kept my job open," Amber said, smiling. "That's really great."

"Kept it open?" echoed Bert. "Course we kept it open. The regulars miss you something rotten. Particularly old Mr Peters. 'Where's Amber with her smiling face?' he says. Think he's a bit gone on you, the soft old bugger."

"I thought you might get someone else in."

"Course not! Why would we want to? We managed without you before and we're managing now. It's just not as easy and the takings have dropped. Mind you, as I'm not paying you that's not the problem it could be."

"Charming as ever, Bert!" laughed Marty. "He can't wait for you to come back." He paused, then added, "Me too."

"Soon as you're better, girl," said Bert, patting her foot under the stiff hospital counterpane. "Start with half days, if you want."

The day after that, Amber was told she could go home.

Chapter Twenty-six

"I've washed the sheets, darling," said Mrs Thornley breathlessly, as they stood together in the door of Amber's bedroom, "and given it a tidy round. . ."

"Oh, Mum, it's lovely!" said Amber. "Thank you!"

Her room was neat and spotless, and there were flowers in a jug on the old chest of drawers.

"Do you want to hop into bed now?"

"I'm fine, Mum, honestly."

"Don't overdo it."

"No, I won't. I'll get a really early night."

"Well, Poppy's making us some dinner, darling. She's really *trying*, you know, Amber – she went out and got the shopping herself." Mrs Thornley looked at her yearningly, desperate for her to approve her little sister.

"That's great," said Amber. "Let's go down, shall we?"

The dinner was a small affair, shepherd's pie with overcooked carrots, eaten in the kitchen, with everyone squeezed round the table. Ben and Kaz were there too, making jokes and complimenting Poppy on her cooking, and Mrs Thornley kept saying what nice house mates Amber had found and thanking Kaz for giving up her bed, so it all went along pretty warmly. Rory turned up as they were finishing eating and insisted on scraping out the pie dish, making Poppy giggle with his loud, lip-smacking noises of appreciation. No one would let Amber help clear up afterwards.

Amber watched her mother and half-sister move around the tiny kitchen with her friends, stacking dishes in the sink, making coffee. She'd got over her bad feelings at them being here; she told herself it was miraculous that, through her illness, the two utterly separate sides of her life had collided, and instead of a hideous crash, there was calm.

"You look tired, sweetheart," said Mrs Thornley, stroking her hair. "Come on, let's get you to bed."

It was like being a child again, young and safe. Her mother insisted on going upstairs with her and tucking her in. She switched out the light and said, "Sleep well, darling. Let's get you a hundred per cent better, eh?"

Amber floated into deep, untroubled sleep. No fear, no noises, no strange disturbing dreams. When she woke next day it was ten thirty and the room was full of sharp winter sun. She went down to the kitchen; Kaz was there, eating toast. "Hey," Kaz said, "want some?"

"Love some," said Amber. "My throat feels almost back to

normal. Better than normal – better than before. Were you OK on the couch?"

"Sure. It's really comfy. Your mum's sweet, Amber. She's so concerned about you . . . we went to sleep talking about you."

"Oh, God. Sorry."

"Don't be daft. She's just so relieved you're OK, after the op . . . *and* pleased it's worked out for you down here. The house and the job and everything."

"Really? She said that?"

"Yeah. She was on about wanting to go to The Albatross, see where you work."

Amber shook her head, smiling. "I can't believe it, you know. The way she's come round. I thought she'd hate me for running out on them."

"Well . . . she doesn't. Sometimes you have to do something dramatic to show your parents you've actually grown up."

Amber laughed, and thought – not for the first time – how wonderfully straightforward the world was for someone like Kaz. Well, maybe she was right.

"Your mum's gone out to get some shopping – stuff we'd run out of. *After* giving the kitchen a real seeing to."

"I thought it looked clean."

"You could eat off the floor! Well, OK, maybe not eat off it but if you dropped some food on it, it wouldn't immediately become dangerously contaminated and have to be binned, like before." They both laughed, and Kaz added,

"We're getting used to this, Amber – we'll miss her when she's gone!"

"Well, it won't be for much longer – I feel so much better."

"You *look* better. *And* without make-up, you cow. Want the last bit of toast?"

"Yes please. I'm going to call Bert today – maybe go in for a half day next week."

"Weren't you told to stay off work for ten days or something?"

"By the end of next week it'll be *nearly* ten days."

"Well I'm sure you're up to it, the way you're putting that toast away. Now – I gotta dash. I'm late for my seminar." And Kaz hurried out.

Left alone, Amber finished her coffee, musing about the way Kaz had eased and oiled the whole situation of her mum and Poppy being there, which was typical of her – it was just in her nature to be generous. And she pondered on how differently Mum and Poppy were behaving now they were down here – more capable, less uptight, more *normal*, at least now they'd got over the trauma of her frantic admission to hospital. And Poppy had mucked in, hadn't she, and cooked, and hadn't turned a hair about sleeping up in the attic. . .

Amber felt a sudden rush of affection for her little sister. If Poppy hadn't sensed anything weird up there, any dark atmosphere, maybe it had gone away. Maybe it was going to be all right in the house now she was stronger, now the rift with her family had been healed. Kaz had said that was how it had happened for her, hadn't she? Just a few bad vibrations at the start that pretty soon left you alone.

On an impulse, she dumped her plate and mug in the sink and went out into the hall. She wanted to see what Poppy had done to the attic room.

Her reflection in the ornate mirror at the top of the main stairs was bright and unwavering as she headed up towards it. She climbed the attic stairs, not looking for shadows, and made her way along the skinny corridor to the far attic. Then she pushed open the door. And jerked back with shock. It had happened again, she was seeing her freakish vision again – the iron bed loured over the room with its black bars gleaming, the junk had melted away from the floor, from the walls . . . the old room had broken through all the clutter concealing it.

"Get sane!" she hissed, shaking her head crossly, as her heart slowed down to its normal pace. Poppy had cleared it, that was all. Poppy's pink drawstring bag was on the chest of drawers, looking oddly at home . . . and her make-up bag . . . and there was her suitcase, under the bed next to a battered old tin box of about the same size. Amber hadn't noticed it in the room before. It had a padlock and the initials I.S. carved into the lid.

Slowly, Amber walked further into the room. The books beneath the runners of the rocking chair had disappeared; she made herself put her hand on the chair's smooth top rung, made herself push it backwards. The sound was the exact sound she'd heard when she was lying in her bed below. . . *Imagined I'd heard*, she corrected herself.

Then the skin on the back of her neck prickled, and she spun round to see Poppy in the doorway. "*God,* you startled me!" she snapped.

"Sorry!" said Poppy. "Like what I've done?"

"Yeah . . . it's . . . what've you *done* with everything?"

"Shoved it in the other two attics, no problem. And then I gave this room a real clean. It's gorgeous now, isn't it?"

"Yes. Yes, it's . . . great. But it's a lot of effort to go to for just a few days –"

"I didn't move any of the furniture. It looked so absolutely perfect, I wanted to keep everything as it was. The bed's comfy, and I *love* the skylight! Last night, I just lay here and gazed up at the stars. . . Hey, you look all funny. Are you OK? I didn't startle you that much, did I?"

"No," mumbled Amber. "It's just that. . ."

"What?"

"Well. . ." Amber hesitated, then decided she'd tell Poppy, there was no reason not to. "Something freaky happened, soon after I'd moved in, when I was still pretty stressed and everything. I came up here, and it was like . . . I *saw* the room like this! I mean . . . I saw it without all the junk in it, just like this. . ."

Poppy took a step towards Amber, an ecstatic smile on her tiny heart-shaped face. "Maybe you were looking into the future," she said, taking her hand. "Maybe you were seeing it when *I'd* come."

Chapter
Twenty-seven

A few days passed, and Mrs Thornley and Poppy showed no sign of going home, despite Amber assuring them that she felt one hundred per cent better. They seemed to enjoy spoiling her and caring for her; a strange kind of harmony existed between the three of them.

On Thursday morning, promising her mother she'd leave right after the lunch time rush and get the bus or a cab back, Amber set off for The Albatross. As she walked down the hill, her pace quickened until she was almost back to her old stride. She remembered her plans to get fit; thought it was once again going to be possible. *More* than possible, because she wasn't under the threat of her poisonous tonsils any more. It felt so good to feel energy again, energy pumping through her legs and muscles. And it was good, she had to admit it, to be away from the house, with her mother fussing over her and Poppy . . . well, for once she couldn't criticize Poppy. Really, Poppy had been OK. She'd tucked herself away up in the attic, and when she'd been downstairs, she'd helped and hadn't got in the way. . .

Amber walked on, breaking into a smile when she saw the vast, flint-grey sea in front of her. She crunched on to the beach. The sun was fighting its way out from behind clouds and at the horizon, the sea was turning blue. Ahead of her was The Albatross, already with its shutters open getting ready for business.

She pushed her way through the wide wooden door, and hurried into the kitchen.

"Amber!" said Bert, straightening up from the dishwasher. "Well – welcome back!"

"Hey!" said Marty. "Great to see you! You look better than ever!" While she was still delightedly processing his words, he meandered over towards her, put his arm round her shoulders, and squeezed.

"All right, all right," said Bert, "less of the kissy-kissy stuff. Get the girl a coffee. How you feeling, anyway?"

"I'm great," said Amber. "On the mend."

"That's what we want to hear."

On the large counter in the centre of the kitchen, fifteen cauliflowers were laid out, cushiony centres creamy white against their dark green leaves. They made Amber want to start cooking. "Don't they look great!" she said, heading for them.

"*Am*ber – you're losing it, darling!" mocked Marty, handing her a mug of coffee. "They're *vege*tables!"

"You shut up – she's right to admire them!" said Bert.

"They're beauties and I got them for next to nothing at the end of the market yesterday. So! Today's veggie special – cauliflower cheese. Amber – how's your white sauce?"

"It's good," she said, "if you've got a good whisk."

"You use mustard powder?"

"And nutmeg. And chicken stock."

"Great stuff. You do two trays of cauli cheese, while I get on with my world-famous chicken casserole. Oh – and you can make some more stock from my bones, OK?"

"That'll be tasty," grinned Marty.

"Idiot. My *chicken* bones. I'll do chicken soup tomorrow. And give you some, girl. Nothing like chicken soup to cure your ills and build you up again. Know what they call it? Jewish penicillin!"

I'm back, Amber thought, picking up a knife, *I'm back, and it's great.*

The day went well. Bert and Marty were so solicitous about her not wearing herself out, fixing her snacks and drinks and making her sit down at every opportunity, that she didn't get a chance to grow tired. She and Marty got on great together and best of all, his mobile stayed in his pocket. No texting at all.

She was unstacking the dishwasher when Bert suddenly said, "He finally did it, by the way."

"Did it?"

"Ditched that little cow. The one that was giving him the runaround. I heard him having a real shouting match with her on his phone last week and when he rang off I said to him, *You want to get out of that one, lad* and *he* said. . ." Bert broke off, because Marty had come into the kitchen. They both watched him as he put down a pile of dirty plates and picked up a basket of bread and exited again. Then Bert went on, "*He* said, *I just did.*"

"Yeah?" said Amber, trying not to show how delighted she was. "That's good."

"You're telling me it's good. He could be a right pain to work with when she'd been putting him through the wringer."

It's possible, she thought. *Me and Marty – it's possible.* Later, she watched him as he stood in front of the sink washing up three huge pans, loving the way he moved, watching his arms, thinking about the easy way he touched her, wondering if it was just friendly, wondering what would happen if she touched him.

At two thirty, when the lunch time rush was ebbing, Bert came up to her with some folded banknotes and said, "Home time. Here's your pay."

"OK, I'll just scrub out those pots and—"

"*Home time!*" She took the money, smiling, and he added, "It's a full day's pay, there. You're worth it."

"Oh, Bert – I *can't*! I've only done just over half!"

"Go on – you take it. It'll . . . what's the word . . . *assuage* my guilt at paying you crap rates for your fine cooking." She laughed, and he said, "I'm serious, girl. You've got a gift. And when you open your first restaurant and get rave reviews in all the glossies, I want it in there that I was the one who trained you up on the job."

"Oh, Bert – come on!"

"I'm not joking!" he laughed back. "I felt bad anyway, not giving you a bean of sick pay. You all right? You need to borrow anything, for rent?"

"That's really kind of you, Bert, but I'm fine, honestly. Mum's paid off two weeks of my rent, and I've not exactly needed to spend much while I've been ill!"

As she'd promised, she got the bus back up the hill, and as she rocked along she thought about how Mum and Poppy had set aside all the hurt she caused them, and come down to take care of her. Maybe, Amber thought, they actually *understood* why she needed to get away, maybe they were moving on too. . . She smiled to herself. Maybe she could have the life she wanted in Cornwall without breaking off from her family. Without having to sever that link.

When she walked into the kitchen at 17 Merral Road, Mrs Thornley was standing at the sink, and Poppy, Rory, and his friend Max were lounging round the table, mugs in front of them. "*Mum!*" said Amber. "Are you washing up again?"

"Oh, darling, you're back!" Mrs Thornley cried, spinning round. "How are you? Have you tired yourself out?"

"Not at all. I feel great. Now come and sit down. Let this lot do that!"

"She won't let us, Amber!" said Rory. "We try!"

"*Sure* you do!"

"I really don't mind," said Mrs Thornley, smiling. "It's the least I can do, help out a bit, when everyone here's been so kind to the three of us. . ."

"We're going to miss you when you go, Mrs Thornley," soothed Rory. "*Not* just because you do loads of cleaning and stuff."

"No – you like her cooking too," said Amber, and everyone laughed, and she went on, "Well, make the best of it, Rors! I'm feeling *so* much better, there's no excuse to hang on to them any more!"

There was a weird kind of pause. Then Mrs Thornley said, "Amber? There's something I want to talk to you about, dear – shall we pop up to your room for a minute?"

Chapter
Twenty-eight

Foreboding invaded Amber as she followed her mother up the wide stairs, but she wouldn't acknowledge it. "What is it, Mum?" she asked breezily, as they went into her bedroom.

"Amber, before we came down here. . ." Mrs Thornley pushed the door shut behind her, walked over and sat on the bed. "Well, you know Poppy was having an absolutely terrible time at college. I told you over the phone."

"I know, Mum. I'm sorry I wasn't there to support you, but—"

"Oh, darling . . . water under the bridge. The thing is, when we got that phone call from Kaz – well, it was almost a relief. It meant we could come away . . . it stopped the awful battle I had every morning, trying to talk her into going in. . ."

Amber reeled under the fact that her mother saw her emergency operation as "almost a relief". Then, like she always did, she shut down on the hurt. *It's OK for me, I'm so much stronger than Poppy. . .*

There was a long pause. Mrs Thornley looked past

Amber and out at the trees in the garden. "She's going to ask me to go back with her," Amber thought, numbly. "She's going to say she can't manage without me."

"I'm thinking of going back the day after tomorrow," Mrs Thornley murmured. "I can't expect poor Kaz to give up her bed for me any more."

"That's probably a good idea, Mum," said Amber, determinedly. "I mean – Poppy needs to get back to college. She's missed a lot of work, but she's bright, she'll catch up – I *know* it's been hard for her, but she's got to get through this! Maybe you could arrange to meet the principal of the college to talk about how difficult she's finding it, she can't be the only one having a tough start, there must be *something* he can do. . ." She trailed off. Her mother's eyes hadn't once left the window.

"She won't go back," said Mrs Thornley, at last. "She absolutely hates it there."

"So what will she do? She can't just hang about at home, can she?"

"She wants a gap year. No – don't look like that – it's getting more and more common for teenagers to take gap years after their GCSEs. Everything's so pressured now, kids can't cope . . . they drop out, then go back when they've had a break, and made sure they're doing the A levels they really want. *I* think it's a good idea."

"It's a good idea if she actually *does* something with her year," said Amber, hotly. "Something that will make her grow up a bit and be more able to . . . to cope with life."

"I know. Obviously, that's what I want for her too."

Amber stared. She'd expected Mrs Thornley to snap at her for criticizing Poppy, but for the first time ever her mother was acknowledging that there was something wrong with the way Poppy was. "The last thing you want is for her to be under your feet all day," she went on, encouraged. "I mean – you talked about going back to work, too, didn't you, Mum? When that job in the art shop came up?"

"I'd like that. Oh, I'd love that – and the money would help . . . Poppy's father gives me a good allowance, but it's never enough. The thing is, Amber . . . the thing is. . ." Mrs Thornley paused, took in a breath, "I actually think it's doing her a lot of good being down *here*."

Amber felt herself go ice cold. Then white hot, ready to explode. She wanted to rage and rail at her mother – tell her *no way*, over her dead body, this was *her* place and Poppy wasn't going to stay down and spoil it.

But she didn't. She had been too well trained over too many long years for that. She stood with her back to the window, and listened.

"I've seen her change," Mrs Thornley went on, "while she's been here. She's a bit in awe of Kaz and the others . . . she's learnt from them, I think. And she fits in well – don't you think she fits in well? I mean – she hasn't got upset, badly upset, you know, like she does, not into a State, not *once* since she's been here. It's been wonderful." Mrs Thornley paused, but she still didn't look at Amber, who stayed silent. "The idea came to me the other day, actually," she rattled on. "Rory was joking about with her, telling her she should pay rent for staying in the attic. I mean – he was only teasing. But it *would* help, wouldn't it? You could all keep it quiet from the landlord – just a casual arrangement – and her rent could pay the basic bills, and all the things like washing-up liquid and coffee. . ."

Amber was fighting her revulsion, her anger, her hurt. Then Mrs Thornley suddenly slumped forward, put her face in her hands, and wept. Amber made herself cross the room, made herself put a hand on her mother's shaking shoulder.

"I can't *cope* any more!" Mrs Thornley gasped out. "Not with it being just the two of us. It's been such a dreadful strain, these weeks since she's started college . . . I *know* I'm bad for her, I baby her, but if I don't she . . . oh, it's worse if I don't. She *needs* to get away from me, that's all."

"It's OK, Mum, it's OK – don't cry. . ."

"It's been so *hard*, Amber! And down here . . . oh, it's been such a *relief* for it not to be just her and me all the time. She's been so *good* with your friends, it's been wonderful to see her acting just like a normal teenager. I know she's been a bit . . . *clinging* in the past but I honestly don't think she'd be like that with everyone else around. I think it would do her so much good, to be here mucking in with the rest of you, I think it would be the making of her. . . It needn't be a whole year. Just for a bit, just to let her find her feet a bit . . . then she could come home again, and things would be different. . ."

Amber knew she was being offered a deal. Oversee

Poppy for a few months . . . then she'd be free. And maybe it *would* help Poppy if she could get her away from home for a bit, maybe it would cure her, teach her to stand on her own two feet. . . She had to help Poppy if she possibly could. Didn't she?

Mrs Thornley pulled a frail little blue handkerchief out of her pocket, and dabbed at her eyes. Amber was overcome with the need to help her, take the burden off her.

"You're the strong one, Amber," whispered Mrs Thornley. "You're so lucky."

Chapter
Twenty-nine

It was agreed that they'd put it to Kaz and the others, and if everyone said yes, Poppy would stay behind while Mrs Thornley went back home the day after tomorrow.

For the other four house mates, it wasn't a big decision. The attic room was empty; the landlord never came to the house; the extra cash would come in very handy indeed. Chrissie was bothered that she was two, maybe three years younger than the rest of them but Ben said she seemed an OK kid and she had her sister there to take charge if anything went wrong. If it didn't work out – she left. No problem at all.

It was only Kaz who sought Amber out in her bedroom and demanded, "This is your decision too, right?"

"What? Of course."

"Well – OK. I mean – I know you were the one who asked everyone if Poppy could stay on. I just wondered if you actually *wanted* it."

"Yes," said Amber. "Really. It'll do her so much good."

*

Mrs Thornley booked her ticket, leaving that Saturday morning. Poppy, almost beside herself with excitement and gratitude, asked Amber to make sure she was home early on Friday because she wanted to give her a "special tea". Afterwards, Mrs Thornley was going to treat the whole house to an Indian meal, as a thank you and going-away present. It was all working out.

At The Albatross, Amber was subdued and explained it away by saying she'd done too much the day before. So it was easy to get off early without explaining about Poppy's special tea. She didn't want to tell Marty that Poppy was staying on. She remembered too well what she'd said to him in the kitchen the night she'd cooked a house meal, when she was getting ill.

She thought he'd be critical. She didn't want to discuss it.

When Amber walked into the kitchen, the table was all laid out with chocolate cake and three mugs, and on the counter was one large present and a pile of little ones, five of them, all wrapped identically in ivory tissue paper tied with lilac ribbon.

"Here you are, dear," said Mrs Thornley, handing her the big parcel.

"Mum – thanks! I wasn't expecting presents!"

"No, but . . . well. We wanted to buy you some."

Amber suddenly felt incredibly chilled. Suddenly, it all slotted into place. Right from the start, she thought, right from when Poppy had moved up into the attic, they'd been planning this. That's why they'd been so sweet to her. That's why they'd made such an effort – cleaning, cooking, fitting in. They hadn't had a change of heart, not like she'd hoped. They weren't reaching out to her, doing it for her.

They were doing it so Poppy could stay on, in the house.

Her mother wouldn't see it that way, of course. A special tea and presents – they're nice things, aren't they? And if they help ease things, make Amber more positive towards Poppy staying on … well, what's wrong with that? Her mother would protect herself, like she always did, from the truth of what she was doing. From the truth of how she quite literally sacrificed Amber, sacrificed who she was and what she needed, to keeping Poppy safe.

Amber felt as if all her energy had drained out of her. It was too much to deal with. She couldn't accuse them, she couldn't make a fuss – it would be too catastrophic. Desperately, she told herself it was OK, it was OK because she was the strong one, she could take it, it was Poppy who needed help, not her. . .

She had to keep going. She tore off the wrapper to find a big, pale blue fluffy dressing gown that said *invalid*. "I thought you needed a new one, something warm for the winter," said Mrs Thornley.

"It's lovely, Mum," said Amber. She rolled it up, set it aside, and sat down.

"Now open mine," said Poppy, picking up the five little parcels and laying them on the table in front of her.

Amber glared down at them, full of grief and hurt.

This is abuse. I don't care how mad that sounds – being forced to do something that feels this sick . . . pretend they're presents when they're not presents, they're bribes . . . fake, false . . . it's abuse.

"Get a grip," she told herself, angrily. Then had the thought that if she accepted them, they'd give Poppy power over her, like when you took a gift from a witch. If she picked them up they'd crumble into bone dust or sag and seep dark blood. . . An image of the split cushion spewing grey feathers and twisted finger-shapes came into her head.

Get a grip.

Poppy sat down opposite her. "Aren't you going to open them?" she urged, in her sweetest voice.

"There's so many, she doesn't know which to open first!" said Mrs Thornley, in a strained voice, as she brought the teapot over to the table.

Amber could feel frustrated tears pressing behind her eyes with the force of hating to touch them, with the knowledge that she had to. She snatched up the nearest parcel, tugged at the bow. It unravelled and the paper slithered away – inside was a pot of chamomile hand cream.

"How lovely!" cried Mrs Thornley.

"Yes – that's great, Poppy," croaked Amber. "Thanks!" She opened the next parcel, revealing a short, chunky purple candle.

"It's not scented," said Poppy, all baby-apologetic. "I just loved the colour . . . this one next!"

Amber took the third parcel, pulled at the ribbon. *Get it over with, get it over with*. And flinched back from what was inside, because her first thought was that it was something dead.

"It's genuine tortoiseshell!" cooed Poppy. "It used to have a lid . . . and it's chipped, that's why it was cheap . . . I bought it to stand the candle in."

"How lovely!" said Mrs Thornley, again.

Amber turned the little shallow brown pot in her hand. She hated it. Hated the fact that some poor tortoise had had to die so it could be made.

"Put the candle in it, dear!" urged Mrs Thornley.

Amber pushed the squat little candle into the pot, made herself say how sweet it looked. The brown and the purple looked vile together, like an old bruise that wouldn't heal.

"Now this one!" Poppy simpered.

Amber felt like someone was holding her down, smothering her. She wanted to jump up from the table and run into the fresh air but she couldn't do that because Poppy was being so *nice*. So generous. *Get a grip*, she told herself.

Inside the fourth parcel was a packet of notelets with autumn leaves on. Nothing Amber would choose or use, but nothing too hideous. Amber took a breath, said thank you again. She felt like she'd said thank you so often her mouth was all puckered up.

There was a pause, then Poppy picked up the fifth present and pushed it slowly across the table to Amber. Her eyes narrowed; a sly little smile tweaked at her perfect mouth. "I wanted you to open this last," she murmured. "It's really special."

Amber tore the paper off and let the contents drop to the table.

"Oh how lovely!" exclaimed Mrs Thornley. "How old are they?"

"Victorian, the woman said. I got them from the same antique shop as the pot."

"They must've cost so much, darling!"

"They did," answered Poppy in a pious little voice. "But I knew Amber would love them."

I loathe them, thought Amber, staring down at the table in revulsion.

A pair of gloves lay there, made of some soft, dead material. Kid, she imagined. There was a traced pattern on them that looked like a skin infection. The fingers were yellow, stained like a smoker's hand, getting browner at the tips. At the wrists, they were fastened by little black beetle-like buttons.

The silence was too long; she had to say something. "Amazing!" she croaked.

Poppy leaned across the table towards her, full of malice. "*Put them on*," she breathed.

"Yes, go on!" said Mrs Thornley. "They look like they might fit you, with your tiny hands."

"That's what I thought," said Poppy. "That's why I bought them."

Amber picked one of the gloves up. Her skin crawled at the touch. It lay in her hand like a dead hand with the flesh sucked out, like a ghost's hand. She dropped it back down.

"Go on, dear," repeated Mrs Thornley. "Let's see if they fit!"

"I . . . I don't want to!" she blurted out.

"Oh, don't be *silly*!"

"It's just – it's creepy. The last person who wore them might've died of syphilis or something."

"Oh, charming," said Poppy, in her teeny-tiny hurt voice, while Mrs Thornley burst in with, "Oh for God's sake, Amber, don't be so horrid!" and nudged her, hard.

Poppy was staring at her across the table, mouth all pouty and hurt, eyes gleaming in what looked like triumph. It was chilling, Amber thought, how often her mouth did something at odds with her eyes.

In despair, she picked up the glove from the table and pulled it on. It felt disgusting to her fingers. Dry, chafing, full of coffin dust. Her nails snagged on the ragged seams; it slid clammily over her palm.

It fitted tight, too tight. She felt like her hand was someone else's.

Poppy leant across the table again and, smiling, did up the beetle at her wrist, and it bit into her flesh.

"There!" said Mrs Thornley. "What a good fit! It's lovely. They don't make gloves like that nowadays. Put the other one on!"

Amber's heart was thudding, fast; she tore at the button, tore the glove off, and then she rubbed and rubbed at her hand, cleaning off the touch of the glove, making it hers again.

"Never mind, dear," said Mrs Thornley, looking at Poppy anxiously, "they're for looking at, really, aren't they? You don't want to spoil them by wearing them."

And she started to cut up the round chocolate cake.

Chapter Thirty

The Indian meal was a great success, with Rory, Ben, Kaz and Chrissie so pleased to be paid for that they courted Mrs Thornley and made a fuss of Poppy, focusing on her and welcoming her into the fold. Amber, still shaken by the furious feelings that had invaded her earlier at the special tea, was glad to hide behind the four of them, crushing down all her feelings of grief and foreboding. Mrs Thornley's face was vivid with relief and hope.

The next morning, early, Mrs Thornley and Poppy cried as they hugged each other when the taxi came to take Mrs Thornley to the station, then Poppy said she was tired and was going back to bed. Amber escaped to The Albatross, and this time, told Marty about Poppy moving in.

He was great about it. He didn't judge – he listened. Over the long day, Amber talked and he questioned her and best of all – he listened. It was wonderful but also so natural that Amber didn't question it. The energy between them flowed and she felt like he was processing all her strange, contrary and disconnected feelings, and it was something he was doing for her – because he wanted to.

When she told him what she'd felt when she'd been presented with all the little gifts, he said, "OK, maybe they were using you. Manipulating you. But I doubt it was conscious, you know? They couldn't . . . I dunno. *Help* it."

"Maybe not. Oh, *God*. D'you think I'm an idiot, letting her stay on?"

He leaned forward then, and looked straight at her. "I think you're generous. Really generous. I don't see what else you could've done. She needs to get away from home, from your mother protecting her the whole time. And being here – it could really help her."

"I hope so," said Amber, overwhelmed by his closeness, and what he was saying.

"You had to give it a go – you had to *try*. And if it gets too much – well, you'll just have to send her home again, won't you? The thing is – you'll've *tried*." Amber evaded her thought that it wouldn't be that easy, it never was, with Poppy. She was basking in Marty's attention; she felt warm, and strengthened.

When she got back to the house, she found that Rory and Max had taken Poppy off with them on a tour of the town, and felt genuinely pleased. She was full of the hope that living at 17 Merral Road might make Poppy change. On Sunday, a crowd of them met up in a local pub for lunch, and the next day, Amber took Poppy shopping, and both times, Poppy was fine.

But then the normal rhythm of the house returned. Rory disappeared for the best part of the next thirty-six hours. Kaz – eyes on Poppy – announced that she thought he had a new woman somewhere. Chrissie asked Poppy if she'd mind hoovering the stairs and clearing up the kitchen as she had so much time on her hands. Poppy did so, but badly and with very bad grace. The next evening, in an effort to smooth things over, Amber brought home leftover lasagne which she heated up and served, somewhat sloppily, with chunks of garlic bread. Only Ben and Kaz joined them; Poppy was sulky and sullen and after asking her a few questions, Ben and Kaz ignored her, and hurried through the meal.

And that night, Amber heard Poppy crying up in the attic.

She pulled on her new blue dressing gown and made herself go to her half-sister. At the top of the attic stairs, she paused. The sound of Poppy's sobbing sounded horribly eerie, drifting along the thin dark corridor towards her. Then the crying suddenly stopped, and there was the sound of something being dragged over the floor. Then a drawer slammed shut, and something was dropped... And the rocking chair started. Back and forward, on the bare boards. Amber felt chilled, appalled, hearing that noise again. She flew along to the end attic, threw herself on the door handle, made herself push the door open. "*Poppy!*" she cried, aghast as her eyes took in the room. "What are you *doing?*"

"*Packing!*" snarled Poppy, savagely, jumping out of the rocking chair. Her clothes were everywhere, halfway out of the chest of drawers, dumped on the floor, strewn across the bed. Her suitcase was in the middle of the room, open, with her sponge bag inside it.

"Poppy – it's eleven o'clock at night!" Amber wailed. "What's *up*?"

"I'm not staying. I'm not staying to be treated like this."

"Treated like *what*?"

"Like a bloody slave! Like I'm just here to bloody clean up!"

Poppy was absurd when she swore, with her tiny china-doll face. "Oh, come on, Poppy," said Amber. "Are you talking about Chrissie asking you to hoover the stairs and stuff?"

"Yes! She's a bitch, I hate her. Before that, I was talking to Ben, and she just *interrupted* me, she just talked right over me. . ."

Amber wanted to tell Poppy not to be so touchy and stupid, wanted to tell her she was damn lucky they let her in the house in the first place, but she didn't. They needed a scapegoat for Poppy's mood, and Chrissie could be that. "Look – you can't expect to like everyone in the house, can you?" she said, as calmly as she could manage. "Don't go off the deep end just 'cos Chrissie was out of order to you. . ."

"It's not just her. It's everyone. *You*. You've been ignoring me and everyone's been ignoring me and I'm going home, OK?"

"Poppy – don't be so stupid! You're tired – it's been a big strain, moving in and everything. Sleep on it – it'll look better in the morning."

"*No.* I'm going now."

"It's past eleven, you can't go anywhere now!"

"I *can*!" shrieked Poppy, her doll-face pulled and ugly. "I'll get a cab to the bloody station – I'll wait there!" And, rigid with fury, she started throwing clothes into her suitcase.

Amber was filled with panic. Poppy meant it, she was crazy enough to mean it, and if she went – well, it was unthinkable that she went. Mum would never forgive her if Poppy set out to go home on her own. She might get killed, raped . . . and even if she made it home safely, it would set her back weeks, leaving like this, she'd have a real breakdown, she'd never go back to college again, and Mum would suffer, *suffer*. . .

"Please, Poppy, don't do this," begged Amber. "Look – I'll talk to Chrissie, yeah? I'll tell her to back off you. Give it a few more days, eh, Poppy?"

"It's not just Chrissie," spat Poppy, but she stopped throwing clothes into her case and sat down on the iron bed. Amber felt a surge of relief. She was winning her round, she was going to be able to stop her going.

"It's you too," Poppy went on. "You've hardly spoken to me. I've come all the way down here and . . . you've hardly spoken to me."

The warped unfairness of this was so absurd, Amber wanted to laugh. But she didn't. She felt like she'd say anything, promise anything, to get Poppy to stay here tonight. "I know," she said, softly, and she sat down beside her sister on the bed. "Look – I've been busy. But tomorrow's Friday – everyone goes out on a Friday. I'll bring some food back from the café and get some wine and we'll have a meal, just the two of us, and we'll have a real talk, yeah?"

"So you don't think anyone's gonna ask us to go out with them, then?" Poppy sniffed. "That's nice."

"It doesn't matter if they do or if they don't. We'll stay in, yeah? Just the two of us. Now come on – you're tired. It's been a real strain, moving in here, getting to know new people. . ." She hated to hear her mother's words in her mouth, but she knew they'd lull Poppy, soothe her. "Come on, you get to bed. We can put your clothes away tomorrow, just get some sleep now. . ." Poppy was subsiding back on to the bed, still with all her clothes on. Amber stood up and pulled the cover over her, tucking her in like she used to do when she was tiny. Then, skin crawling, she made herself stroke Poppy's hair until the sniffling and sighing stopped. Then she stepped back from the bed, took the sponge bag and the frantic heap of clothes out of the suitcase, and started folding the clothes up on the chest of drawers. "That's it, you go to sleep," she crooned, "it'll look so much better in the morning. . ." Poppy's eyes were closed now, and she was breathing steadily. Amber closed the suitcase and pushed it under the bed, next to the large, battered tin box with the initials I.S. carved into the lid.

Something connected in her brain.

"Poppy," she said, in a low voice, although it was madness to talk again now her sister was going off to sleep, "didn't that old box have a padlock on it?"

In an instant Poppy was sitting up again, eyes alight. "Yes," she said, "but it wasn't shut properly. Honestly, Amber,

I fiddled with it and it just kind of . . . fell open! It's full of the most amazing stuff. Have a look!" She scrambled out of bed, and crouched on the floor in front of the box. It was as if all her grief and anger had never happened. "Look – these blouses, and lace collars, and this old hat . . . and look! Look at this ebony mirror, and this brooch. Isn't it fabulous?"

She handed Amber a tiny dark-silver pin, with a sludgy green stone set into it. Amber turned it over in her hand and said, "You didn't buy that stuff, did you."

"What stuff?" Poppy was focusing on the tin box, tracing the initials I.S. with her forefinger.

"The stuff you gave me just before Mum left. The gloves, and the little tortoiseshell pot. . ."

Poppy let out a giggle. It was a horrible sound in the dark attic.

"You found them in this box, didn't you," Amber went on.

"Oh, so what!" exclaimed Poppy. "So what if I did? I didn't have much money, and I was going to sell the gloves to get you something, but when I got to the antiques shop, I dunno, it just seemed so *stupid* to sell them for a couple of quid and let the shop owner get a huge mark-up when they're so lovely . . . don't you think they're lovely?"

Amber didn't answer. She couldn't say it. She couldn't say she hated them and they belonged to someone dead.

Someone who used to live here, someone who might not have left.

If you said it, it became real. It came into the room with you, and was real.

Poppy was silent, smiling at her.

Chapter
Thirty-one

"Girls' Night In," Amber thought, stirring the spaghetti sauce as it simmered gently on the stove top. "God, what a farce."

At last, Poppy came into the kitchen and sat down at the table, making no eye contact with Amber. "Hi!" said Amber warmly. "You hungry?"

Poppy shrugged, making a little moue of disgust. Amber fought down her desire to say *Piss off if that's how you feel!* and poured her a glass of wine, which she put down beside her.

Poppy ignored it.

Amber turned back to the stove. Her whole day had been overshadowed by her promise to spend the evening with her sister. She was officially back to full time now, and today Bert had talked about a rise, but the day was spoilt. When Marty asked her how it was going with Poppy she'd snapped "Fine," and walked away, loathing the idea of talking about her. Then she'd regretted it, but it was too late, and there was a kind of rift between them for the rest of the day.

Poppy continued to sit silently at the table looking at, but not touching, her glass of red wine. The Routine's started, thought Amber – a routine they used to follow all the time at home. If Poppy acted like this, it meant she was in a State. And if she was in a State, you had to gently coax her to tell you what was wrong. Then you had to listen, like her slave, for as long as she wanted you to listen and you had to soothe and support her. If you didn't do the Routine, or skimped on it, she'd flip out and it would all be a hideous nightmare and Mum would suffer, *suffer*. . .

"Mum's not here now," thought Amber, savagely. "She's not here, and I'm not doing it." She tasted the sauce, added salt, and announced, "I think I might be getting a rise!"

Silence from Poppy.

"Bert talked about it today. He said profits have gone up a lot, he's really glad I'm back to full time now. It's great, isn't it?"

More silence. Amber got out two dishes and a colander from the cupboard next to the sink, and crashed them on to the counter. She forked out a strand of spaghetti from the pot, pinched it, and said "*Ouch!* That's done."

Silence, silence.

She bashed the colander into the sink and tipped the spaghetti into it, then divided it between the two dishes, and spooned over the sauce. It steamed fragrantly. She grated over a rich scattering of Parmesan, picked the two dishes up, marched over to the table, and put them down.

Poppy ignored them.

Say something, bitch! thought Amber, raging. She sat down, snatched up her fork, twirled pasta on to it, and pushed it into her mouth. "Mmmm . . . s'good. Though I say so myself." Poppy sat like a stone. "Tuck in!" urged Amber. A large tear dripped off the end of Poppy's nose, and into her pasta. Amber forked in another mouthful, but it felt like mud in her mouth. She dropped her fork, and groaned. "What's wrong?"

Poppy had won.

Chapter Thirty-two

"Come on, Poppy, it's obvious you're upset," said Amber. The words were well worn, used often – she knew exactly what she had to say. "Is it still what you talked about last night that's bugging you, or has something else happened?"

Poppy remained silent, but her hand moved slowly to her wine glass. She picked it up and took a small sip.

"Come on – tell me what's wrong. Has someone said something to you?" Amber glared at the top of her half-sister's head. An image of grabbing her by the hair and pushing her face forward into her plate came into her mind. "Come on – I can't help if I don't know what it is, can I?"

"You should've let me go last night," Poppy said at last, in a tight, twisted little voice. "You should've let me go home."

"Oh, come on, Poppy," said Amber, relieved, because at least they'd got past Stage One, the silent suffering stage, and were on to Poppy talking. "We went over that last night, I haven't had time to talk to Chrissie yet but—"

"It won't make any difference. Everyone'll still leave me out."

"Poppy, that's just not true. What about that meal last night?"

Poppy's mouth screwed up. "No one talked to me."

"They tried to!"

"Did they?"

"Yes! You have to talk too! You have to make an effort!"

"I'm new here!" Poppy hissed. "They should make the effort to me!"

"They have been! But you can't go on being *new* for ever – I mean, they *tried* to include you, they asked you what you wanted to do—"

"They were criticizing me. For not getting a job."

"No they weren't. They were just asking you what you were going to *do* now you're down here. . ."

"I wish I wasn't. I wish I'd never come."

A longing to say *Well sod off then!* seized Amber, but she resisted it. She couldn't go through Poppy packing again, and having to beg her to stay. . . "You've got to give it a chance," she murmured. "Give *them* a chance."

"Oh, *I* see! You're on their side, aren't you? You think it's me."

"Poppy—"

"*Don't* you?"

"No!" Amber lied. "Of course not. Look – maybe they could've made more effort. But once you've got to know them . . . they're fine, honestly. Just give them a chance."

"It wasn't just them. *You* were leaving me out, too."

"Oh, Poppy – I wasn't!"

"Chatting and laughing with *Kaz*." She sneered the name, bitterly.

"I wasn't," repeated Amber hopelessly, and she forked some more pasta into her mouth. She chewed and swallowed, barely tasting it. Poppy still hadn't touched hers. In the silence, the window rattled and the curtains billowed out over the sink.

"I'm cold," whined Poppy.

"I'll turn the heat up." Amber got to her feet, glad to move from the table, and said, "Do eat, Poppy. You'll feel better if you eat."

By the time she got back from the thermostat on the wall in the hall, Poppy was begrudgingly transferring a few strands of spaghetti into her mouth. "Like it?" Amber demanded.

Poppy nodded slightly, and took another sip of wine. "I don't like this house," she muttered. "It's cold. And . . . *creepy*."

"It's *not*!" exclaimed Amber loudly, to smother the flutter of fear she'd felt.

"The windows are always rattling, and the floor creaks. . ."

"It's an old house, that's all."

"And I've heard this *scratching* sound, on the roof."

"Birds, that's all."

"It's all right for you, sleeping downstairs, with Ben right next door. The attic's really *creepy*. I feel weird up there."

"I thought you loved it?" said Amber, desperately. She

couldn't bear Poppy talking this way, digging up things she'd pushed down and buried.

Poppy didn't answer. Suddenly, the curtains billowed out once more, dislodging a knife on the draining board that rattled into the sink. Amber shot to her feet, went to the window, pulled out the bit of cardboard wedging the loose frame, folded it over, and jammed it back in. She glanced out at the garden; it looked dank and gloomy, with a sliver of moon giving a thin, cold light. Spooked, she pulled the curtain tight against it, but the night still pressed in through the long glass door.

When she got back to her seat, Poppy was staring fixedly at the half-open door into the hall. "Finish your dinner," Amber said, forcing warmth into her voice, "before it gets cold."

"It's cold already," Poppy muttered.

"Well, eat some of it – *Poppy*! Why are you staring like that?"

"I heard a noise."

"No, you didn't."

"There's someone out there."

"There isn't! Poppy – stop doing this!"

"Doing what?"

"*Staring!* Making out there's someone out there!"

"There is!"

"There *isn't*!"

"Well, if there isn't, you won't mind going to see, will you?" Poppy shot a triumphant look at Amber.

This was another old controlling game. When they were

181

children, sharing a bedroom, Poppy would tell horrible stories about being buried alive, the undead, evil coming to get you. Then, both of them terrified, she'd want Amber to comfort her, and if Amber couldn't do this well enough, she'd scream and wake their mother, whose white, wretched face would blast Amber with guilt. "You *know* how nervous Poppy is," she'd say, "you're the elder, you *know* you mustn't let her get so scared. . ."

Once, Poppy had grown convinced that something "like a big lizard" was slithering down the chimney. "It's coming in!" she'd squealed. "I can hear it! I can hear its claws, scraping down!"

"Shut up!" Amber had begged. "There's nothing!"

"Go and look! Go and look up the chimney!"

"*No!*"

"Why not, if there's nothing there?" wailed Poppy, voice rising. "You can hear it too, can't you?"

"No!"

"It's *coming down!*"

In terrified desperation, Amber had stumbled over to the chimney, and peered up, and a sudden draught of cold air had hit her face like lizard-breath, and she'd screamed. Screamed and screamed, Poppy joining in.

Her mother had spent the whole of the next day in bed, with Poppy beside her. Amber had brought their meals up, on a tray.

"What are you thinking about?" demanded Poppy, querulously, bringing Amber back to the present.

182

"Just remembering how scared you used to get, as a kid."

Poppy went rigid. "Can't you *hear* it?" she hissed. "Something scraping along the floor, in the hall . . . like something being *dragged. . .*"

Amber stood up and went to the door, heart racing, even though she knew nothing was out there. It was Poppy making her afraid. Poppy had the power to create horror out of nothing.

Amber stepped into the hall, and looked round. Nothing. Of *course*. The door to Kaz's room was shut but just the sight of its bright stickers and signs comforted her. She pushed the kitchen door to behind her, and walked down the hall. It was so good to be away from Poppy. She meant to go to her room, brush her hair, then tell Poppy she'd been doing a thorough check of the house. . .

She started to go upstairs, watching her reflection come to meet her in the great ornate mirror at the top of the stairs.

There was something behind her in the glass.

Chapter Thirty-three

With animal speed, Amber spun round. Nothing there. *Of course*, nothing there. She turned back to the mirror. It was still there behind her reflection, a shape, a shadow, long, thin, shifting, and as she watched, it faded. Just a trick of the light, she told herself, firmly. Light on dust. She took another step upwards, then stopped. A feeling of hopelessness had flowed into her, a feeling of pure, dark misery. It was so strong and sudden she thought she must be sensing what Poppy was feeling, sitting alone and scared in the kitchen. Amber thought she did sometimes pick up on Poppy's feelings. She turned, and hurried back to her.

Poppy was waiting, eyes huge. "Was there anything?" she whispered.

"Nothing!" said Amber. "Obviously!" She sat back down at the table. Poppy's plate was practically untouched. "Aren't you going to finish it?" she asked.

"It's cold."

"I can bung it in the microwave."

"No, thanks, it tastes weird when you do that," Poppy said accusingly.

Amber stood up again, clearing the plates, tipping Poppy's pasta into the bin. "Want some coffee? Some pudding? I've got some chocolate here. . ."

Poppy first ignored her, then she sobbed out, "You don't understand, I hate it here! They don't like me!"

"They do, Poppy. They do, honestly. They're just a bit . . . insensitive. I didn't. . ." Amber swallowed. "I didn't feel welcome when I first came."

Lying to Poppy, to make her feel better – it was second nature to Amber. The words slid easily out of her mouth.

"I'm going to go back," whined Poppy. "I'll make the arrangements tomorrow. I'm going to go home."

Amber thought of their mother's face the last time she'd seen her, driving away in the back of a cab as her daughters waved her off, transformed by relief and hope. "Don't do that, Poppy," she said. "Please. I *want* you to stay."

It was ten past three in the morning. Amber could see that on her little illuminated travel clock. She'd put it next to her on the floor where she was lying wrapped up in her duvet. She kept waking up, because the floor was so hard.

They'd sat in the kitchen until nearly midnight while Poppy sobbed and complained and Amber persuaded her not to do the one thing she most wanted her to do – leave the house. Poppy had cried and said she was too scared and upset to sleep alone up in the attic, so Amber had gone up there and fetched her pillows and duvet and put her to sleep with them in her bed. Poppy, used to being looked after, hadn't protested; instead she'd made Amber promise to lie beside her all night, like when they were little and had beds only a couple of hand spans apart.

Now Amber craned her neck up towards the bed, listening for Poppy's breathing. Silence. Earlier, Poppy had been whimpering and snuffling in her sleep, but she must be deep asleep at last, because now there was deep silence.

But some sense of emptiness made Amber sit up and peer across at the bed. It was pitch dark, but she could just see the duvet bunched up on the far side, in a shape that could be Poppy . . . she reached out, prodded the duvet.

It collapsed on air. The bed was empty.

Amber lay back down on the floor and told herself Poppy had just gone to the loo. This was good – normally, after an evening like the one they'd had, she'd be too jumpy to go on her own, and she'd wake Amber up to go with her. "She'll be back in a minute," Amber told herself.

Several minutes went by, and Poppy didn't appear. The silence hummed. And then it hit Amber that there was no light. If Poppy had gone to the bathroom, why wasn't the light on?

Shivering, Amber made herself stand up. She wrapped the duvet round her for comfort as much as warmth, and hobbled to the door. The landing was dark except for a glimmering of moonlight coming down from the skylight at the top of the attic stairs.

Amber looked, not wanting to look. A thin shape was there again, but this time it was dense, solid.

Amber snapped the landing light on. It was Poppy.

Chapter
Thirty-four

Poppy was standing with her back to the attic steps, smiling.

"What're you doing?" hissed Amber, heart hammering.

"What d'you mean, what am I doing?" Poppy said, calmly. "I've just been to the bathroom, that's all."

"Well, why didn't you turn the light on?"

"Because I didn't want to wake you and Ben! Some people have something called consideration!" Her voice had changed – changed completely. The querulous whine had gone; she sounded harsh now, confident. "God, Amber, haven't you ever peed in the dark before?" she barked, and grinned. It looked ghastly in the thin moonlight, like a skull's grin.

"*Stop it!*" Amber blurted out.

"Stop what?"

"You're being weird – stop it!"

"Oh, Amber, I'm not weird," said Poppy, smiling still and coming towards her. "You're still half asleep."

Amber made herself stand there and not dart back into her room and lock the door on Poppy, which is what everything in her was telling her to do. She made herself smile back. "Are you coming back to bed?" she asked.

"No," said Poppy, and pushed past her into the room. She went to the bed, and gathered up her duvet and pillows.

"What are you doing?"

"It's your bed, you have it. I'll be fine in the attic."

"But – you said you were scared, you said—"

"I'll be fine. Night!"

And without a backward glance, Poppy strode past her and went up the steep narrow steps into the attic, trailing the duvet behind her like a cloak.

A week went by. Poppy spent most of her time up in the attic, and when she came downstairs to eat she was quiet and self-contained, and coolly indifferent to everyone around her. When Kaz asked her what she was doing up there all day, Poppy looked straight back and said, "Research."

"Oh. Into what?"

"I'm looking into doing different A Levels, when I go back. I'm just checking out which ones."

"Great! Well if you want to come up to the college library, they've got loads of stuff on—"

"I'm fine," said Poppy, firmly. "Thank you."

"I'd like to know what Poppy's doing for money," grumbled Kaz to Chrissie, later.

"An allowance from her dad," said Chrissie. "I think he's pretty generous."

"And Amber's dad isn't?"

"Obviously not. You'd think her mum would make it up, wouldn't you."

"Maybe she can't afford to?"

"Maybe."

"Amber's better off, working, anyway," Kaz went on. "I'd go out of my mind if I was on my own all day, like Poppy. I mean, she can't only be doing research, she—"

"Oh, for God's sake," broke in Chrissie, impatiently. "As long as she's out of our hair and pays the rent, who cares?"

On the surface, Amber more or less agreed with Chrissie. Poppy was behaving herself, so why worry? But underneath she felt deeply uneasy. It was so unlike Poppy to behave this way, making no emotional demands on her sister. Amber had the disturbing sense that she was *waiting*, biding her time. But she pushed this down and told herself that things were working out; that the break from home was having the effect they'd hoped for.

After all, things were OK, weren't they? Poppy still joined in for house meals, and came out to the pub, especially if Rory was going too. She did no more than her share of the clearing up but she did do it; and even Chrissie couldn't complain about that. And if she didn't seek Amber out to spend time with her, she was pleasant enough when they met in the kitchen, or on the stairs . . . maybe, Amber thought, she really was just growing up at last.

The atmosphere in the house was calm, too. Nothing

eerie, nothing weird – even the windows had stopped rattling. Because there was less wind, Amber told herself, like she told herself she'd imagined most of the spooky stuff before because she'd been raw, leaving home, then on the edge, getting ill . . . and after she'd got out of hospital, there'd been the tension of Poppy staying on, and Poppy acting up and freaking her out. . . .

And *why* the shapes and shadows and gloom had been there didn't matter now, because they'd gone, and it was fine. It really was fine. Now, if she saw the sinister old woman in Merral Road, she just waved brightly and hurried by.

The one thing she couldn't rationalize – the obscene finger-like talismans in the cushion – she simply set aside and refused to think about.

The next time Marty asked Amber about Poppy, she really opened up to him. She told him about Poppy spending all her time up in the attic, alone, and he shrugged and said he thought that was fine. "Maybe she's on some kind of *retreat*, you know? Taking time out. She must be seeing things about your old life that make her pretty uncomfortable. Maybe she's reading stuff or . . . or just *thinking* about it."

Amber liked that idea. She loved Marty endorsing what she was hoping against hope was the truth. She went on to tell him about her mother almost weeping with relief and gratitude on the phone, over Poppy settling in, and he said again what a great thing she was doing for her family. She talked about her childhood, analysing all that was skewed in it. He asked thoughtful questions that dismissed any embarrassment. Not wanting all the conversation to be about her, she asked him about his alcoholic dad, and he talked about it and said he'd done what he could to try and help but after a certain point you just had to stop wasting your energy. When she asked him if he wasn't bitter about it, being raised by someone half-pissed all the time, he said no. He said he was free of all that crap in his past and then he looked at her and said she was getting free of her past, too. She loved hearing him say that, that she'd *got free*.

They were getting closer all the time. Amber now admitted to herself that she was half in love with him, but thought maybe he just wanted to be friends. He was so open with her – people who fancied you weren't that open, were they? But then she was open with him and she fancied him so much she couldn't breathe properly when they stood up close. . .

When Marty suggested that she should ask Poppy down to The Albatross to have lunch, to "get her out", she felt a wave of repulsion at letting her half-sister invade yet more of her life – and then went home and invited her. She wanted to be the brave, generous person Marty thought she was.

Poppy, however, was pretty indifferent to the invitation, and took a couple of days to turn up, then when she did she sat in the corner, keeping a low profile. Three days later, she came down to lunch again, unasked, and chatted with Bert and Marty, and was as usual low-key with Amber, as if Amber was just someone she knew, nothing more.

Later that day, as they worked side by side in the kitchen, Marty said, "Look, tell me to shut up if I'm out of order here, but your sister seems to have a really strange attitude to you. I just wondered if you'd fallen out or something."

"No," muttered Amber. "It's just . . . like I told you, she's . . . keeping herself to herself."

"You know – you should talk to her. Tell her how you feel, tell her the things you've told me. And give *her* a chance to talk about it all, too."

So that evening when Amber got home, she dumped her bag and went straight up to the attics, full of determination to do just that. The skylight was gloomy with rain clouds and the thin stairs were dark as she hustled up them, eyes focused down on each step as she climbed. She went along the skinny corridor to the door at the end. Three old framed sepia photographs had appeared on the wall beside it; Amber examined them uneasily. They were depressing-looking Edwardian family groups; all the faces, even the children's, were grim, all the bodies stiff and formal through having to keep still too long. Amber lifted one of them away from the tobacco-coloured wall; it exactly fitted the pale rectangular shape underneath. She checked the next one; it was the same. Poppy must have found the photos that used to hang here, and put them up again.

She turned to the door, and knocked.

"Yes?" said Poppy sharply.

"Poppy, it's me. It's Amber. Can I come in?"

There was the sound of Poppy crossing the bare floorboards, then a key turned in the lock, and she opened the door. She had a webby-looking black shawl round her shoulders.

"Hi," said Amber, slightly creeped out by the lock and the shawl, "what are you locking yourself in for?"

Poppy shrugged. "No reason."

"Can I come in?"

"Sure."

She followed Poppy into the room. The old tin box was in the centre of the room, and clothes and little boxes and bundles of letters were arranged round it on the floor. Amber thought uneasily about the gloves Poppy had given her. She'd shoved them right to the back of a drawer, under a jumper that she hardly ever wore, and tried to forget about them. "Found anything else in that old chest?" she made herself say.

"Not really," said Poppy. "It's just interesting, that's all. I like old things." She perched on the end of the iron bed, near the pillows, and Amber sat down opposite her.

"So," said Amber. "I just – I dunno. I don't seem to have had a proper chat to you for ages."

"You're busy."

"Yeah . . . well. I just thought I'd come up."

"Fine," said Poppy coolly.

"I phoned Mum yesterday – she was asking after you. Said you hadn't called for a bit."

"I'll phone her tomorrow. She knows I'm OK."

"Yes. You are, aren't you? You're liking it here?"

"It's fine," said Poppy.

"You're not getting bored? I mean – have you thought about getting a job, or something?"

"I don't think it's worth it. I mean – I'm not gonna stay here for ever, am I?"

"No," said Amber carefully, "but . . . I was just wondering if you'd thought about what you'll do when you leave?"

Poppy stared at her. "Go home, of course. I'm not sure I'll go back to college, but. . ."

"Do you want to go home?"

"Well, what else would I do? *Dad* won't have me to stay, will he? Not with his precious new family. And Mum – she'll expect it, won't she?"

"Yes. But we can't always do what she wants us to do."

"Well, we can't both run out on her," said Poppy, acidly. "Not like you did."

"D'you know why I left like that?" Amber demanded, stung.

Poppy shrugged.

"Because I had to. I had no other way of leaving. Not like a normal teenager." Amber took in a deep, shaky breath, and decided that the only way to talk to Poppy was to jump straight in. "Poppy, Mum's got *problems*. I've only begun to see how bad those problems are, now I've been away from her for a bit. Our childhood was just *weird*, wasn't it? Not like other people's. Mum was – she was crippled by fear and suspicion, and she made us that way too. She treated you like some kind of invalid and she. . ." Amber trailed off. No need to go into how *she* was treated, not now. "Poppy, we might've been cared for but we were starved of normal things. It wasn't healthy. D'you remember what she used to say when we'd cuddle up together on the sofa looking at books? 'How lovely, just us three together, and the big, bad world locked out. . .' It was literally locked out, too. Three bolts on the front door, and at least two locks on every window. . . We were *terrified* of anything outside of us, terrified of letting anyone else in. It was . . . *warped*, it was wrong."

Amber paused, breathless with her own courage, and risked a glance at Poppy. Whose face was like a little white mask hovering in the half-light. It gave nothing away, no emotion moved on it.

Amber took another deep breath, and plunged on. "Poppy, you've – you've got to decide what you're going to do. Maybe you shouldn't go back home. Maybe it wouldn't be the best thing for you . . . *or* Mum. I mean – look. You can stay in that old world if you want to, you can be like that, live in that twisted-up way. It's what we're used to; it's how we were brought up. Or you can try to *leave*. That's what I'm doing. It's hard, and frightening, at the start sometimes I just wanted to get back to that old cage we'd built round us, you know – keep everyone out, we're safe here, don't let anyone else come in."

Another pause. Amber leant forward on the bed, close enough to reach out and touch Poppy, but she didn't touch her. "If you want to get out," she went on, low and urgent, "like I did – I'll help you. It's so hard, seeing what we came from, what we *were* . . . sometimes I feel like I've got wires woven right into my flesh, holding me back, tearing into me . . . but I've got to go forward, I've got to *get away*, and you have too." Amber stopped, looking at Poppy's white face with its slash of red mouth, and her heart was thumping with the sheer importance, the truth, of what she'd been saying. She had no idea how her words had fallen on her half-sister.

The light from the room was almost gone, just a soft dusk from the skylight above them falling on Poppy's face. It looked like a puppet's face on a dark stage. And suddenly it opened its wide red mouth and said, "Honestly, Amber, what a load of melodramatic crap you come out with sometimes."

Amber collapsed back, punctured, while Poppy went on, briskly, "I mean, *wires, honestly*! We had a *lovely* childhood – you know we did! It was lovely, just the three of us – it wasn't a *cage*, it was special, not just being like everyone else. It wasn't *warped – you're* warped, saying it was."

Amber closed her eyes. "So you think it was normal, do you," she said. "All that fear, and suspicion, and you always being put first, wrapped up in cotton wool, treated like you might ignite at any moment. . ."

"Oh, now we're getting to it! You know what your problem is, Amber? You're just so *jealous*. *Still*. You still can't bear it that I'm closer to Mummy than you."

"I'm not," croaked Amber. She suddenly felt tired, completely defeated, unable to go on with this. "I'm not jealous. I'm just—"

"I mean, all that stuff about *not letting people in*. What nonsense. Mummy got people round sometimes, but they'd just spoil things, like that Christmas the cousins came and ruined everything. And *I* let people in now – Rory, all the people in the house, and –" she broke off, and her white face swam closer to Amber. "Marty. I've let Marty in."

Chapter Thirty-five

Amber got to her feet. A toxic mixture of jealousy and repulsion and huge disappointment were coursing through her. She wanted to hit Poppy, hit her hard, but she didn't, she just got to her feet and walked towards the door. "OK," she said. "OK. I wanted to help, but *you* don't want help, do you. You and Mum – you're both as weird as each other. Fine. You look out for yourself, Poppy. I'm going."

She pulled the door shut behind her. Outside the door, she stopped for a minute, thought of going back in, demanding to know what Poppy meant by saying she'd let Marty in. And then she heard – felt, almost – a soft *haaaa*, right near her face. Like an exhalation of breath. A sweet, sickly smell surrounded her. It was flowery, but with something underneath . . . like flower-scent covering rot, decay. . . . Amber felt faint. She put her hand out to the wall to steady herself and it hit one of the photos, which juddered and swung on its hook. Then she hurried for the stairs and scrambled down them. The smell still seemed to be clinging to her when she got to the bottom. She grimaced, shook her hair, rushed into the kitchen. At the sink she ran a glass of water, and gulped it down in one.

"You all right?" said Ben.

She turned to see him sitting at the kitchen table. "Yes," she breathed. "Yes . . . sorry. Just had a row with my sister, that's all." The smell had gone. God, what was it? A dead mouse or something, under the floorboards?

"Want something stronger than water?" asked Ben. "I've got some beers in the fridge."

Amber didn't especially want a beer, but she wanted to stay near Ben and his easy kindness, his *normality*, until she'd calmed down again. "Yes, please," she said.

"Get me one too, yeah? After all, the sun's beyond the yardarm or whatever that justification is for knocking back an early drink. . ." Amber took two beer bottles from the fridge and decapped them, and Ben said, "So! What were you and Poppy rowing about?"

"Oh . . . you know," muttered Amber, sitting down opposite him. "Just sister stuff."

"Wouldn't know about that. Grew up with brother stuff, which is mainly just about beating the shit out of each other." Amber laughed, took a sip of beer. "Maybe that's what you should do with Poppy, eh?"

Amber didn't answer. She could half-hear Ben chuntering on about his two big brothers, then about going to see a motorbike that was up for sale, and she was saying the right responses like "Really?" and "Yeah?" while her mind was full of what had happened in the attic. She tried to ignore her jealous curiosity about Marty while she processed all that Poppy had said. She tried to absorb the fact that, far from seeing its faults, Poppy loved where they'd come from and who she was. She wasn't going to change. Then another thought slithered in. If Poppy wasn't taking time out in the attic to readjust, to think about who she was and how she could change . . . then what, exactly, was she doing up there alone for hour after hour. . .?

"That old girl was asking about her today."

Ben's words broke through her reverie. The skin on her spine crawled. "What?" she whispered.

"You know – the old girl from number eleven. She collared me as I was coming back from college. *I see you've got another guest in the house, dear* – wanting to know who Poppy was, when she'd moved in."

"Did you tell her?"

"Well – yeah, why not? She just wants a chat, doesn't she? She must get lonely, all on her own. . . I explained about you being in hospital, and your mum and sister coming down – she was dead concerned about you being ill. . ."

"She should mind her own sodding business!" snapped Amber.

"Hey – no need to get so narked! She's harmless enough, just incredibly nosy!"

"Yeah, well – she gives me the creeps."

"That's what Kaz says. She'll do anything to avoid her . . . she'll go out the back door if she has to."

"I didn't know Kaz did that," croaked Amber, fear beating away in her.

"Extreme, eh? The poor old cow – she just wants to chat. She's losing it, though, I reckon. Kept on about *where was the new girl sleeping*, got all upset when I said up in the attic –" Ben broke off. "Are you OK?" he said again. "You look a bit odd."

"I'm fine," Amber gritted out. "*Fine.*"

Amber finished her beer slowly, willing Ben to stay in the kitchen with her, but he downed his beer fast and said he was going to take a shower. She was longing to ask him if he was doing anything that night and if she could tag along with him but couldn't bring herself to ask. She'd been taught never to make demands on anyone.

Soon, she was alone in the kitchen. It was only ten to eight. I'll go for a walk, she told herself. I'll work all this shit off and get myself tired and then I'll sleep.

She grabbed her coat from the hooks beside the front door and pulled it on. Something made her look out of the narrow hall window before she opened the door.

Behind the skeletal shape of the bare plane tree, the old woman was there, across the street. Standing there half-lit by the street lamp, half in deep shadow.

Watching the house.

Chapter
Thirty-six

The next morning Amber marched down the hill towards the seashore telling herself everything was all right, she'd just lost her grip for a while, that was all. Poppy was a loser bitch and the old woman was barking, and she'd got upset and imagined stuff but it was all right now. The sun was out, and seagulls wheeled and called in the sky.

Last night, cheated of her walk, she'd gone to bed early, wanting to get to sleep to stop the fear growing inside her. But all she'd done was lie awake, listening to the noises above her head. Poppy was moving about, dragging something across the floor. Then – to Amber's horror – she started talking to herself in a high, complaining voice. Amber had lain rigid in bed, determined not to go up and comfort her. The floorboards creaked as Poppy paced up and down; the rocking chair moved. Amber put her pillow over her head to shut it all out, and into her mind came the old woman, watching the house. She thought of going downstairs and looking out of the front window again, because it would make her feel better to see the road empty. But she was too scared to, in case the old woman was still there. She spent the rest of night huddled under the duvet, chasing sleep, half-sleeping, waking, listening, *listening*. . .

Just night terrors, she told herself now in the daylight, marching on. When she was little, there'd been a lot of night terrors. And in the morning Mum had poured out their cereal and said *See? It's all better in the morning, isn't it?*

And it was better – until the next night came round.

"If Poppy's gone when I get back," she thought, "if she's packed her bags and gone home, because of what I said to her, too bad. No, not bad. Good. I've had enough. Mum can just deal with it. I can't be responsible any more. . ."

She strode on.

She knew Poppy would still be there when she got back.

The Albatross was already busy when she arrived. A couple of small boats had come in early, promising Bert cheap fresh fish if he pulled his finger out and got the coffee and eggs on. Amber got straight on with frying eggs and bacon while Bert rushed in and out with coffee, gloating over the good profits they'd make today and moaning about Marty always being late.

As soon as Marty arrived to take over the frying, Amber started gutting the fish for lunch. Amid the healthy business of the café, the horrors of the past night continued to dwindle. There wasn't a lull until about midday when the fish, blanketed in spinach and fresh herbs and laid in trays, started to go into the oven to bake. Amber and Marty hurried out to clear tables. They'd barely had a chance to talk but there was a good feeling between them. Amber was rehearsing in her head how she'd tell him what had happened when she went to talk to Poppy, she'd find out what Poppy meant about "letting Marty in". . .

She looked up as two lovers in their early twenties came into the café. Their pleasure in each other radiated out; they were giggling over whether they wanted a late breakfast or an early lunch. Full of envy and longing, she watched them choosing the table over by the far window and sit with their heads bent close together.

Then she got on with her work. The next time she looked up it was to see Poppy walking in.

She watched, stunned, as Poppy, ignoring her, walked straight up to Marty and put her arms around his neck. He laughed, and seemed to draw back; but then she craned up and kissed him on the cheek. He smiled, said something to her that Amber couldn't catch. Then Poppy flounced off happily and sat down at a table for two. Marty turned and looked over at Amber, but before he could say or signal anything she ducked her head down to the table she was clearing. Her eyes fixed on the plates she was piling, burned into the old pine wood. She turned her back and cleared another table, then laid two fresh ones.

When she at last looked up, Marty was sitting opposite Poppy, and they both had mugs in front of them, and they were laughing.

*

Amber didn't know how she got through the rest of the day. Anguish boiled inside her. When Marty tried to speak to her, she pretended she hadn't heard and turned away.

If there was a God and He wanted to hurt her, she thought, He'd do exactly this. He'd arrange for Poppy and Marty to fall for each other, and make her watch. Poppy was the screwed-up, twisted past that she was trying to get away from and Marty. . .

Marty was where she wanted to go.

She admitted that now. Maybe she didn't have a chance with him, maybe he saw her just as a friend, but that had been enough for now, just to see him day after day, just to work alongside him and feel what she felt for him. . .

Until this. The worst that could happen.

At twenty past five that afternoon, Amber left The Albatross and headed along the beach to the phone box. She felt numb, suspended, but it was one of the days she usually phoned home and she was determined to keep functioning, keep things going. She still hadn't told her mother about her mobile phone – the thought of being contacted at any time filled her with horror.

"Amber! How are you, dear? How's *Poppy*? She hasn't phoned me for ages. . ."

"She's fine, Mum. I mean, I'm not seeing a lot of her, what with working. . ."

"But you're keeping an eye on her."

"Of course. She came down to the café again today, for a coffee."

"Oh, how nice! I do worry about her getting isolated, you know. . . Are the other people in the house looking after her too?"

"They're OK with her, Mum. She's included."

"Oh, *good* – that's so good! It's wonderful it's all worked out so well, Amber . . . and I've got some great news too! That job in the art gallery – it came up again, and I'm starting on Monday! Just three days a week, but it'll do me so much good. . ."

Soon afterwards, the pips went, and Amber said that she'd remind Poppy to phone, and put the receiver down. Then she trudged on up the hill.

Her mother had a job. That was excellent. It meant she could start to have a life of her own, away from Poppy. . .

But it put pressure on her to keep Poppy down here longer.

She turned into Merral Road, and what she saw sent a sick jolt to her heart. Instinctively, she stepped back into the cover of an overgrown hedge.

Poppy and the old woman from number eleven were coming out of the trees at the end of the road. The old woman had her face turned to Poppy, talking earnestly, but Poppy was looking straight ahead, expressionless. They walked slowly towards number seventeen, and stood talking outside the gate. Amber drew further into the hedge, watching. She could hear nothing of what they were saying, and she could only see Poppy's face. It still had its deadpan, doll look on – giving nothing away. But even from the back, the old woman looked upset, or angry, or both. Her hand was beating the air, her head wagging, and suddenly she reached out, and grabbed Poppy's arm.

And at last, Poppy reacted. She opened her perfect red mouth and laughed, a wide-mouthed, mocking laugh. Then she shook the old woman off, opened the gate and went up to the front door and in, without a backward glance.

Amber stayed hidden. She watched as the old woman, muttering like a witch, went along to number eleven and disappeared inside.

The whole scene had seemed unbearably sinister to her. She waited until her breathing had gone back to normal, smoothed down her clothes rumpled from the hedge, and headed towards her house.

"Hey!" called Kaz, from the kitchen, as Amber let herself in. "That you, Amber?"

"Yeah," Amber called back, walking through.

"Did you manage to scrounge any tomatoes?"

"What?"

"*Tomatoes!* Poppy said she was dropping by the café, and I asked her to tell you I was gonna cook moussaka tonight, and I'd do a. . ." Kaz took in Amber's face. "She didn't tell you, did she. Didn't she turn up?"

"Yeah, she was there. But she . . . she must've forgotten. Sorry."

"Oh, no problem. I was just going to make a tomato salad to go with it, that's all. Are you up for a meal?"

"That'd be great, Kaz. Can I help?"

"Yes. You can make some tea and then sit there and talk to me."

Gratefully, Amber filled the kettle as Kaz went into a long moan about how mean and unreasonable her tutor was being, just because she was a few days, well OK, *weeks*, late with this big essay she was writing. . . Part of Amber was longing to tell Kaz what she'd just seen outside the house, but she knew the old woman was taboo for Kaz. What did she want with Poppy, though? Why had they been in the woods?

She made the tea, and sat down at the kitchen table just as Poppy appeared in the doorway. "Like the look!" sneered Kaz. "Tacky goth."

Poppy looked extraordinary. She'd ringed her eyes with black liner, and her hair was wound up on top of her head in a kind of mad chignon, stuck with combs. She had a short skirt on, a torn lacy chemise, the old webby shawl, and high knee-length boots. She should have looked ghastly but somehow, she didn't. She was kind of freakishly sexy; she made the other two girls look safe and dull.

"What time are we eating?" demanded Poppy.

"Soon as it's ready," bridled Kaz.

"Only I'm going out. *Rory's* asked me out."

"What, to an early Halloween party?"

"A party with his drama crowd," Poppy snarled, then she turned on her heel, and left.

"I'm going to deck that little cow some day soon," Kaz exploded. "Sorry, Amber, I know she's your sister and all, but if she comes on to Rory any more with her *open invitation* act, I swear I'm going to deck her."

Amber laughed, and felt her mood lift a bit. "Has he really asked her out?" she said.

"Probably. He has *no* morals – he's like a dog, following his dick around – and she's coming on to him really strong, so what's he *gonna* do? She's . . . I don't know, there's something about her now, even Ben was saying how sexy she was. . ."

"Don't tell me Ben fancies her too."

"I dunno. He said girls like her used to be called 'jail bait'."

"Except she's well over sixteen."

"Yeah, but she's still *young*! Rory should be a bit more *responsible* . . . it's not just the way she looks, it's her *energy*, she's all focused and up for it. She's gonna get burnt, badly burnt. I had a real go at Rory last night for playing along with her but of course he just had a horrible knowing *sneer* on his face the whole time. He said: 'Are you telling me your whole agenda, Kaz?' *Agenda*. I wanted to bite his face. *Agenda*. He knows what I feel about him, and he just trashes it and abuses it. . ." Suddenly, Kaz was crying. Amber shot to her feet, and nervously put her arm round her, and Kaz engulfed her in a warm, sweet-scented hug. Then she pulled away, and kind of shook herself, like a fox coming out of a wet ditch. "*Bugger* this," she said. "I'm not letting that shit upset me any more."

"Good," said Amber, fervently. "You're worth about ten dozen of him."

Kaz smiled. "Oh, you're sweet. I am, though, aren't I?"

"Yes. All he has is looks. That's not enough."

"It's enough for most people. Aren't you worried about him messing with your little sister?"

Amber huffed out a sigh. "Yes. But – I'm worried about so many things to do with Poppy, that . . . well, her coming on to Rory doesn't exactly stand out."

Amber was hoping Kaz would ask her what else she was worried about. But she didn't, instead she asked, anxiously, "So you think it's that way round? Her coming on to Rors?"

"Yes. Rory's probably too much of a slag to say no, but I bet most of it's coming from her. You remember Marty?"

"The guy you work with? Course I do."

"Well, I like him . . . I really like him."

"Well, we all guessed that, sweetie! That night he came here – *definite* magnetism between the two of you!"

"Really?" Amber squeaked. "From him too?"

"From him, to him, all over both of you. Can't understand why you're not an item yet."

Amber flushed up with pleasure, and the anguish that had twisted her stomach into a knot, ever since she'd seen Poppy kissing Marty, started to loosen its grip. "Poppy's coming on to Marty too," she muttered. "Maybe she's already pulled him – she's certainly trying to make out to me that she has. . ."

"What a bitch! Does he like her?"

"Dunno. He seemed to. I was really upset about it, earlier."

"Oh, *Amber*!"

Amber grinned ruefully. "I dunno, maybe I've got it wrong. I hope I've got it wrong. Thinking about the . . . *gloating* way she looked at you when she announced that Rory had asked her to a party – maybe she's just on some kind of nasty little power trip."

"*Jesus.* For all we know she's been trying it on with Ellis, too, to get at Chrissie!" said Kaz. "And if Chrissie catches her, I wouldn't rate her chances! Chrissie does karate. She will sodding *paste* her."

They both burst out laughing, then Kaz said, "Hey come on, get serious, Amber, there's no contest between you and Poppy. You and Marty should get together."

Amber looked down at the mug in her hand, smiling. "Oh . . . I think he's out of my league."

"*Wha–at?* Are you kidding? He's a *geek* compared to you, Amber, honestly. I mean – he's got a great smile and a nice arse, but he seriously needs a haircut and his nose is too big, he'd be over the *moon* to go out with you. . ."

"Oh, *Kaz*!"

"I'm *right*! You should speak to him – what have you got to lose? I bet he's just in total awe of you, that's why he hasn't made a move on you. He's shy."

"He didn't act shy with Poppy."

"Oh for Christ's sake! If he prefers that scraggy, slutty sixteen year old over you he needs his brain sorting. Sorry, Amber, I know she's your sister, but – I can't stand the little cow. She's sly and she gives me the creeps and you're right – I think she's really getting off on rubbing my nose in Rory slobbering over her. Look – is it OK to be totally frank here?"

Amber nodded, on edge for what would come.

"Well, I have to tell you something. Chrissie agrees with me. *And* Ben. None of us like her – we don't want her to stay on. She's beginning to . . . I dunno. Get on everyone's nerves. She kind of *lurks about*. . . And it's just weird, having her hanging around not doing anything. It's been great having the extra money but it's just not worth it."

Amber was shocked. Then she laughed, because it was so exhilarating to have Kaz put into words what she was always trying not to think herself. Then she thought of her mother's happy voice talking about the job in the art gallery. "D'you want her to move out right away?" she croaked.

"Oh, no – it's not *that* bad. Look – when she moved in, there was a kind of understanding that it would just be for a couple of months, so she could get her head together. We all think we should stick to that. You're gonna be going home for Christmas, aren't you? Well – when you come back afterwards, don't bring Poppy with you. Sorry if that sounds harsh. But we talked about it and we all agreed."

There was a pause. Then Kaz said, "I've upset you, haven't I?"

"No, honestly," said Amber. She was thinking: Up until Christmas – that'll still give Mum and Poppy a real break from each other. It'll give them a chance to make changes, if they're up to it. But if the house decides Poppy can't stay, it's out of my hands. It's not my fault. Mum won't blame me.

"Actually, I think you're right," she said. "That's the best solution. It really is."

"Brilliant!" cried Kaz. "Come on – I'm opening a bottle. Sod Poppy, and sod Marty, and especially sod *Rors*."

Just as she was pulling the cork, Rory swaggered in, towing Poppy, who ignored her sister and stared gloatingly at Kaz. "How d'you like her kinky outfit?" Rory crowed.

"Not much," snapped Kaz.

"Oh, but the drama crowd'll *love* it. She looks like a living voodoo doll."

"And that's good?"

"It's different. Hey, Kaz – are we gonna get to eat any time soon? Only I don't wanna be late."

"Oh, Rors – I've got bad news, I'm afraid. There's not going to be enough for you and Poppy too."

"*What?*"

"Yeah – sorry! Poppy forgot to tell Amber I needed tomatoes from the café and without them – well, it just won't go round!"

"Oh, come *on*! *Tomatoes?* You're having me on – you can stretch it!"

Kaz beamed. "Sure I can. But I'm not going to. Now sod off and buy your living doll some chips."

Amber and Kaz were still laughing as Ben and Chrissie and Ellis wandered into the kitchen. Kaz started dishing up her moussaka, and Amber fetched the plates. She was on a high of complete exhilaration at the way Kaz had dispatched Rory and Poppy. She knew she'd pay for it later with Poppy, but for now she didn't care. She and Kaz were allies, and things were beginning to crack and break apart. She knew she'd be able to talk to Kaz more about Poppy; get help with it all. And most of all she loved Kaz's courage, the way she said just what she felt. She wondered if she could start to be that way, too.

Her one regret was that she couldn't talk about the old woman – and about the fear in the house. But she knew that was off limits. When Kaz had visited her in hospital, they'd made a kind of pact that things were fine now. To talk about it – well, that would make it real.

Keep it unspoken, Amber thought. *Keep it unreal.*

Chapter
Thirty-seven

Amber went up to bed around eleven thirty, mellow with the wine she'd drunk, and knew immediately that Poppy had been in her room, probably looking for something to go with her party outfit. Back at home, she'd often go through Amber's things and borrow stuff without asking. Amber hated it, but to protest was to make Poppy burst into tears and bring down accusations of being mean spirited from their mother.

The wardrobe door was swinging open, and two skirts were on the floor: the little drawer in the mirror stand had been pulled out, and a tangle of chains and rings were strewn across the top of the chest of drawers. Swearing, Amber scooped everything up and put it back, mentally running through what she owned. A couple of pairs of earrings had been "borrowed", and a wide bone bangle. Amber slammed the drawer shut, undressed, and got into bed.

*

Rory and Poppy didn't get back until very late that night. Amber heard Poppy giggling as she and Rory stumbled up the stairs.

Rory's bedroom was on the ground floor. He didn't need to come upstairs.

She heard Rory saying something slow and slurred and persuasive, then she heard them both edge their way up the attic stairs, feet shuffling and knocking as though they were wrapped up in each others' arms. The far attic door opened, and banged shut. The iron bed above her head creaked and twanged.

Amber sat up in bed. "Shit," she muttered. "*Shit.*" A bit of her was glad, because if Poppy had taken Rory up to her room like that then maybe she hadn't got anything going on with Marty. But most of her felt responsible. Poppy was just a kid – a virgin.

What should she do – go up there and bang on the door? Shout at Rory, tell him Poppy was too young and unstable to be pushed into sex? Sure, that would really go down well, wouldn't it? Poppy would fly at her, scream at her for interfering; Rory would sneer, accuse her of being jealous, like Kaz was. . . Amber drew up her knees, wrapped her arms round them tight and tense. She couldn't just do *nothing.* Despite the way she was acting, Poppy was almost completely inexperienced with boys. If Rory had sex with her, then acted like it was no big deal or just plain dumped her, God only knew what it might do to her. . . Amber scrambled off her bed, then realized that, over her head, there was complete silence. She held her breath, listening. She heard the sound of the door being pulled open, and someone rushing out, along the corridor, down the stairs, past her bedroom door, down the main stairs. . .

Rory. Rory, going back to his room. Why had he fled? Was Poppy all right?

Amber pulled her dressing gown on, and edged slowly to her door, but before she could reach it, the talking started over her head. Poppy, talking in a whining, sing-song voice. Then she stopped, as though she was listening to someone talking back to her. Then she started talking again, and stopped again. Even though Amber knew Poppy was alone she found herself straining her ears in the silences, trying to hear what Poppy was listening to.

Amber sat back down on her bed. She had heard this before, heard the way Poppy's voice rose and fell and *persuaded* . . . she cast her mind back, then with a sick jolt remembered exactly what it was. It was the way Poppy sounded when she was talking to their mother, when there'd been some kind of upset and she was over the crying stage and together the two of them would reinterpret reality so that none of it was Poppy's fault. Poppy would whine "I can't help it if. . ." and "If only she hadn't. . ." and "If only they'd. . ." And their mother would soothe her and assure her and agree with everything she was saying, say anything, anything at all, to make her feel better again.

"Jesus, she's sicker than I thought," Amber muttered to

herself, and she opened her door, deciding she had to go up and comfort her. "She's pretending Mum's there, telling her it's all OK, telling her it's everyone else's fault, not hers –"

A laugh filtered down from the attic. It wasn't like anything Amber had ever heard come out of Poppy's mouth. It was gloating, crowing, *cruel*. It chilled Amber to the bone. She got back into bed and pulled her pillow over her head.

As she was getting ready to go to The Albatross the next day, Amber made a decision. She was going to ask Marty if she could talk to him after work, find out what was going on with him and Poppy. And then take it from there, wherever it led her. At the back of her mind were Kaz's words: *You should speak to him – what have you got to lose?*

When she arrived, Marty was already there, sitting down on the boardwalk outside with his long legs stretched out in front of him and his feet scuffing in the sand. He stood up as she got nearer and called out, "Hey, Amber! I've been waiting for you!"

"Yeah?" she called back.

She walked over to him. "I got to talk to you," he said, eyes searching her face. "You were acting so weird yesterday. What's up?"

"Nothing," she muttered. "Well, OK. I didn't know you knew Poppy so well."

"So *well*?"

"Marty – have you been meeting her? Have you been seeing her outside of the café?"

"No! Of course not. Well. . ." An almost guilty look crossed Marty's face, and Amber felt her heart constrict. "Look – can we sit down for a minute?" he said.

The sun was climbing the sky behind the sea. Bert was nowhere to be seen. They sat down on the boardwalk together. "Only," Amber went on, stiffly, "I ought to warn you that she's not exactly stable at the moment. I mean – if you get involved with her, you're playing with fire."

"Get *involved* . . . there's no way I want to get involved with her! Hey, are you—"

"Am I *what*?"

"Nothing," said Marty, but he was smiling, and Amber knew he'd been about to say "jealous". Somehow, she didn't mind. "Look," he went on, "yesterday, when she came into the café – I don't know what game she was playing. Throwing her arms round my neck and everything. I kept trying to get your eye and you wouldn't look at me. She said she had something to tell me, she asked me for a coffee. When I sat down with her she . . . she was all jokey, she was coming on to me. You saw her."

"Yeah. I thought you were getting on really well."

"Well – we were, I s'pose. I was kind of fascinated. *Intrigued*. I asked her what she had to tell me and she said she couldn't talk about it here – she said she'd come back at the end of the day. I wanted to ask you what she was up to but you wouldn't talk to me. You seemed really mad at me, I didn't know what was going on. You went off along the beach – I hung around. She was waiting behind the café, watching you go. We walked along the beach together, sat down on those rocks over there." He paused, hung his hands loosely between his knees. "I asked her what was up, she asked me for a smoke. I had a bit on me, so we sparked up."

"Great," said Amber. "She's only sixteen."

"I know, I know. Sorry."

"Why did you say you'd meet her?"

"Because . . . because she's your sister. Because I thought I might be able to help. Because I thought she might have something to say about *you*."

Amber wanted to let this sink into her, like honey into bread, but she was afraid to. She was afraid to trust it.

"She had nothing to tell me, anyway. She was just – *flirting*, and getting stoned, saying all this weird stuff. . ."

"What stuff?"

"You don't want to know. It was pretty nasty. About you, and Kaz . . . she's not a nice girl, Amber. I can't believe you're sisters."

There was a silence. Amber hugged her arms round her knees and let her face sink on to them.

"Look," said Marty, in a low voice. "Look – there's something else. There's something else I got to tell you. I get these feelings sometimes. Hunches."

"What d'you mean?"

"I get hunches about people."

"I see. And you've got one about Poppy?"

"Amber, something happened. Something rank."

A shadow fell over them, across the boardwalk, and they

looked up to see Bert grinning above them. "So we're taking breaks before we actually do anything, now, are we?" he demanded.

"You weren't here to let us in!" said Marty.

"No, OK. Well I'm here now. Come and help me unload this beef from the truck, will you?"

There was no chance for further talk that day. Amber was longing and dreading to hear what Marty had to say. The three of them worked flat out, and took lunch on the run. At the end of the day Bert was jubilant; he gave them a tenner bonus on top of their generous tips, and he hung around chatting and planning the menu for tomorrow so that in the end Amber felt she had no choice but to just say goodbye and go.

Chapter Thirty-eight

When Amber went into her bedroom, she pretended she couldn't smell anything at first. She slammed the door shut behind her and, heart thudding, marched over to the window and threw it open, wide. Dank, chilly air flowed round her.

But the smell was there, in the room with her. Sweet, sickly, like rotting flowers. She knew it, she'd smelt it before, up on the landing that night she'd rowed with Poppy about not going home to their mother again and she'd heard this *haaa*, felt it on her face...

Don't think about that. Think what the smell was. It couldn't be a dead mouse, like she'd thought before. It wasn't lavender, or roses ... *violets*. That's what it was, sugary, sickly violets. Her mum had given her some violet-scented drawer liners once, she'd hated the smell, she'd tried to cover it up with pine disinfectant but it had made the flower-pictures run and it had smelt even worse and her mother had been hurt...

Violets. And something else, underneath. Flowers covering up decay and rot.

There was something on her pillow.

She didn't want to look over at it, she was filled with a sense of something vile, like the finger-shapes in the cushion. But she made herself look.

It was the gloves. The creepy old gloves that Poppy had found in the tin chest and given her, and she'd loathed putting on. They'd been arranged on her pillow palms down and fingers spread, with the thumbs folded round each other like you do when you make a shadow picture of a bird on a wall.

Amber picked up her waste paper bin, picked up the gloves, and threw them into it, heart thudding. It could only be Poppy, Poppy fiddling about in her room again, playing stupid tricks. . . "I need a cup of coffee," Amber thought, "coffee with sugar." She went to her door, and pulled it open.

Poppy was standing right outside.

"*God*," squawked Amber, "you made me jump! What the hell are you doing?"

"I just came to see you, that's all," said Poppy, pouting.

Amber shielded the waste paper basket with her arm, so Poppy couldn't see the gloves. "You've been in my room, haven't you?" she demanded. "Last night, and now. Did you take anything?"

"I don't know what you're talking about."

"Yes you do. And what d'you want to put those gloves on my pillow for?"

Poppy smirked. "To remind you."

"Remind me *what*? And why d'you need to lay them out like some kind of relic?"

"I *didn't*."

"That's what it looked like. You went through my *things*, Poppy – those gloves were right at the back of the drawer."

"Yeah – nice, Amber! Hiding away a present I bought you!"

"You didn't buy them, did you. You—"

Poppy suddenly snatched the waste paper basket from her hands. "You can't throw them away!" she spat. "How dare you? *How dare you?*"

"Jesus, don't go over the top! *How dare I?* Easily. Look – I'm sorry, but I don't like them, OK? You take them if you like them."

Sullenly, Poppy pulled the gloves from the bin, and handed it back to Amber. Then she wandered into Amber's room and sat on the end of the bed, cradling the gloves as though they were kittens, smoothing and stroking them. Amber felt cold just looking at her, cold and repulsed. "What are you *doing*?" she snapped. "Look – can you go, please? I was just going down to the kitchen."

Poppy's eyes grew huge, as though her sister had slapped her. Then she slumped forward, and started crying.

"Oh, for goodness' sake," said Amber, "all I said was I was going down. You can come with me, can't you? Can't you? *Poppy!*"

It was the old manipulation again. Poppy wouldn't answer, just cry, until Amber went over to comfort her, until

Amber would do or say anything to comfort her. But Amber couldn't bear the thought of touching her – of even getting close. "Poppy," she begged, "*please* – let's go down and make some tea. . . Poppy, stop nursing those bloody gloves, you're giving me the creeps, you look mad or something!"

"*I feel mad!*" Poppy wailed. "I think I'm *going* mad!"

"Don't be stupid," said Amber, fighting to keep her voice steady. "Look – come on, come downstairs, put the gloves down and—"

"I s'pose you heard what happened last night?" Poppy screeched.

"What, you and Rory? Yes. But he wasn't up in your room long enough to get up to much, was he?"

Poppy burst out crying again. "He was horrible," she sobbed. "He treated me like shit – like a piece of meat."

"Well you hardly gave him a good message, did you? Hauling him up there like that. . ."

"It wasn't *me*, it was *him*. He pressured me, and. . ."

Amber felt like she couldn't bear to look at Poppy for another minute. Like a toxic stew, hatred and love and compassion and loathing were all mixed up together inside her. She had to get away. She had to *do* something. "OK," she barked out. "I'm gonna see him. I'm gonna shout his balls off."

Amber raced downstairs. She was pretty sure Rory was in; she'd seen his leather coat hanging up in the hall. She'd never been to his room before, only ever caught a glimpse of the masculine, somehow stylish, mess inside when the door was left open. But now she flew at the door, and hammered on it. No answer. She hammered again, shouted, "Rory? It's me, it's Amber – I gotta speak to you!"

There was a groan from inside. "Whaaa?"

"It's Amber – I need to speak to you!"

"Yeah . . . OK . . . come in."

She pushed open the door, and went in. A musky, fuggy, male smell hit her; he'd been asleep. He sat on the edge of the wreckage of his bed, jeans on, shirt off, scrubbing at the sides of his head to wake himself up. "I bet I know why you're here," he muttered.

"Well – good," snapped Amber. "That'll save us some time. I've just left Poppy really, *really* upset in my room. 'Cos of what *you* did last night."

"Amber, I know you're her big sister and everything, but don't try and pin all this on me. It was mutual."

"*Mutual?* She's *sixteen*. Couldn't you have been a bit more responsible, a bit more *caring*?" Rory picked up a litre bottle of water from the floor beside his bed, and drank. Amber watched his throat work as he swallowed. He was so sure of himself, she thought, so sure of his place in the world because of who he was and how he looked.

"I mean – she's just a kid," she went on. "I know she went after you, maybe even threw herself at you, but she's a kid, she's naïve, she's completely inexperienced. . ."

Rory barked out a laugh; water spilled out of his mouth. "Oh, *right*," he said, "she's completely inexperienced. Well let me tell you she's pretty bloody *pervy* for someone who's completely inexperienced."

Amber felt her face grow fixed, white. "What do you mean?" she whispered.

Rory shook his head, groaning, like he didn't want to remember. Then at last he focused on her face. "OK," he said. "I'll tell you. Look – OK, I was out of order. I take your point that I was out of order to let it go on. But once it's started, sometimes it just has to *go on*, you know?"

"Spare me that rocker shit. Just tell me what happened."

"OK, OK. We started fooling around at the party and . . . you say she's inexperienced but she can really *kiss*, your sister. Tongue like a sodding eel, it was amazing. She was really coming on strong. And it just got . . . you know, *going*. *She* wanted me to come up to her room. I told her she was too young, we were making these jokes about me just coming up to read her a bedtime story and tuck her in. . ."

"Funny," said Amber.

"Anyway, we get on the bed together and fooled around a bit – and. . ." Rory stopped. He bit down on the side of his mouth, looked down at the bottle in his hands.

"What?" she croaked. "What happened?"

"What she did – she lay back on the bed, and laced her hands together over her chest, and shut her eyes. And I said *Oh right – asleep already?* and *she* said. . ."

"What? What did she say?"

"*I'm dead.*"

"*What?*"

"Straight up, that's what she said. Really quietly, hardly moving her mouth – she was playing dead, wasn't she? So I said something like, *Oh right – if you're a corpse I can do what I want then, can't I?* I got on top of her and stuck my tongue in her mouth . . . I thought she'd start laughing or kissing me back – but she didn't move. Her skin felt really cold . . . even her mouth was cold. It freaked me a bit, up in that bloody creepy attic. So I really went for her."

"What do you *mean* you *went for her*?"

"I was just messing around, for Christ's sake! I was trying to get a response. I had one hand on her tit, the other up her skirt and she still didn't move. And then. . ." Rory broke off, wet his lips with his tongue.

"Then *what*?" said Amber.

"She said *I'm dead* again only this time I swear to God I didn't see her mouth move. I was completely freaked out. I was bricking it. I told her she was a screwed up little slag and I scarpered. God, I was so freaked out."

He looked up at Amber, expecting her sympathy. She looked back at him stonily. "The others are talking about getting her to move out, and after this I agree with them, frankly," he said. "She's gotta go, Amber – she's not right in the head. You know what? I really think she wanted me to do her, like that." He laughed. "Maybe I should've done."

"Or maybe you should just choke on your own vomit and die," said Amber, and walked out of his room.

Amber stood in the hall, trying to slow her breathing. She

was too angry, too disturbed, too shaken and scared, to face Poppy again. She knew without question that Rory had been telling the truth, which meant that Poppy was either lying or inhabiting some mad half-world where her delusions were real, where she didn't know how crazily she acted.

She grabbed her coat, and ran out of the front door into the dark, and as she ran she scanned the street for the old woman from number eleven, relieved to see no sign of her. Away from Merral Road, she flicked her phone to *Marty*, pressed *call*, and let it ring.

Praying.

Chapter Thirty-nine

"Sorry it's such a tip. And sorry it's pitch black. They turn the electricity off – that's the problem with squats."

Amber stumbled on down the corridor. Marty was leading her with one hand and holding a candle in a jam jar in the other. "I didn't know you lived in a squat!" she laughed, negotiating her way round a pile of cardboard boxes.

"Didn't want you to look down on me, did I? Actually, we're doing a deal with the council right now. Gonna get it all kosher, the power on and everything. Here's my room."

Marty's room reminded her of Kaz's room. It was hung with drapes like an Arabian tent, and full of stuff – there was a guitar propped against the wall, and clothes, plates, books and mugs strewn on the floor. But it was mainly the feeling in it that was the same. Amber felt safe here.

There was nowhere to sit but the floor or the sagging bed, so she perched on the edge of that and said, "Thanks, Marty. For letting me crash into your evening like this. I just. . ." She could feel her throat tightening. *Don't let me cry.*

"Hey," said Marty. "What's up? Come on, tell me." He sat down beside her and put his arm round her. She burrowed her face in his shoulder and sobbed. "*Sorry!*" she wailed.

"S'OK," he said. He was stroking her hair, her arm. "Go on, snot all over my shirt if you want. It's OK, it's OK."

Amber sucked in a big breath, and stopped crying. "You shouldn't have been so *nice!*" she hiccupped. "It started me *off!*"

"Well, *sorry!*" he grinned. "Will it get you going again if I ask you if you want a cup of coffee?"

"No," she said, smiling back at him. "But I'm fine. I just . . . oh, *God,* it's so good to be here."

"Stay as long as you want," he said. He let his arm slide down from her shoulders, but stayed close beside her on the bed. "So – you want to talk about it? Is this about your little sister?"

"Yes. And the house. And Rory. And the scary old woman from number eleven. And the fact. . ." She took in a breath. "The fact that I sometimes think there's something evil in the house. Something affecting Poppy. Which means I'm losing it, doesn't it. Going mad. I can't hold it together any more." She drooped her head. This was going to put Marty off her for good, acting like some messed-up nutter, but she couldn't help it. It felt so good to be here, with him beside her. It felt so good, the way he was *listening.*

"I don't think you're mad," he said. "I think your little sister's got problems, and I don't think you're mad."

"She's acting so *weird,* Marty! She scares me. She's

spending all her time up alone in the attic. When she's not trying to pull Rory or . . . or *you*. In this . . . *weird* way. She needs help. I mean serious, psychiatric help. But how do I do that? I can't just haul her off to the doctors', can I? I tried talking to her . . . telling her how screwed up it was, the way we were brought up . . . she won't have it. She always thinks everyone else is wrong."

There was a silence. Then Marty said, "Who's the scary old woman from number eleven?"

Amber laughed, and told him. Then she told him what had happened with Rory and Poppy, and then she went on to tell him everything, however freaky and insane it sounded, about the gloves and the attic and the cushion and the noises and the smell of violets and the shape on the stairs, in the mirror. . . She was no longer scared that things became real if you talked about them; she knew they were real now, and some part of her was getting ready to face them.

At last, she wound down to silence. Marty sighed.

"You think I'm barking, don't you," she muttered.

"No," he said.

"Oh, great. So there's something in the house then."

"Maybe. Maybe something did happen in the past, maybe the vibes from it still hang about. . ."

"Maybe. Whatever it is, the house is bad for Poppy. She's getting worse, she. . ." Amber trailed off. She felt suddenly cold. "Oh, God. You had something to tell me, didn't you? Something horrible, about Poppy. You said you got hunches. . ."

"Yes."

"And you got one about Poppy?"

"No. That's what creeped me out. I told you I met her after work. . ."

"Yes," said Amber. The thought of it still stung.

"Well, we sat down on the beach and everything was fine, I thought she was an OK kid who'd had some problems, and being here was helping her sort herself out, and then. . ." Marty looked sideways at Amber, as though he was weighing up whether to go on or not. Then he went on. "We were . . . just smoking and I was waiting for her to talk to me, tell me what she had to say, but she was coming on all flirty and then, like I said, saying this nasty stuff about you and Kaz, and then . . . she put her hand on top of mine."

Amber shook her head, confused. "And?"

"It was her hand. It freaked me completely. It didn't feel human."

"*What?*"

"I'm serious. It felt all knotted up and hard, like . . . claws. Like a dried monkey's paw, or something."

"A *dried monkey's* paw. . .?"

"Seriously, Amber, it totally freaked me. It felt *horrible.* I know I was smoking but even so. . ."

There was a pause, then Amber said, "Maybe she caught you with her nail or something. . ." She trailed off. *Why do I always have to stick up for her?* she thought.

Marty shook his head. "It was more than that. Worse. It was the feeling *of* it. I can't explain." He started to laugh.

"There was this book that used to scare the shit out of me when I was a kid. It was about shape-shifting. This evil creature – it used to change into good things, nice things like cats or dogs, and get taken into someone's house – but something always gave it away. It would move wrong, or sound wrong . . . mostly it would feel wrong. Because it would kind of – retain a memory of the shape it had been before. One bit that really scared me was when it had shifted from a goat into a little girl and when the boy helped her up a tree they were climbing, her hand felt like a hoof. And he was stuck there with her, in this tree."

There was a silence. Amber tried to laugh, and found she couldn't. "You're not saying Poppy's shape-shifting," she said at last.

"No. But I've got so I trust my instincts on these things. You can sneer if you like –"

"I'm not sneering."

"– but I'm good at sensing someone's energy. If I get bad vibes off someone I'm usually right."

"But you said you *didn't*. Get bad vibes off her."

"No, I didn't, not at first. That's why I'm spooked by it. I dunno. It's like she's got really clever at hiding it."

"Hiding it?"

There was a pause. Then he sighed and said, "Who she is."

Chapter Forty

Marty made more coffee, and found half a packet of digestive biscuits. They talked on, round and round, then Amber looked at her watch and said, "It's so *late*. Oh, God, I really don't want to go back there tonight."

"So stay here," Marty said.

"What?" she gasped, heart skidding.

"You can have the bed, I'll kip on the floor. And if you get a nightmare, I'll wake you up."

"Oh, right," she laughed, trying to sound casual. "And if we turn up together in the morning, both of us coming from *your* direction, what's Bert gonna say?"

"It's Sunday tomorrow, Amber."

"Oh. Oh, right."

"But if it wasn't, he'd say . . . he'd say what took you both so long."

This was so unexpected and so completely wonderful and what Amber wanted to hear, that she couldn't deal with it. She huffed out an embarrassed laugh, and got up to go. "I'll be fine," she said. "Honestly."

She didn't look at Marty, she didn't see his face fall.

"Well, let me give you a lift back," he said.

"You've got a car?"

"An old Beetle. Not always reliable, but we can see if it starts. . ."

"I'll be fine," she insisted. "I'll walk fast. Thanks for listening to all my psychotic crap, Marty."

"Look – Amber – you *sure* you want to go back there tonight?"

"Yes," she said, and her voice came out like a little bark. "I've got to go back sometime. If I leave it, if I duck out of it. . . Anyway, I can't. . ."

"Can't what?"

"I can't leave Poppy all on her own, can I?" she muttered, and she left.

It was frightening walking up the dark, deserted hill on her own, but Amber was rolling over and over in her mind the way Marty had listened, and made her feel good, and what he'd said at the end, the amazing thing he'd said in the end about them being together, and she only began to get really scared as she got closer to her house. All its lights were out, and the Chubb lock had been turned, which meant everyone was back and thought she was, too.

She'd got used to climbing the main stairs without looking in the huge, ornate mirror, used to not glancing towards the skinny attic stairs. She told herself that her room was a haven, and when she got to it, she'd feel safe.

She opened the door. Poppy was in her bed, with her dark hair spread out over the pillow.

Sickened, she snapped on the light.

It wasn't Poppy. A black shawl was draped across her pillow – the cobwebby, lacy shawl that Poppy wore, the one she'd found in the old tin trunk in the attic.

Then Amber registered with a thump to the heart that her room had been trashed. She made herself walk forward, into the mess. All three drawers had been pulled out of the chest of drawers and dumped, all her clothes strewn about. The little drawer in the mirror stand lay broken on the floor, with all the jewellery she kept in it, bracelets and necklaces and rings, scattered about. The wardrobe door was gaping, clothes pulled out of it. The huge white vase she'd salvaged from the middle attic lay on its side, cracked, with the grasses that she'd collected from the cliffs by the sea bent and broken. The Bakelite radio lay by the wall as though it had been hurled against it.

She went to her bed, plucked up the shawl, and threw it towards the door, then she flipped her pillow over in disgust. And stood there, heart thudding.

Poppy. This wasn't just going through her things. Her room wasn't safe any more.

Poppy.

She raced out, and up the attic steps, snapping on the light at the top so that the bare bulb flared along the corridor. She was going to wake her sister up, she was going to yell at her, let fly at her, smash her to a pulp –

A white face jumped at her, sudden and violent as an attack.

It was one of the faces in the photographs, on the wall outside Poppy's room.

Transfixed with terror, Amber stared. The face belonged to a woman. She had a high lace collar pinned with a brooch and severe, pulled back dark hair. She looked grim, ageless.

What had made it jump out like that, catch her eye like that?

The woman was smiling. A hateful smile, full of malice. It was only a tiny face in a photograph but it was clear, vivid, far more vivid than it should be.

Its narrow eyes looked alive.

Amber turned and fled back to her room that wasn't safe any more – it had never felt safe – and, for the first time, turned the key in the lock.

Amber couldn't lie in bed the next morning, even though it was Sunday. She got up and put her room back to rights as much as she could. She picked up the radio first and found that, miraculously, it still worked. The little mirror-unit drawer slotted back together again, although she needed to buy glue to strengthen it. The crack in the big white vase didn't show if she turned it to the wall; she could pick more grasses. When she hung and folded up her clothes again, she found three things with tears in them – well, she'd mend them later.

She went down to the kitchen, locking her door after her, taking the key with her. She'd switched off inside; banned all thoughts. Poppy was cracking up, but she couldn't deal with it now. She'd sorted and locked her room; now she'd make a sandwich, head out to the cliffs, and spend the day walking.

But when she got to the kitchen, it was full. Ben, Kaz, Rory, Chrissie – they were all up and dressed, unheard of for a Sunday, and sitting grouped round the table. Rory and Chrissie were smoking, even though Kaz had banned it from the kitchen and Chrissie hardly ever smoked anyway. Their faces were set; it looked like a formal meeting.

"Hi," said Kaz, guardedly, as Amber sidled into the doorway.

"What's going on?" she croaked.

"Three guesses," said Rory.

"You're talking about Poppy."

"Yes," said Kaz. "Amber – she's got to go. *Soon.*"

Amber thought of her mother's stricken face. "You said Christmas. . ." she whispered.

"I know, but things have changed. For a start, she's stalking Rory. OK, he behaved like a stupid, irresponsible, paedophile prat, leading her on, but now she follows him – she watches him –"

"It's started to seriously give me the creeps," said Rory. "I stayed round Max's last night. Slept on the floor."

"Oh *diddums!*" erupted Kaz.

"You try it!"

"I've tried to talk to her, Amber," Kaz went on, ignoring Rory. "I tried to get her to come out for a drink with me. But she won't talk, she just shrugs me off, or looks at me with those weird eyes . . . I think she needs help – professional help."

"She just lurks up in the attic the whole time," put in Rory. "When she's not following me."

"Or on the stairs," added Ben. "I seem to keep passing her on the stairs. It's starting to get to me."

"She's obsessed by that mirror," said Rory. "She's always looking at herself in that bloody mirror."

"She's more vain than you are, mate," said Ben.

"Basically," snapped Chrissie, "she's acting like some kind of deranged nutter, and it's making this horrible *atmosphere* in the house, and we want her out of here."

"I'm sorry, Amber," murmured Kaz.

"I mean – we want her out before she gets any *worse*," Chrissie went on. "She's taken to wearing all this horrible old stuff she found up in the attic – did you see her yesterday? She's got this old bunch of keys on a chain round her waist."

"A bunch of keys?" echoed Ben.

"Yeah – you know, a big silver ring with loads of keys on it, like—"

"A jailor," said Rory.

"Yeah, well, I was gonna say like housekeepers used to have. Some of the keys are pretty impressive, now she's polished them up. Elaborate, like jewellery. And *big*, some of them – the whole thing must weigh a ton, but she doesn't seem to mind."

"So – any of these keys work?" demanded Rory. "Any of them open doors or cupboards in the house?"

"Dunno. Probably."

Kaz stood up and took her empty mug over to the sink. "My bedroom's got a brand new lock, thank God, and only *I've* got the key."

Ben looked over at her. "So you've started locking your door, have you?"

She shrugged. "I've come back a couple of times and . . . well. Stuff has been moved. It could only be Poppy. I don't want her poking around in my room, do I?"

Amber stared at the floor, and her hand closed round the key in her pocket. A vision of Poppy had come into her mind, so strong she thought everyone else must see it too: Poppy in the middle of the night outside her bedroom door, poking wire through the keyhole, the key falling silently on to the carpet, then Poppy lifting her ring of keys and finding a key that fitted and unlocking the door and creeping in, creeping in. . .

"I don't think any of the doors on this floor have their old locks," said Ben. "Maybe the old larder. . ."

"My door's got an old lock," said Amber.

"Mine too," muttered Chrissy. "The key's lost but I'm getting Ellis to put a bolt on the inside."

Suddenly, there was real fear in the kitchen, real vibrating fear. But no one commented on it, no one said, "Why are we talking like this?"

Then Ben shifted in his seat, and said, "Come on, let's not get paranoid. She's just wearing 'em for the look of it."

"Christ knows why," snapped Chrissie. "Basically those keys look ugly. *Nasty.*"

Rory blew a thin stream of smoke up at the ceiling. "Keys," he murmured. "Old keys. Keys mean power. You got the only key, only you can lock and unlock a room, or a cupboard, or a chest. You can keep people in, or out, you can keep stuff hidden, controlled, *secret. . .*"

"Hey," said Kaz, "any chance you might end this bout of free association?"

"I was just thinking," Rory said, "just wondering why she likes them so much. Maybe she likes what they stand for."

"Yeah, well, you said it. Secrets."

"Power. *Control.*"

"*Shut up,*" snapped Kaz, shoving back her chair from the table, getting to her feet. "I'm going out," she said, "I need some fresh air." And she went.

The whole table shifted and broke apart then, and everyone wandered off, subdued, not really looking at one another.

Amber was left on her own, standing against the door frame. She hadn't mentioned the fact that Poppy went in her room too, and on her last visit, she'd completely trashed it. She'd barely spoken a word.

Chapter Forty-one

Amber kept to her plan to walk along the cliffs. She strode along for hours with autumn sun above her and the wind in her face, making little detours into civilization when the cliff-top path gave out, walking, walking, until it became meditation, until she was almost in a walking-trance, her body moving by its own will.

Everything that had happened spooled through her mind, and she began to make patterns of it, and then, decisions. One – she had to confront Poppy with what she'd done to her room. Two – she had to tell her she thought she needed help. Three – she had to tell her the house wanted her to leave. The malevolent face in the photo jagged into her mind suddenly, but she blanked it, blotted it out, telling herself that the anxiety and stress were getting to her.

She stopped to eat the sandwich she'd made and rest for a bit, then set off again, wanting to get back to her walking-trance. But she couldn't get beyond her third decision, telling Poppy that the house wanted her to leave. She'd be sending her back home in a far worse state than she'd arrived in – sending her back to their mother who'd just begun to find a new lease of life, with space away from Poppy and her new job. However much Amber told herself it wasn't her fault, she felt responsible. It felt like a terrible failure.

She walked on. A light rain started. She had no idea where she was, but she'd followed the line of the cliffs, so it must be possible to find a bus that would take her back the way she came. She stopped at a small town, went into a café, ordered tea and toasted teacakes, and sat waiting. The place was empty apart from two old ladies, sitting bored with each other in the window. Then a family pushed in through the door, laughing, shaking off the rain. Two little boys, an older girl, Mum and Dad . . . textbook happy family. They did look happy, too. Years ago a family like that could bring a lump to her throat, but she was over all that now. . . She watched the man jokily swat his oldest son on the side of the head with the menu, and thought: *Poppy's dad. Tony. Why don't I get in touch with Tony?* This would have been unthinkable back at home, this would have been treachery, treason of the first order, but *now. . .*

He can take care of her, Amber said to herself. *He can take her away*.

Her tea and teacakes arrived, and she ate them hungrily. Then she asked the waitress about buses, and set off for the bus stop, to go back home.

As the bus was toiling up the hill on the homeward stretch, Amber's phone bipped, with a text from Kaz. *We're at The George xxx*. The George was an easy-going, relaxed pub that they sometimes met at before going down for some seaside nightlife. If Amber got off the bus now, she'd be about five minutes' walk away. She stood up, hit the bell, and went straight there.

Kaz and Ben were sitting at the large table in the corner, with Rachel, the girl with long auburn hair and the wonderful, loud laugh, and two boys that Amber knew by sight. Kaz greeted Amber warmly, moved up to make space for her, dispatched Ben to buy her a drink. She asked her what she'd done with her day, then by finding out where she'd got the bus back from, worked out exactly how far she must have walked – around ten miles – and announced it to the table. Everyone was loudly impressed, and this started a discussion on what slobs the rest of them were, and how they ought to take more exercise. . . There was a melancholy, early-Sunday-evening feel to the pub, but Kaz's group were loud and upbeat. Amber realized early on that Poppy wasn't going to be mentioned, not when half the people at the table didn't live at Merral Road, and she felt hugely relieved, and relaxed into almost enjoying herself.

The house was deathly quiet when Kaz, Ben and Amber got back there. There was no one in the kitchen; no music playing. Amber thought of Chrissie bolted into her room, and Rory, probably away, sleeping on Max's floor again.

And, gripped by anxiety and guilt, she thought of Poppy. Tucked away up in the attic like a madwoman. She'd probably spent the whole day on her own, not eating properly, bored, miserable. . .

Amber said goodnight to the others and went up to the first floor landing. "I ought to go up and see her," she thought. "I ought to go and confront her with what she did in my room, talk to her about needing help. . ."

She looked towards the thin attic stairs; the darkness seemed to clot and twist on them.

She felt full of dread at the thought of going up there, walking into the black silence, not knowing what she'd find. She hurried into her room, and locked it behind her.

Let sleeping dogs lie, she thought. *Let whatever's sleeping . . . lie.*

Chapter
Forty-two

It was different in the morning, of course. Monday, Amber's day off. The sun was up and there was noise from downstairs as everyone got ready and had breakfast and went off to college. Amber showered, dressed, made tea and marched without pause up the stairs to the end attic, where she banged on the door. "Poppy, are you awake?" she called. She tried the door, but it was locked. "Poppy, come on. I've got tea for you."

More silence. Maybe Poppy wasn't in there. Maybe she'd gone out, locking the door behind her, and that sinister old girl from number eleven had taken her into her house. . .

"*Poppy!* Come *on*! We need to talk about what happened! What you did to my room! Look – I'm not cross. Not any more. I just need to talk to you."

There was a faint noise from behind the door, as though someone was turning over in bed. Then Poppy's voice, muffled and sleepy, said, "Later, yeah?"

"All right. D'you want this tea?"

"Leave it outside. Please. Thank you."

Amber plonked the mug down on the floor, and as she did, she glanced at the three old photos on the wall. There was nothing weird about them, she thought. They were just boring old photos streaked with dust.

"OK, Poppy – we'll talk later. Don't lie in bed too long. It's a nice day. We could go out, we could—"

"Oh, Amber – let me just have another half-hour's sleep, yeah?"

Amber felt let off the hook by the normal note to Poppy's voice. It had been like this all Poppy's life – if she was "OK" you could leave her, if she was in one of her States, you couldn't. And she sounded "OK" – at least for now. . .

Amber went straight down to the kitchen and found Kaz sitting there, drinking tea. "Hey," Kaz said, looking up, "ever been to Merton market?"

"No – never even heard of it. What's it like?"

"It's amazing. People go to it from miles around – it's getting bigger all the time. It's held the last Monday of the month, in Merton Town Square, and it has *the* most amazing stuff there – jewellery, leather stuff, and the *clothes* – all these stalls with dirt cheap, end-of-line outlet stuff – or maybe it's nicked, I've never liked to ask – and remade stuff, and second-hand stuff, you never know what you're gonna find. . ."

"Sounds fantastic!"

"I got this bag there," Kaz said, pointing to her lovely,

squashy turquoise bag. "Eight pounds, that's all. And it's real leather and I've never seen another even a *bit* like it. Anyway –" she checked her watch – "if you fancy coming, we've got twenty minutes before the bus goes from Alton Street."

Amber hesitated. She ought to phone Tony, Poppy's dad – she ought to get on with it. But she dreaded doing it, she dreaded getting in touch after all these years . . . maybe an extra day wouldn't make a difference. . . "I'd love to come!" she said. "But haven't you got college?"

"Not on Merton Market Day," replied Kaz, grinning.

As Amber rushed to get ready, it struck her that Kaz had orchestrated this trip because she thought Amber should get right away from the house on her day off. Or, more particularly, that she should get right away from Poppy. That Kaz could be so generous towards her made her feel even happier about the trip.

Kaz was in high spirits as they set off, full of jokes and gossip, and Amber, infected by her mood, joined in. It was so easy to have fun with Kaz. No snide, no agenda, no fear of a sudden switch – nothing of the stuff she was used to with Poppy. They climbed to the upper deck and sat right at the front like a couple of kids, swaying along the narrow roads. A group of four lads got on, and Kaz flirted hilariously with them, but refused to give them her mobile number because she said she was engaged to a media magnate. Then the two girls got off the bus at Merton Town Square, and the market swallowed them up. Amber had brought with her about seventy pounds' pay and tips that she'd been planning to pay into her bank account, but when she saw the fantastic array of stalls laid out, she gave herself permission to spend the lot.

Kaz really knew how to work the place. She towed Amber first to an outlet stall where tops were being sold out of a grab-bag for a fraction of their high street cost. They rummaged happily and came out with two each. Amber was doubtful about one of hers – a stunning low-cut sea-green one – because she wasn't sure how often she'd have the guts to wear it, but Kaz insisted she'd look great in it. Kaz seemed to know that Amber was out to drop her quiet, tame image, and she had a real feel for what would suit her. On a remade stall she found the perfect skirt to go with the sea-green top, then she made Amber try some second-hand jeans on behind a blanket hung in front of the stallholder's van doors, announced, "They make your bum look magic," and got her to buy them, too.

Amber was having huge fun, and she still had twenty-three pounds left. Around two o'clock, starving, they stopped at a Mexican food stall and ordered filled tortillas, then sat side by side on a low wall devouring them. "It's Rachel's birthday the week after next," Kaz said, between mouthfuls. "We're making her seriously celebrate – have a big night out. You can wear your new skirt and top."

"You sure she'd ask me?"

"Positive. People *like* you, Amber. You know," she leant her shoulder against Amber's, warm and heavy, "you mustn't worry so much. *She'll* be going home soon, won't she? Then you'll be free."

"I hope so," muttered Amber. "I thought – I thought I'd try and get in touch with her dad, see if he can help. . ."

"Good idea. It's time it was taken off your shoulders. Now!" Kaz scrumpled up her tortilla wrappers, looked around for a wastebin, "are you up to a bit more shopping?"

It was getting dark when Amber and Kaz got off the bus at Alton Street. Amber couldn't help seeing that Kaz got quieter and slower the closer they got to Merral Road, and that she kept glancing towards number eleven, as though she was dreading to see the old woman.

"Are you hungry?" asked Kaz, artificially loud, as she unlocked the front door. "I'll make some cheese on toast if you like. . ."

"Great. I'm just gonna nip upstairs and dump this stuff, OK?"

There was no need for Amber to take her new clothes upstairs, no need at all. She could have left them in the kitchen, and helped Kaz with the food. . . But something impelled her to go up there.

She put her key in the lock, but it wouldn't turn. The door was already unlocked.

Poppy! she thought, with a surge of loathing. *Poppy's got another key to my door, she's wearing it on a ring on a chain round her waist. . .*

She went into her room. There was no doubt that Poppy

had been in there again. The bed was rumpled up as if she'd been lying on it, clothes were strewn about, and Amber's jewellery had been tipped out again, all over the top of the chest of drawers. Necklaces and chains were traced into strange shapes; her earrings were in a heap, her rings lined up like an undulating snake.

Somehow, Amber felt more disturbed by this than when Poppy had trashed her room. She stared down at the strange shapes, reluctant to touch them, and realized her tiger-stone pendant was missing. It had been an eighteenth birthday present from her three friends at sixth-form college, before she'd had to cancel the holiday with them. . .

"*Sod you, Poppy!*" she hissed, slamming the little drawer shut. And suddenly, like a miasma around her head, there was that smell again. Sickly, decaying violets. Rottenness. *Corruption.*

Amber ran from her room and down the stairs, then rushed into the kitchen. She'd tell Kaz, she'd tell her everything, all about the weirdness in the house, she'd *make* her listen –

Poppy was sitting at the kitchen table.

Kaz was slicing cheese on the kitchen counter. It was like a stand-off, neither of them speaking or even looking at each other.

"You've been in my room again!" Amber erupted. She felt braver with Kaz there, listening, like a judge. "And not only that, you've got a key to it, haven't you?"

"No, I haven't got a key," said Poppy. "You didn't lock your door. You were in such a rush to go out with *Kaz* that you forgot."

"So you admit you've been in there, then? And if you know you haven't got a key to my door on that stupid bunch round your waist you must have *tried them all*!"

"Kaz was calling up the stairs . . . *Amber! Amber! We're going to be la–ate!* . . . and you forgot to lock it."

"What the *hell* are you playing at, Poppy? First you trash it, smash all my things up—"

"The other night? I was angry with you."

"Oh, and that makes it all right, does it?"

"You said you were going to shout Rory's balls off, and then you just . . . went," whined Poppy, mouth trembling. "You went out. I watched you go. I was really upset. I was all on my own. I didn't know what I was doing . . . I just, I went *mad*, OK?"

Behind Poppy, Kaz pulled a face at Amber. It said a lot of things: *God, she's madder than I thought* and *Hang on in there* and *Don't weaken*. Then Kaz walked quietly out of the kitchen, closing the door behind her. Four slices of cheese-on-toast lay on the counter, uncooked.

"Kaz is just being tactful," thought Amber. But she felt drained of strength by her going.

"OK, Poppy, so you went mad," she went on. "Let's not go into that now. My tiger-stone's missing. The pendant, on a chain."

Poppy smirked, and her hand went to her neck and

pulled it from the collar of her shirt. "You only just missed it?" she sneered. "I borrowed this days ago."

"Give it *back*! *Now!*" Amber lunged, full of wanting to grab the chain and twist it into Poppy's thin, white neck, but Poppy undid the clasp fast and pushed it at her.

Amber pocketed her tiger-stone and demanded, "What did you take today?"

"*Borrow*," said Poppy. "I only *borrow* stuff. Honestly, most sisters are fine about lending each other clothes and things. You can borrow my stuff any time you want."

"I don't want. I hate your stuff," snapped Amber. She wanted to add *And we're not really sisters*, but Poppy's eyes were filling with tears, so she didn't. "Just give me back what you took today, Poppy, and then *ask* in future, OK?"

"I didn't take anything today."

"Oh don't *lie*! You've admitted you were in my room—"

"I went in your room because I was lonely. I just lay on the bed . . . I didn't touch anything!"

"You *liar*! You make me sick, Poppy. I don't want you touching my stuff, OK?"

"I didn't!" Poppy wailed, and slammed her face down on to her folded arms on the kitchen table, sobbing.

Amber felt like grabbing her hair, dragging her up by her hair, hauling her up the stairs and into her room to face the mess she'd made. "OK," she shouted, "you come up now, you come and see it now, and tell me who did it if it wasn't you! The chains are making all these weird shapes, my rings are lined up . . . you saying Chrissie or Kaz or one of the boys did? I'm sick of it, Poppy! I know you go in my room – you pinch things, you fiddle with things – just stay out, OK? Stay *out*!!"

Slowly, Poppy lifted her head from her folded arms. She looked straight at Amber, and the expression on her face made Amber go cold. It was gloating, curious, excited; it seemed to come from her deepest self but at the same time it was unlike anything Amber had ever seen on her face before.

"What?" Amber faltered. "Stop *smiling* at me like that. I'll bloody slap you, Poppy, I mean it."

Poppy stood up, still smiling. "I won't ever go in your room again," she said, calmly, starting to walk out of the kitchen. "I promise."

Chapter Forty-three

That night was still and uneventful, but Amber barely slept. It was a relief to get to work the next day, and lose herself in chopping and stirring and serving out. Marty seemed uncertain with her, almost cool, and she knew it was because she hadn't stayed the night with him on Saturday. But she couldn't find it in herself to talk to him, to put things right. She felt taut as wire. Everything inside her was closed down, waiting.

When she got back to the house, the old woman from number eleven was waiting by the gate. Something inside Amber snapped, and she was filled with fury. She marched over, and the old woman turned towards her, wringing her hands.

"What are you doing here?" Amber snarled. "Who are you waiting for?"

The old woman was rigid; anxiety covered her like a fog. "I'm just. . ." she croaked. "I'm making sure things are all right, dear . . . I'm just. . ."

"You're just *what*? You're an interfering insane old *bat*, that's what you're *just*!" Amber screeched. "*Leave us alone! Stop acting like such a lunatic!*" Then, without a backward look, she marched inside.

She'd taken great care to lock her door that morning. But somehow, she knew what would be waiting for her. She unlocked her door and went in. The wardrobe door was swinging open, the duvet was humped up – Poppy had been in her bed again. The drawer under the mirror had been tipped out; her jewellery tangled up in a heap beside it. All her shoes and boots were in a pile, in the corner. And the tall sea grasses had been pulled from the cracked white vase and broken, one by one, and laid out like a huge, damaged fan on the carpet.

Amber turned on her heel and stamped up to the attic, rage sparking from her. She hammered on the end door and when Poppy unlocked it she shoved it open and slapped her, hard, right across the face.

Poppy screamed; Amber pushed her back into her room. "*Liar!* You sodding little pervert *liar*! What kind of sick, creepy game are you playing, eh? Trying to psyche me out? You *have* got a key to my room – you've been in there again, messing with everything! *God*, you're sick, Poppy!"

"You're the one who's sick – blaming me for stuff I don't do!"

"Give me those keys. *Give me – !!*" Amber lunged forward, and snatched at the ring of keys hanging from Poppy's waist.

The chain snapped; and with it, Poppy.

"*You've broken it! You've broken it!*" she screeched, face contorted like a vampire changing. "*How dare you? How dare you?*"

"You want me to slap you again?" yelled Amber. "I will – you hysterical *bitch*!" And she shoved Poppy hard again, so that she tottered back and collapsed on to the bed, where she sprawled, wailing.

"Oh, shut *up*!" shouted Amber, pulling her room key from her pocket, and holding it against all the keys on the ring, one by one. "OK, it's not here, is it? Why did I think you'd leave it on this ring, where I can get at it? Where have you hidden it? Come on – where have you hidden it?" She grabbed Poppy's hair, yanked her head back.

"You *wait*!" Poppy hissed, through gritted teeth. "You *wait* till she finds out how you've treated me. . ."

"Oh, yes, you're gonna split on me to Mum, aren't you – like you always do? Well, *sister,* I don't *care* any more. You can go back home, and tell her what you like. You're leaving. You're leaving here. Now *where's the other key*?"

With a weird kind of shucking movement, Poppy got free from Amber's hand. She bounded to the far side of the bed and faced Amber, spitting like a cat. "*Look at the ring!*" she shrieked. Her voice was gloating, cruel and gloating. "*See if you can undo it!*"

Amber looked down. The large silver ring had been welded shut; nothing could be put on, nothing taken off. "That doesn't prove a thing," she muttered, but she was shaken. "Not every key in this house has to be on this ring. . ." She trailed off. She felt drained, and horrified by what she'd done. She'd yelled at the old woman, she'd stormed in and slapped Poppy, she was losing it, losing control. . .

"I'm going," she mumbled.

As she left, she thought Poppy hissed something, something that sounded like, "You wait. *Sister.*"

Chapter Forty-four

Even though she felt there was no point to it, Amber locked her door that night. She'd thought of going down to Kaz's room; she'd considered phoning Marty, and asking if she could see him. In the end she'd just gone to bed, and pulled the duvet over her head, and berated herself for not phoning Poppy's father yet, for putting it off. She resolved to do it first thing in the morning. She knew his surname – Basketer – and it wasn't a common one. There couldn't be that many of them in the small town where he lived. She'd phone work, and say she was ill, and spend the day . . . *dealing* with it all.

Having a plan allowed her to sleep, at least for a few hours. But suddenly, she snapped awake, wide awake. Something had touched her hair, moved over the top of her head like a caress. *Spider!* she thought, in disgust. The old house was home to hundreds of large spiders that hid in dark corners and shrouded the cornicing with cobwebs. She flicked frantically at her head, then lunged at her bedside table and turned on the lamp. In the pool of light, she peered all around at the pale pillow and undersheet, but there was no black scuttling shape to be seen.

"*God* girl, you're getting jumpy," she told herself. "Nothing touched you."

She had a sip of water from the glass beside her bed, then switched off the light and settled down again. Soon, drowsiness lulled her. Her mind floated, almost calm . . . the house was silent, and she was drifting, drifting. . .

She jerked awake. Her scalp was crawling, her hair was stirring as though it was being gently tugged. She shot upright, turned on the lamp again, started desperately scanning the pillow and sheet, and though she didn't admit it to herself she was hoping, desperately hoping, to see a great ugly spider stalking away, legs entangled in one of her hairs. . .

Nothing. Nothing visible at all.

She sat for a minute, trying to calm her breathing, then she made herself turn off the light, and she lay rigid in the dark and tried to sleep. But she knew she was waiting.

Stop it, she breathed.

And waited on.

A full five minutes later, it came again. Soft and slow, just grazing the top of her head, passing over it like a bird's wing, like a trailing hand. She shook her head furiously. *Imagination. I'm just spooked, that's all. Your skin crawls when you're scared, doesn't it?*

It came again, a soft sly stroking just above her ear. She

banged her head down on the pillow. It came again, on the other side. Like a hand teasing her, playing with her terror. She lay stiff and tense, barely breathing.

And then she screamed, but the sound was strangled in her throat. Something had stabbed her. Like an animal's claws, or the tines of a huge fork, jabbed into her scalp. In terror she bucked upright, rubbing at her head, and she was stabbed again – a line of sharp stabs on the side of her neck.

She thought her heart had stopped. She couldn't move, breathe.

Fifty long seconds passed as she waited to be stabbed again.

It's my nerve-endings freaking out, she told herself desperately, *the nerves in my skin, I'm all messed up, it's like when you get flu and your skin gets hypersensitive. . .*

Then into her mind came the vision of a hand, evil and teasing, fingers like claws, jabbing at her, stabbing at her with five pointed nails, and she froze, she literally nearly passed out with terror.

Leave me alone, leave me alone, she begged over and over, mouth dry with terror, *leave me alone!*

Long, long stillness. Horrible stillness, waiting for the next touch, screwing her eyes tight but still seeing the sharp-nailed fingers darting at her. She held her hands covering her face. She thought of the nails clawing at her eyes, at her mouth. *You won't get my face,* she thought.

The smell of violets covered her, like a veil over her face, smothering.

There was a voice, muttering, outside, and the key turning . . . and above her head, she heard Poppy laughing, gloating, mocking, and then the rocking chair started up, back and forth.

Back and forth.

Back and forth.

Chapter
Forty-five

Amber wasn't sure how she survived that night. She lay, rigid with fear, unable to move, just like the old days when Poppy had scared her sick with some horror tale and she was caught between terror of being in their crypt of a bedroom and terror of getting out of bed. Then the winter dawn began to drift past the curtains and into the room, and she felt she could breathe again. She scrambled out of bed, yanked back the curtains, threw the window open wide, and breathed in the clean, cold air. Then she went to the bathroom, washed her face and cleaned her teeth, and pulled jeans and a T-shirt on.

She knew she had to deal with this now, today. She had to confront Poppy, talk to her, make her talk, tell her she had to leave. Before the next night came.

She hurried down to the kitchen, made a mug of strong, sweet tea, and stood drinking it, too anxious to sit down. No one else was up – it was too early, barely eight o'clock yet –

and anyway, everyone hid away in their rooms for as long as possible nowadays.

Poppy wouldn't be up.

Amber poured the rest of her tea down the sink, and headed upstairs.

Early light was wavering through the skylight at the top of the attic stairs; it put strength into Amber as she climbed them and walked silently along the thin corridor. The end door stood ajar, as if Poppy was waiting for her, inviting her in. She took in a deep breath and entered the room.

Poppy wasn't there. The bed was empty. Where on earth had she gone this early? Amber hadn't heard anyone leave, and yet her nerves had been so taut and strained last night that she'd heard every movement in the house, every little creak and scuttle. . .

She thought of the old woman at number eleven. Maybe she was involved, Poppy had gone to her, or she'd got hold of her somehow. . . "I'll have to go round there," Amber thought. "I've put it off long enough. I'll make that old cow tell me what's going on, with her watching the house, and everything. . ."

Her eyes fell on the tin travelling box that Poppy was so obsessed with, sticking out from under the bed. She crouched down, pulled it out further. The initials I. S., gouged into the lid, looked brighter, deeper, as though Poppy had been polishing them. Slowly, she lifted the lid.

The box was packed full, right up to the rim. On top was

laid Poppy's black lacy shawl, the one she'd spread out over Amber's pillow. Fingers shrinking, Amber pulled it out and dropped it on the floor. Next, she took out a long, grey woollen skirt that she'd seen Poppy in a few times. Beneath that, the torn, lacy chemise that Poppy teamed up with a short skirt and long boots.

"Why," thought Amber, "doesn't Poppy hang these things up with her other clothes? Why does she return them to the chest each time?"

Next, she pulled out a plum-coloured felt hat, some disintegrating lace collars, and a brush, comb and mirror set in ebony. They were all things she recognized from the time Poppy had gleefully shown her the tin box, when she'd realized where Poppy's presents – the old gloves and tortoiseshell pot that she was supposed to put a candle in – had come from. She lifted out two embroidered blouses, and found herself staring at the gloves, and nestled alongside them, the tortoiseshell pot.

Amber grimaced. She'd shoved that pot right to the back of her wardrobe, in a shoebox with some high heels she rarely wore – but Poppy had managed to find it. And reclaim it, along with the gloves. Amber peered into it, thinking she might find some of her jewellery inside. But there was only the little dark-silver pin with a muddy green stone, and a worn gold ring. Poppy wore both of them a lot. Amber couldn't bring herself to even touch them. The ring looked like a wedding ring off a corpse.

Underneath the pot, was a book. *The Thrifty Woman's*

Guide to Housekeeping by Agnes Steadman. She opened it. A name had been written inside, the name of the book's owner. A kind of chill settled round her as she deciphered the crabbed writing:

Ivy Skinner.

Ivy Skinner.

I. S., the owner of the box.

Ivy Skinner. It was as though someone had said the name right next to her, into her ear.

Clinging Ivy, she thought. *Poison Ivy.*

Under the book was a packet, tied with frayed, stained green ribbon. It was made up of letters and old faded photographs. Not wanting to, Amber picked it up, and the ragged bit of ribbon came undone, and slithered away, and the letters and photographs separated like dry scales in her hands.

Her heart was racing in panic. As she looked down, words like "disappointment" and "your fault" and "wicked treatment" and "never forgive" floated up to her. *How dare you?* had been underlined, twice. Amber couldn't bring herself to read more. As she shuffled them in her hands, she saw that they were all in the same crabbed handwriting, and they'd all of them been signed with the same name: Ivy Skinner.

They must all be letters that had never been sent.

A fading sepia photograph had fallen on to the bare boards of the floor. Amber picked it up, and looked at it. It was of a woman with three small children standing in front of her. She was thin, with dark hair in a bun. She could be any age, Amber thought, her face was set and sour – her *face*...

It was the face in the photograph in the corridor, the face that had jumped at her . . . the same malevolent smile, and hooded, hateful eyes . . . and her hand – *her hand*!

Amber knew it, she'd felt it. The pointed fingernails, the hand like a claw hooked on to the little boy's shoulder – she knew it. She knew the way his whole body seemed to be straining away from that hand in hatred and fear and revulsion.

Faint, sick, Amber dropped the photo and raced from the attic. She ran straight down the attic stairs, grabbed her purse with her key in it from her room, then ran down the main stairs, and out of the house, slamming the front door behind her. She ran down the road, up the path to number eleven, and banged on the door.

It glided open almost immediately. "Hello, dear," said the old woman. "Oh, you've come. Oh, you've come at *last*."

Chapter
Forty-six

"Is Poppy here?" Amber gasped.

"No, dear, of course not!" said the old woman. "She won't talk to me. She won't have anything to do with me."

"Something's going on. In our house. Something horrible's going on, and Poppy's involved . . . I want . . . I want to know what you know about Ivy Skinner."

The old woman was silent, searching her face.

"You seem to know something," insisted Amber. "You've been hinting at all this stuff, and watching the house, scared of something, scared for us – it's about Ivy, isn't it. *Isn't it?* I want to *know*."

"Come in, dear," the old woman said. "Come in and I'll make us some tea."

Amber hesitated. She felt like a witch was inviting her over the threshold, like if she crossed over there'd be no going back. "OK," she mumbled, and stumbled in. The old woman closed the door behind her, then led her down the long corridor to the kitchen. It was the same shape as the kitchen at number seventeen, with similar pine units, but it was tidy, with old-fashioned china plates decorating the walls and a tablecloth on the table.

Through the half-glass door, Amber could see that the garden was overgrown beyond hope, and thought that the old lady must be very much on her own in life. "I'm sorry I was so rude to you," she muttered. "The last time we met. I was on edge, and you freaked me out, the way you kept kind of *lurking*. . ."

"It's all right. I understand. You must have thought me very odd indeed."

"Yes. Look – I don't know your name."

"Miss Bartlett."

"I'm Amber."

"I know."

Silently, Miss Bartlett filled the kettle, and laid out a tea tray with cups, saucers, and a tiny rose-patterned milk jug. Amber watched, rigid with fear and impatience.

"Shall we go into my front room," said Miss Bartlett, "or shall we stay here and catch the sun before it moves round the house?"

"Let's stay here," said Amber.

"Sit down, then, dear. Make yourself at home."

Amber sat at the little table, and Miss Bartlett poured the tea, then said, "So. You've found out about Ivy at last."

"I found some stuff. In the end attic. A book and letters and stuff. And . . . and a photo. And weird things have been happening. My sister . . . she's getting affected by it all. And that's getting through to me, 'cos we're . . . 'cos we're . . . close. I don't know what's going on but . . . I dunno, sometimes things from the past can have a hold on now, can't they?"

"Yes, they can, dear. Oh, they can."

"It's like . . . there's some kind of energy in the house, and I'm sure it's about this woman Ivy Skinner. . ."

Miss Bartlett put her cup down with a chink. "Do you know," she murmured, "I hate hearing her name, even now. It makes my blood run cold."

"*What?* Why?"

"She was still alive, when I was child. An old woman with a thin bent body and a face that was . . . oh, so bitter and mean looking. She lived with her nephew – he never married. We were all terrified of her, all us children. I hated living so close – you didn't dare go by number seventeen on your own. Of course, there were all sorts of stories about her – some of them just foolishness, about her stealing babies and cooking them, or meeting with the devil down in the woods, some of them maybe with more truth in them. . ."

"What stories had truth in them?"

Mrs Bartlett took a tiny sip of tea. "She'd . . . lived in the house for years. Since she was a young woman. She'd come to help her sister . . . well, her half-sister . . . care for her children. Then the sister died, only a year or two later – well, you can imagine the rumours. They said Ivy was jealous of her, wanted her out of the way, wanted the father for herself."

"What – enough to do away with her?"

"So people said. And the children she cared for, the nephews and nieces . . . people said they were never quite right, they always looked terrified. Stories like that, they don't go away, they still cling, don't they? The oldest nephew never married, never left home. After the father died, he stayed on in the house, with just her. . ." Miss Bartlett put down her cup, and looked at Amber. "It's so strange, talking about these things, dear," she said. "After so long."

"But you wanted to," said Amber, "didn't you. You've been trying to tell me."

"Yes. Yes, I have."

"There's more, isn't there. More than just rumours from the past."

"Yes, there's more. When I was about eight, there was a big to-do at my school. I can remember it as if it was yesterday – it was like a kind of mass hysteria that got hold of everyone, about Ivy, parents coming in, and meetings, and then finally the headmaster standing up in front of the whole school and saying that from now on Ivy Skinner was not to be so much as *mentioned* in school. Anyone even saying her name would get the slipper and get sent home. He said we were moving on, leaving all the nonsense, as he called it, behind us. But the thing is . . . it wasn't nonsense."

Amber felt as though an icy hand was tracing down her backbone. "What happened?" she whispered.

"One of the worst things you could say to another child was that you'd got something of theirs and you were going to give it to Ivy Skinner. Because then, you see, she'd have power over that person . . . she'd make a wax model, she'd make evil come to them. Anyway, some of the lads were persecuting this little boy – Michael Draper was his name. They told him they'd given his scarf to Ivy, then one day after school they grabbed him and dragged him up here, up to Merral Road, and pushed him through the gate of number seventeen, shouting for Ivy – and she came to the door. Michael was so terrified at the sight of her, he passed out. The other lads were pretty terrified too – they left him and ran."

"And?" croaked Amber. "*And?*"

"She dragged him inside. She got hold of his feet, and dragged him in through the door. His head was banging on the step, on the threshold. . ."

Amber's mind was filled with the pitiful, horrible picture. There was a silence. Then she mumbled, "You saw it, didn't you?"

"I was in the woods, at the end. I heard the boys coming, and Michael screaming and sobbing, and I hid. There was nothing I could do, they were big lads – they'd've thrashed me. When Ivy had . . . *taken* him, I ran and told my mother, and she went down to number seventeen, and knocked on the door. I waited by the gate. I was terrified, I was terrified for Michael but most of all for my mother. Anyway, the nephew opened the door – Mr Alcock, his name was. He said he didn't know anything about a boy being taken in. My mother insisted – she pointed to me – she said her daughter didn't lie. Then she went into the house with Mr Alcock, and what felt like hours later, but it can't have been long I suppose . . . he came out, carrying Michael Draper in his arms. Ivy had dragged him all the way up to the attic. . ."

"Oh, God," shuddered Amber.

"He carried him over to our house, and Mother called his parents and the doctor. . ."

"What'd she done to him?"

"We never found out. Not a mark on him, except bruises on the head from falling, they said. He'd had a . . . nervous collapse, I suppose you'd call it nowadays. He never talked, and he was never right after that. His parents – well, you can imagine, they were out for blood. They went round to number seventeen demanding to see Ivy – the police had to be fetched. Hysteria took hold of everyone – rumours were rife about what she'd done to him. Children at school were getting too terrified to go out, mean children were using Ivy to frighten others, stealing bits of clothes to leave for her, and gangs of boys were talking about storming her house . . . and that's when the headmaster put the ban on it all."

"Did it work?"

"Well, it all died down, but then it would've done that anyway, wouldn't it? In the end. No one ever saw Ivy after that. Except my mother, that is."

"Your mother? What happened?"

"Mother always wanted to believe the best of everyone. She worried that we never saw Ivy any more, started saying Ivy was just a poor old woman, not being treated right by her nephew. Why did she live in the attic, for a start, she said. She said maybe Ivy was scared of the nephew, and she was just trying to help, taking Michael Draper up to her room. . ."

"But you'd seen what she did. You'd seen the way she dragged him into the house, with his head banging on the step."

Miss Bartlett's head drooped forward. "Yes, I had," she whispered. "I still see it. Her *hands* – they were thin, with huge knuckles. . ."

"Why didn't you tell your mother?"

"I don't know. Some things are just . . . too awful, aren't they. They're so bad you shut them out, you can't speak about them, you just lock them away, you pretend they're not there. I don't know. Oh dear, excuse me. . ." She dabbed at her eyes. "I haven't spoken about this for years."

"Are you OK?"

"Yes, dear, yes, just a bit. . ."

"What happened? When your mum went round?"

There was a long silence. The sun had moved round the house, and the kitchen was suddenly drab and dark, and filled with melancholy. "If you don't mind, dear," said Miss Bartlett at last, "I'm going to have to ask you to go now. I'm very tired."

"But –"

Miss Bartlett lifted her face. She looked worn, exhausted. "Please go, dear. I can't talk any more about this. Not now."

Unsteadily, Amber got to her feet, whispered *goodbye,* and left.

Chapter
Forty-seven

Amber let herself into 17 Merral Road.

Poppy was standing on the main stairs, in front of the great, ornate mirror. Her hair was piled in a wild bun on the top of her head. She was wearing the black shawl, and the torn chemise, and her shortest skirt with the ring of keys dangling against her bare leg.

"*You've been in my room!*" she shrieked. "My tin box was open, all my things were chucked about, how *dare* you go up into my room without asking, how *dare* you just—"

"Oh, cut the dramatics, will you?" Amber shouted back, although her heart was hammering with fear. "I went up to see you – the door was open – you weren't there. And anyway," she added, stalling for time, "what about all the times you've been into my room, eh? What about the damage *you* caused?"

"Where have you been?" demanded Poppy.

"Where have *I* been?" Amber blustered. "You were the

one who was out at seven forty-five in the morning. Maybe you were out all night, I don't know."

"Maybe I was," leered Poppy. "Not your business, is it."

"No. Not any more."

"You mean you've given up caring about me."

"Oh, for *Christ's* sake – look, Poppy, you need help. I'm going to –" she broke off. If she told Poppy she was going to contact her father, God only knew how Poppy would react.

"You're going to what?" sneered Poppy, in a sing-song voice. "*Help* me? Be a bit more of a *sister* to me? Spend some *time* with me? Not keep putting *Kaz* first?"

"Look, Poppy – you need to leave here. It's not doing you any good, this place."

"Oh, that would suit you, wouldn't it. Get rid of me. Well, you're not going to. I like it here. I'm staying!"

Amber's eyes slid from Poppy to the reflection in the mirror behind her. There was something strange about it. It was wavering . . . then growing denser. As though it had its own reflection, behind. "Stop it!" she wailed.

"Stop what?" sang Poppy.

"Stop . . . stop what you're doing!" She took in a terrified breath. "You're doing it . . . all of it . . . *you're* . . . *letting* . . . *it* . . . *happen!*"

Poppy took a step towards her, and shrieked, "*Where were you? Where were you?*" Then she turned and fled along the landing, and up the narrow steps to the attics.

*

"Don't *think*," Amber said to herself, furiously. "Don't think, don't react, don't angst, don't brood, don't backtrack, just *do*. Two phone calls. *Two phone calls*."

She went into the kitchen, slammed the door shut behind her, pulled out her mobile, and phoned Bert. "Hey, Bert? I'm really sorry – I'm not well . . . yeah, well, I did have a bit of a good night last night . . . I'm sorry . . . I will, I'll take it easy. I'll be in tomorrow. OK?"

Then she collected a pad of paper and a pen from the counter by the oven, and sat down at the table. Directory Inquiries gave her seven Basketers in the town Poppy's father lived in. She didn't give an initial because she didn't know if he listed himself under Tony or Anthony.

Methodically, she worked down the list, phoning each number, trying not to dwell on the thought that Tony might well be ex-directory. Most people were out – gone to work, she imagined. She marked their names to phone again later unless their answerphone messages eliminated them. The two people who did answer were not very happy at being disturbed. When she finished the list, she grabbed her purse and her coat and left the house.

She didn't admit it to herself, but nothing would have induced her to go upstairs again, past the mirror, past the attic steps, into her room beneath Poppy's.

Amber walked into town, tried to absorb herself in window shopping, while the wheels of her mind turned. She wished she'd actually read Ivy Skinner's letters, horrible as they'd looked. Maybe Poppy had cracked up reading them. And because she was so close to her, she was imagining all this stuff too . . . and Miss Bartlett, she'd added fuel to it all, with her horrible memories of the past, her obsession with number seventeen. . .

Or Ivy was still in the house.

Ivy was real. Ivy had touched her.

Clawed her. Her scalp crawled. *Don't think of it. Don't think of it*.

She walked on. Take care of Poppy first, she thought, then you can get out. Maybe Kaz will want to leave too . . . maybe we can find a new house together. . .

She realized she'd eaten nothing all day, and ordered food in a small, scruffy café – one of the ones that hadn't given her a job when she'd first arrived. She didn't eat much.

Then she walked some more along the seafront. It was only four o'clock, but it was already getting dark. She'd made up her mind to go back to the house at six, when people would begin to get back from college, and phone through the list again. She knew she could find somewhere quiet to phone from her mobile, but making the decision to phone from the house would make her have to go back there.

She knew she needed something to make her go back to 17 Merral Road.

When she let herself in the front door, she could hear Ben and Rory arguing in the kitchen about Rory's "genetic inability to wash up *ever*", and she headed for them like you head for a fire when you're freezing.

They both seemed very eager to be loud and cheerful, and very solicitous about her. Neither of them mentioned Poppy, though it seemed to Amber that she hovered in the air between them. Rory asked her if she wanted a cup of tea, and Ben said that – "owing to Rory's genetic inability to cook *ever*" – he was going out in half an hour or so for fish and chips, if she wanted some.

She agreed, gratefully. The local chippy's cod and chips weren't a patch on the food from The Albatross, but it was comfort she wanted, the chance to sit with these two boys and be normal for a while. It would be her reward for dialling all those numbers again, trying to get through to her stepfather. Maybe Kaz would turn up to eat too, and Chrissie, all of them crowded in the kitchen together. . .

Safety in numbers.

Amber ran up to her room, eyes fixed on the floor in front of her, unlocked her door, went in, switched on the light, and locked the door behind her again. Fearfully, she scanned the chest of drawers, the wardrobe, her bed . . . it all seemed to be untouched. But there was that smell again, that sly scent of sweet violets in the air. . . *I'm imagining it,* she thought. Recently, she'd started thinking she could smell sickly violets everywhere. She sat on the edge of her bed, and started dialling methodically through all the numbers still uncrossed-out on her list. If the phone was answered, she asked her prepared question: "I'm sorry to bother you, but does Tony Basketer live here?"

She got two polite negatives, one phone slammed down; then a woman answered. The woman didn't answer Amber's question, just said, sharply, "Who's calling?"

"It's . . . it's Amber Thornley. It's about Poppy." There was a pause. "His daughter," Amber prompted.

"I know who Poppy is," said the woman, warily. "Hang on a moment."

Amber hung on. She could hear voices at a distance from the receiver; the woman sounding upset, accusing, a man placating . . . and then a baby started crying. . . .

Then, right into her ear, Tony Basketer said, "Amber?"

Amber wasn't prepared for the gulp of old emotion that seized her by the throat when she heard his voice, heard him saying her name. It was ten years, more, since she'd heard it, but she still knew it.

"Yes," she said. "Tony . . . hello."

"Hello. How did you get this number? Did your mother give it to you?"

"No. It was trial and error. Tony . . . Poppy's not well."

"What's wrong with her?"

"She's just . . . she's . . . I'm afraid she's going *mad*. She's living with me in Cornwall, and she's . . . she's just so *unbalanced*. I can't cope any more. And I can't send her home, to Mum, 'cos she can't cope either. We need . . . we need someone else to help us."

There . . . there, it was out.

Amber felt as though a great weight had rolled off her soul. Now Tony would take over, he'd ride in and take Poppy away and the house would normalize and it would all be all right. . . .

At the end of the line, Tony cleared his throat. "By the someone else, you mean me, of course."

"Well . . . yes. You're her dad."

"I know. But Amber, I haven't spoken to Poppy at all for . . . what? Seven years now? And I hardly saw her before that, not since I left. Your mother saw to that. They accept my monthly cash injection, and that's about all. Birthday cards, presents . . . all returned unopened. I've given up trying, to be honest."

"I know," said Amber, "I know, but it's . . . it's *different* now. It's all . . . it's all kind of *broken open.* She's away from Mum, she's having some kind of breakdown . . . if you could see her, talk to her – help get her some professional help. . ."

"*What?*" He barked out a laugh. "I've been saying that for years. Ever since she was tiny. That's why your mum threw me out."

"What?" croaked Amber. "She *threw you out. . .*"

"Yes. Oh, I'm sure you were told the version where I walked out because I'm a selfish, uncaring man. But the truth is, she couldn't accept there was a problem with Poppy. She hated me – I mean *seriously, violently* hated me – for suggesting it. She'd turn on me like a tigress, if I ever brought the subject up."

"But . . . but you were trying to *help* Poppy. . ."

"That's not how she saw it. She couldn't bear to have her criticized. She made out her behaviour was normal, that it was other people – me, you, Sonia—"

"Who's Sonia?"

"The little girl next door she stabbed with nail scissors. . ."

"*What?*"

"Oh, yes. It was just after Poppy had started school. She and Sonia would go together . . . Sonia's mum and your mum taking it in turns to walk there with them . . . you'd go too, don't you remember?"

"No," said Amber, weakly. "I don't remember it at all."

"Well, Sonia was a popular kid. Poppy wasn't. And one Saturday morning . . . Amber, Poppy *planned* it. She stole the scissors from the bathroom cabinet – she had to drag a damn *chair* out of our bedroom and climb on it to get to them. Then she trotted next door and asked if Sonia could come out to play, all sweetness and light – and then she stabbed her. Twice. Once on the neck, once on the arm the poor kid flung up to protect herself. Sonia's mum . . . *understandably* . . . went ballistic. She wanted to get social services involved, get Poppy a psychiatric assessment – she was ranting on about how Poppy needed to be put away, somewhere safe where she couldn't hurt people and your mum went on and on about how Poppy had been driven to it because Sonia had been teasing her and leaving her out at school. . . It was a nightmare. God, it was awful."

Somewhere deep inside herself, Amber had started to

shake. As if the truth was at long, long last coming out, about her mother and the way she was with Poppy. What was it they said about the truth?

That it set you free.

But Amber didn't feel free.

"What . . . what happened?" she whispered.

"Well, Sonia hadn't been really hurt . . . just deep scratches, really . . . so we avoided the Social Services being set on us. But all the kids at school – and more to the point, their *parents* – got to hear of it, of course, and after that we were pretty much ostracized. Your mum convinced herself it was a one-off, that nothing like that would happen again, and what we had to do was move, move away and make a fresh start."

"Was that to the flat in Waterstead Lane?"

"Yes, d'you remember it?"

"Yes. I thought we had to move 'cos of your job. . ."

"That's what we decided to tell you. I'm not proud of how I behaved, going along with it – how I buried what I *knew*. I knew what Poppy was like. I wanted to get her help – assessed, analysed, *anything*. But your mum would go insane if I even suggested it. She'd scream that I was on 'their' side – on Sonia's mum's side, the teachers' side, the side of anyone who'd ever criticized Poppy. . . She was in real fear that Poppy would be taken away from her, put into care, you see. She'd do anything to protect her."

There was a silence down the phone line. Then Tony sighed, as though he was bone-weary, and said, "Sometimes

I think that would have been the best thing for her – getting put into care. Look – this is all a bit heavy. Sorry."

"It's OK. I want to know . . . I want you to go on."

"Well, after we moved, all your mum's energy was devoted to keeping Poppy on the level. She'd do *anything* to keep her happy. So, of course, Poppy got worse and worse. She thought the universe revolved around her. You, Amber – you were just *set aside*. Oh, your mum loved you and took care of you and everything, but really, she couldn't see beyond Poppy. If you had friends round and they upset Poppy – they were bad friends, and you weren't allowed to see them again. If *you* upset Poppy, you were punished. It was like . . . the point of all of us was to serve Poppy."

"But you were her dad, and I was the strong one," Amber muttered, repeating an old, worn-out mantra. "Poppy needed help."

"Yes. She needed help not to behave like an insane self-centred little monster. She didn't get it. One night it all came to a head. I put my foot down about something, and we had the mother of all rows – I insisted Poppy get professional help. . . The house was like a war zone, things smashed, broken. . . You – you poor little scrap – were sat there halfway up the stairs, peering through the banisters at us . . . then Poppy woke up and started wailing and you ran up to her."

"I have no memory of that. None at all."

"No? Probably just as well. Your mum was hysterical, *forcing* me out through the door . . . in the end, I gave up and went. I couldn't bear leaving Poppy like that, I knew she'd just get worse. And God, I couldn't bear to leave *you*, Beady, with those two, it tore me apart, but you weren't *my* daughter, I had no say in your welfare whatsoever. . ."

Beady. It had been his word for her. Amber Beady. She'd forgotten. He'd said he was going to buy her some amber beads, when she was older. "Couldn't you have told someone?" she whispered. "Contacted someone . . . for help?"

"I went to our GP the next day, told him all about my fears for Poppy. He clearly thought I was unhinged by the breakdown in my marriage but got the Social Services to call round. Who of course saw two nice little girls, well turned out, mother a bit anxious maybe, but taking care of them . . . they closed the case before it was opened. Poppy . . . *got by.* She didn't do anything else as bad as stabbing Sonia – your mother's constant vigilance took care of that. You had to live with her to know something was wrong. God, it's weird talking about this after so long. I've kind of . . . got used to accepting I can't change anything. Accepting I had to leave her and your mother to get on with it."

"Even if it was damaging Poppy?" *And me*, she thought.

"Amber, the child abuse the papers are full of – the sex abuse and the violence and the criminal neglect – that's just the tip of the iceberg. All kinds of other abuse goes on, parent to child. Indifference. Coldness. Sneering. *Falseness*. Children everywhere don't thrive the way they should, the way they've got a God-given right to, because of mean or crippled or otherwise bloody inadequate parents. And there's sod all we can do about it."

"But . . . if you'd stayed in her life. . ." *If you'd stayed in our lives.*

"You think I didn't try to? Your mother blocked access. Women who want to mess up access can do a pretty thorough job of it. It was exhausting. And Poppy turned colder and nastier on each visit because of the excellent job your mother was doing on her, lying about why I'd left . . . it really messed me up. I took her to court in the end, did you know that?"

"No."

"No, you wouldn't. After that, Poppy refused to see me at all. It was a terrible time. If I hadn't met Annie, I don't know how I'd've got through it."

"Is Annie the woman who answered the phone?"

"Yes. She helped me walk away from the whole sorry mess. She saved my life. We've got two kids of our own, now."

"But . . . but Poppy's still your daughter!"

"Yes, she is. But I can't come back into her life now. Too dangerous."

"But she's in danger *now*. . ."

"I don't mean for her. I mean for me."

There was a long silence. She could hear Tony breathing, into the receiver. It came into her mind to beg him to help, to tell him everything, all about the house and Ivy Skinner – and then Ben shouted from downstairs: "Amber? The fish and chips've arrived!"

"I'm not . . . I can't risking getting embroiled with your mother again," Tony went on. He sounded exhausted. "Or . . . this sounds harsh – or *Poppy*. I'll pay for her – if she wants to see someone, a counsellor, a psychiatrist, anyone – I'll pay for it, happily. But I can't do more. I've promised Annie. I've got a new family now."

Amber's throat ached from trying not to cry. In the background, on the other end of the receiver, the baby started wailing.

"I've got to go, Amber. You understand, don't you? Phone me if you think she might . . . you know . . . see someone, and you need the cash. . ."

"OK, Tony, bye," she mumbled, and put the phone down.

Chapter
Forty-eight

The three of them – Amber, Ben and Rory – were silent as they sat down to their fish and chips. Amber registered that she was hungry, having left most of her café-lunch, and ate methodically. The crashing of her plan to take care of Poppy had yet to sink in. She knew, too, that she'd revisit all that Tony had told her about the past, process it, *own* it . . . but she wasn't up to that now. Any more than she was up to going round to Miss Bartlett's again, to hear the rest of her grisly story.

For now, she pushed it all down.

Ben stood up to get a beer from the fridge and said, deliberately casually, "Did Kaz say anything to you, Amber?"

"What about?"

"Or leave you a note?"

"A *note*?"

"She's left," said Rory, through a mouthful of chips.

"*What?*"

"Yeah, midday today," Ben said, frowning, as he sat back down. "I got back from college, there she was with her bags in the hall. I asked her what the hell she was up to and she mumbled something about going home for a few days. But she had, like, *all* her bags with her. I asked her what the hell was going on, was it Rory pissing her off –?"

"Not me," said Rory. "I've steered clear."

"Or was it Poppy, 'cos she really was going to be moving out soon – but she wouldn't say. She wouldn't even look at me. Then the taxi came and she just . . . went. I thought she might've said something to you, seeing as you're close."

"No," whispered Amber. "Nothing."

"I went in her room, and . . . well. Go and see for yourself."

Shakily, Amber got to her feet. Sensing she needed company, Ben stood up too. Rory reached across the table, started finishing off Amber's chips.

The two of them crossed the hall, and went into Kaz's room. "See?" said Ben, walking over and pulling open the wardrobe door. "Just about all her clothes have been packed up. Summer gear too. Why would she do that if she was going to come back?"

"But . . . a lot of her stuff's here. I mean – the bed's still made up . . . there's make-up and stuff over there. . ."

"Maybe she just left in too much of a hurry to sort that all out," said Ben, gloomily. "I've tried calling her – she's not answering. Not texts, or anything."

Amber looked around. "I wonder what happened?" she muttered.

There was a silence. Then Ben said, "Amber, it's gotta be

to do with Poppy. You know it has. This used to be a *great* house, really fun, great to live in, and now, since your sister moved in. . ." He trailed off, walked towards the great bay window, and looked out at the dark street. "She's really been getting to all of us, Amber. Chrissie's been staying more and more with Ellis, and Rory's out all the time. . . We've got to get her out."

"I know," said Amber, "I'm working on it."

"Maybe Kaz just snapped. She's like that. She comes over as really strong, you know, an earth mother type, but if something freaks her . . . well, you know. You know what she was like when we found those . . . you know. Those things in the cushion."

Fear was in the room with them. They both moved towards the door, and back into the hall. Night was waiting, crouching, waiting, coming nearer, like a madman with a knife. . .

Ben jumped, nudged her. Someone was at the front door – they could see a dark shape through the blue and yellow stained glass. Neither of them moved to open it. "It's that old girl," hissed Ben, "leave it."

"It's too tall for her," Amber hissed back.

The knocker sounded. Ben kind of gathered himself, then stepped forward, and pulled the door open.

Marty was outside. "Amber, you all right?" he said. "I thought something was wrong when you phoned in sick. I've been getting my . . . you know . . . my *hunches*. All day."

Chapter Forty-nine

Sharing a bottle of red wine that Marty had brought with him, sitting in Kaz's room because she was too scared to go upstairs, Amber told him everything. About the tin chest full of Ivy Skinner's things, about Miss Bartlett and all she knew of Ivy Skinner's past, about Poppy's further disintegration. She even told him about feeling something clawing at her head, and he didn't try and explain it away, he just listened.

She cried when she told him about the phone call to Tony, her stepfather, and he put his arms round her and held her. "Come back to my place," he said, gently. "Get away from here, at least for tonight. You're exhausted."

Amber took in a great, shuddering breath. "I'd love to," she said. "Trust me, I'd love to. But Poppy – how can I just leave her? She's right on the edge. Suppose she does something stupid, suppose she harms herself?"

"When did you last see her?"

"This morning. She'd been out somewhere . . . God knows where. She was waiting for me when I got back from

Miss Bartlett. She was furious that I'd been through her things . . . well, Ivy's things . . . kept demanding to know where I'd been. . ."

"Shall I go up there, see if she's OK?"

Amber turned to stare at him. "You're a bit of a hero, aren't you?"

"Well . . . it doesn't scare me like it does you. . ."

"'Cos you think it's all in my imagination."

"No!" He hugged her, tight. "That's not what I meant. Just . . . I haven't had such a basinful. And she's not my sister. And . . . I'd do it for you." Then he kissed her on the mouth, quickly, and stood up, and left the room.

Amber sat there, stunned, suspended in time, still feeling the kiss.

Marty came back down barely five minutes later. The first thing he did was pick up the bottle of wine and empty the remainder into their two glasses, while Amber scanned his face. "*Well?*" she said.

"Well, she's all right. But Christ, you're right, there's something going on. That whole top corridor . . . her room . . . I didn't want to be there. *Really* nasty vibes."

"What happened?"

"Well – I knocked. And she said, *Piss off, Amber.* So I said – *It's Marty.* Then there was this weird scrambling and knocking noise, like *knock, knock, knock. . .*"

"The rocking chair. She'd jumped off the rocking chair."

". . .and then she unlocked the door. She had this . . . *thing* on, like a nightie, all torn, rotting lace hanging off it . . .

like coffin clothes. And she *came on to me* . . . Jesus, she was like a cartoon whore. *Marty, hi . . . how lovely . . . come in . . . come and see my room. . ."*

"Did you go in?"

"Not bloody likely. I stood in the doorway, didn't move an inch. Although. . ." He took a fast swig of wine.

"Although what?"

"I dunno. I *wanted* to go in. Not 'cos I wanted to go in her room . . . I just felt this . . . *urge* to get out of the corridor. Kept wanting to look behind me."

Amber shuddered out a sigh. "What did you say to her?"

"I said – 'I've just come to see if you're OK, Poppy. Amber's worried about you.' She didn't like that. That's when it clicked that I was with you, downstairs. Her face went really nasty, she started swearing about you being a slag, sleeping with different guys every night. . ."

"*What?*"

"So I left. Fast. Look – she's barking, Amber, she needs help. But she's OK. I mean – the room looked OK, all tidy, and on the bed, there was food . . . a sandwich or something, a bottle of juice. . ."

"She must have gone out to buy some."

"Yeah. Hey . . . you look so tired. Sweet, but tired. I'll kip over here, shall I? On that sofa."

And Amber took in a deep breath and said, "No, sleep in the bed. With me. Please. I want you to hold me."

Chapter Fifty

They slept with most of their clothes on and he held her, all night. Once, when he shifted position, she could feel how hard he was, against her hip, through his jeans. Wanting her. The fact of this flowed into her like honey, strong and sweet, nourishing her. She wanted him, too. She knew it could happen – *would* happen, later. When they'd got through this. All was quiet from upstairs; there were no disturbances that night. In Kaz's sweet-musk-smelling sheets, she fell asleep a long time before him. He cuddled his body round hers, and watched her face in the light from the street lamp outside, until it was switched off in the early hours and he, too, fell asleep.

When he woke, she wasn't beside him any more. She was standing by the window, with the curtains drawn, letting the sun stream in, and she was running her fingers over something, some mark, on the huge old mahogany table that stood in the window.

"Morning," he said, softly.

She turned towards him. Her face was alight with energy, and something like triumph. "The *furniture*," she said. "Oh, why didn't I *realize*? The *furniture*."

"*What?*"

"Ivy's real. She's real, she's here, she's *real*."

"Amber, what are you talking about?"

"I thought, like I always think, 'It's you, Amber, you're going mad, you're affected by the stress, by Poppy, it's in your mind, it's *you* –'"

"*Amber?*"

"Kaz felt it . . . you felt it last night . . . but that could have been, like, sympathy, or mass hysteria or something, after all, Ben and Chrissie and Rory, they didn't feel anything, did they, they're *normal*, they're not weird and messed up like me – oh my God, I don't believe it took me so long!" She glared at him, eyes wild. "Look at these! Just look at these!"

He got out of the bed, walked over, and stood beside her. "What? Those rings on the table? From glasses and stuff?"

"Yes. On a beautiful mahogany antique. And in my room – my dressing table's walnut, I think. Ben's huge oak chest of drawers. And the mirror, at the top of the stairs. They all must be worth a fortune. Why would our landlord – who like most landlords is pretty canny when it comes to money – just leave them, these valuable antiques, in the house?"

"Maybe he's waiting for their value to go up even more. That's how it works with antiques, isn't it."

"Not if they get damaged. You really think a student house is the best place to store fine antiques? Just look at these rings!"

Then she pounced on him, and kissed him, and was off out of the room, shouting, "I'm going to see Miss Bartlett. Don't move!"

Amber ran up the front path of number eleven, and hammered on the door. Miss Bartlett opened it, dressed in a faded blue candlewick dressing gown. "He bought the stuff with the house, didn't he?" Amber demanded. "Our landlord? The old furniture – it came with the house?"

Miss Bartlett showed no anger at being knocked up at ten to eight in the morning – not even surprise. "Yes, dear," she said. "I remember asking him. He bought it in a job lot."

"And – I'm sure I remember Rory saying some of it had been there since the house was first built. . ."

"Yes, to my knowledge, some of the pieces have always been in the house. Passed on from owner to owner. Now come in, Amber. I was just making some toast. Would you like to join me?"

Amber thanked her and followed her into her tidy, old-lady kitchen. She sat down at the table with its check cloth and watched impatiently as Miss Bartlett got another cup and saucer from the cupboard and laid more bread under the old-fashioned, eye-level gas grill. "Marmalade, dear?" Miss Bartlett asked. "I make my own."

Amber nodded. "Please."

Miss Bartlett sat down opposite her, and poured the tea, and said, "The house was sold a couple of years after Ivy Skinner died. I was about ten at the time. And it's been sold on . . . oh, at least three times since then. And to my knowledge, the mirror at the top of the stairs, and the huge table in the front room, and all sorts of other stuff too . . . it was never moved out."

"That's not normal, is it," said Amber. She felt scared, but exhilarated, too.

"No. People take stuff with them, or they sell it – old stuff left is sold or cleared out. I remember talking to Mrs Marshall, back in the 1970s, it would have been . . . she wanted to make the attics into playrooms, but. . ."

"Ivy stopped her."

"Yes, dear. I don't know how – though I've got my suspicions – but yes, I think Ivy stopped her."

"The end attic . . . Ivy's attic . . . it's the same as it was when she lived there. The bed, the rocking chair. . ."

"It was her home," murmured Miss Bartlett. "She wanted it kept the same."

Amber scraped some yellow butter on to her toast, and then some of the glowing marmalade. It tasted delicious. *It wasn't just her. It wasn't just her. The Marshalls, the people before them . . . the furniture proved it.* She swallowed, and said, "Miss Bartlett, I wish I'd listened to you earlier. Are you up to finishing the story now?"

"The story. . .?"

"You were going to tell me what happened when your

mum went round to see her – after all that trouble with the little boy she dragged into the house, and the headmaster banning her name being mentioned. . ."

Miss Bartlett sighed. "Oh, it was terrible. Mother came running home, and she was white faced, and shaking, and she went into the scullery and I heard her retching, retching and retching, like she wanted to be sick and be rid of something bad but she couldn't make herself. And when she came out of the scullery. . ." Miss Bartlett stopped.

"What?" urged Amber.

"I saw her arm, where she'd pushed her sleeve back. She had these scratches up it, as though someone with sharp nails had grabbed her, and just gouged, gouged. . . I asked her. I said, 'Mummy, what've you done, what's happened?' And she wouldn't look at me. She said she caught her arm in the brambles by the gate."

"Ivy," whispered Amber.

"Yes. I think she attacked her. Mother never spoke about it. I heard her and Father arguing, a few nights later, because Mother wanted us to move. But she wouldn't tell him why. I can remember him shouting, 'You want us to move and you won't tell me why?'"

"But you didn't move."

"No. We didn't move. And not long after that, a few months maybe, it was the winter of 1939, I'll never forget it, I saw a thin, plain little coffin being carried out from number seventeen, and taken away. Just the funeral men there, no mourners. Not even the nephew went further than the gate.

She'd died alone, Amber – an old woman living on bitter and secret, up in the attic, dying there. . . I remember my mother talking about it, to a neighbour. They were saying they didn't know how long it was before the nephew realized she was dead. Oh, awful. She had a vile life, a vile death . . . all her life had been leading to that lonely, awful death on her own in the attic."

"And you think. . ." Amber paused, took in a deep breath. "You think she's still around."

Chapter
Fifty-one

Miss Bartlett took a mouse-bite out of her toast.

"You think she's a ghost, you think she haunts the place, don't you?" Amber said.

"I think she's there as something. Something that makes the house unhappy, that makes people who live there *not thrive. . .*"

"Why didn't you move away, Miss Bartlett?"

"Well . . . I never married. And then my father died, quite young, and my mother was distraught . . . and then all too soon, she was an old woman. . ."

"I mean after she died," said Amber, bluntly. "Why didn't you just sell this place, and put it all behind you?"

"Oh, I'd love to. There's some flats, sheltered housing they call them, near the sea . . . with a warden and everything, and a community room, and gardens. . ."

"So do it. Sell up, and go."

The old woman stirred her tea, slowly. "I told you I ran to my mother, didn't I? When I saw Michael Draper being dragged inside. Well . . . I didn't. I was too scared to move. I hid in the woods . . . those woods, at the end of our road. I . . . I just curled up, and blocked it all out. I *fell asleep*. It was dusk by the time I got home, told my mother. He'd been in there . . . *hours*. I should have spoken out. I never told anyone what I saw. I should have spoken out."

"You were scared to."

"Yes. I thought she'd come and get me."

"So . . . staying here . . . watching. This is some kind of way to . . . make amends?"

"I don't know. I just felt this . . . *need*, to be close. To try and warn people, I don't know. Year after year I've hoped the curse had gone, but I've seen families broken up and people destroyed and. . ."

She trailed off, mouth trembling. Amber leant over and squeezed her hand. Then she said, "It's her, isn't it. In the mirror. I told myself it was a just a shadow, just a trick of the light, but it's her, *her*. And on the attic stairs."

Miss Bartlett put down her cup with a rattle in its saucer. "You're telling me you've seen her?"

"It doesn't look like a woman. Just a shape, a long, thin shape. But it's Ivy. I know it's Ivy."

"Oh, Amber, you've seen her. Oh, that can't be good." Miss Bartlett wrung her hands, and her breath came out like gasps. "It means she's getting stronger. I thought . . . I thought she'd fade, with time. I thought you young people would . . . *exorcize* her. But she's getting stronger."

"All this time," said Amber, "all this time I've been

thinking it's me, I'm going mad, I'm picking up on Poppy being weird – it's not me, it's *her*. She's in the house. And I know how she does it."

"How?"

"How she stopped the attics getting turned into playrooms, how she stopped the furniture getting taken away. She can make you feel . . . awful. Like – really sad, *despairing*."

"She's done that to you?"

"Yes. Yes, looking back, loads of times. It's vile. It's like she gets inside you, you're . . . *steeped* in her, like a foul smell . . . that's her, too. The smell's her, too. The violets, the sickly violets."

"Parma Violets."

"What?"

"It's a sweet, an old-fashioned sweet – they used to be very popular, they covered up the smell of decaying teeth . . . she used to suck them, even as an old woman, she sucked them all the time."

"Oh, God. Oh, *God*. Her breath. That's . . . vile." Amber half stood up, as though she was going to start running. "Oh, God, she must be so close to me . . . when I smell it, she's right up close to me, *breathing* into my face. . ."

Miss Bartlett reached out, took hold of Amber's arm, pulled her down into her chair again. "It's all right, dear. It's all right. Breath – it's life, isn't it. It's all she's got left of life. Breath, and a bit of a shadow. . ."

"And the *feeling*! She's got that left, too! God – it's so

obvious, it's so *obvious*. She can't affect just anyone. Rory –
she couldn't get him. Or Ben, or Chrissie. It's if you're weak
in some way . . . Kaz isn't weak but she got her when she'd
split up with her boyfriend."

"But all the other people, dear . . . the people who've
lived in the house since it was first sold . . . it's been such an
unhappy house. . ."

"They must have had weak spots, too. How many
families are totally happy? She just . . . made it all worse.
Like she made Poppy worse. And the furniture . . . well,
maybe the landlord was going to sell the mirror or
something. . . I bet she focused like hell and made the buyer
feel bad. Just – *bad*. Nothing specific, but just gloomy and
miserable, so he didn't want the mirror any more, or he
thought it was ugly, or couldn't be bothered. . ."

"Yes. Yes, you've got it."

"In the end, the landlord would give up trying to sell
stuff, wouldn't he? Anyone would."

"Yes, they would. And that's what Ivy wants you to do."

"Give up trying?"

"Yes. Give up trying to help your sister. She wants her,
Amber. She wants to claim her. Poppy's living in her room,
wearing her clothes . . . that's how she's got stronger. She's
feeding off her, somehow. You've got to stop it, Amber!
You've got to stop it!"

Chapter Fifty-two

Amber went back to 17 Merral Road. Marty was sitting at the kitchen table frowning into a mug of coffee; his face cleared when Amber walked in. "Do you trust me?" she asked.

"No reason not to," he replied.

"Then phone Bert and tell him neither of us will be in today. Tell him my sister's collapsed – had a breakdown. Tell him to close the café if necessary."

Marty saluted. "Will do." He pulled out his mobile.

Amber ran upstairs to Ben's room door, praying he'd still be in, and found him coming out of the bathroom, wrapped in a huge brown towel. "The landlord's number," she said. "Do you have his number? I never dealt with him – it was all through Kaz. . ."

"That's 'cos as far as Mr Tilson's concerned, the less he has to do with this place, the better," said Ben. "He's happy to leave it all to Kaz. What d'you want his number for?"

"It's . . . it's to do with getting Poppy out."

"In that case, I'll fetch it right now," said Ben. He

disappeared into his room, then re-emerged with a scrap of paper. "That's his work number," he added. "He's always at work."

Amber headed back to Kaz's room, punching in the number she'd been given. A man's voice answered. "Mike Tilson here!"

"Hi!" she purred. "It's Kaz Cooper – you know, from 17 Merral Road?" She was trying to sound as much like Kaz as possible, banking on him not knowing her voice that well.

"Oh, Kaz, yes, hello. Problems?"

"No . . . not at all. Everything's fine. Just . . . this is going to sound silly."

"Fire ahead."

"A friend of ours . . . he was round the other day . . . his dad's in the antique business. He was looking at that old table in my room? He said it was worth a fortune. And the thing is, Mr Tilson . . . I'm scared I'm going to damage it. I was painting my nails on it the other night, and. . ."

"Yes, yes," snapped Mike Tilson. "I know it's a good piece, a damn good piece. I've just never got round to flogging it. I mean, I've tried, but. . ."

"Well, Leo said his dad would definitely buy it."

"He did?"

"No problem. *And* the mirror, the big one at the top of the stairs." She giggled, with Kaz's throaty giggle. "Someone fell against that the other week. We had a bit of a party, not a big one, but I was scared this guy had cracked it, and. . ."

"Kaz, I'm really busy," said Mike Tilson. "Look – get me

a price for the things, OK? Get me an offer from this friend's dad, and phone me back."

"And will I get a bit of commission?" cooed Amber. She had to sound convincing. Had to sound as though the money was a big part of the reason she was doing this.

"Ten per cent," said Mike Tilson, and put the phone down.

"What are you up to?" said Marty, smiling. He'd come into the room behind her, sat down close to her on the bed.

"I'm seriously pissing off a ghost called Ivy Skinner," said Amber. "Trust me, Marty. We've got to move *fast*." She darted over to Kaz's bookcase, pulled off a copy of the Yellow Pages. "Here – second-hand and antique dealers. You take this page –" she tore it out, handed it to him – "I'll do these. Tell them eleven o'clock's viewing time, for the table, and chair, and a mirror, and a chest, and . . . and *an old iron bed*. With the idea that they take them away *today*. OK?"

Amber loved the fact that Marty seemed to take a psychic leap and understand what she was up to. He grinned and got on with the phoning, happy not to ask questions, happy to follow her lead. Thirty minutes later, they'd made appointments for three dealers to come round in just over an hour's time. Most were suspicious, so they'd offered Mr Tilson's number as proof that the owner wanted the stuff to be sold. If anyone did get in touch with him, Amber planned to tell him she . . . or rather Kaz . . . had got a few more dealers involved so as to get the best possible price.

It was Marty's idea to say the owner wanted the place cleared fast because the house was about to be converted into three flats. Amber loved that idea. "That would really sort her out," she said.

"Her. So you're convinced it's a ghost? An objective . . . *ghost*?"

"A very objective ghost. You know that feeling you had last night, when you were checking on Poppy? You felt this urge to get in the room? That was her. That was Ivy."

Marty shuddered. "Creepy."

"You felt it . . . but the point is, you didn't go with it. She's got no real power. She just kind of . . . hangs about, like a bad smell. Like the violet stink of her breath. The only power she's got is what you give to her, because you're scared. It's the same with Poppy." Amber got to her feet, eyes alight. "Jesus, it's so clear now. Poppy's been the one with power ever since she was born. But only because we *give it to her*."

Marty looked at her. She was almost incandescent with energy, with purpose. He wanted to grab her and hold her to him, but he thought he might just bounce off, like you'd bounce off a forcefield. "Want another cup of coffee?" he laughed.

"Yes please. Decaffed, I'm wired enough. Now – I've got to go and wake up Rory." And she left.

There was no answer when she banged on Rory's door, so she marched straight in.

Luckily, he was alone in the big, tousled bed. "Rory!" she hissed. "Rory – wake up – you gotta do something for me!"

"*What?* What the *hell*—"

"Just listen, OK? I'm sorting Poppy out. She'll be leaving . . . today. But I need your help. I need you to get her out of the way for a few hours while I . . . while I sort it."

"*Whaaaat?* You are *kidding*? You expect me to have anything more to do with that psycho?"

"She won't be psycho if you charm her, Rors. Come on. You could charm the Wicked Witch of the West, you could charm Medusa if you put your mind to it. Just go up, and say . . . say anything. Say you want to take her out for lunch, give your relationship another try."

"Our *relationship* – you are *kidding* –"

Amber leaned forward and got hold of his forearm, where it lay all smooth and brown against the off-white sheet. "No, I'm *deadly serious*. You've got to get her out of the way, OK? *Trust me*. You've got to. If she's here and finds out what's going on . . . well, she'll make her earlier behaviour look quite rational. *Restrained*."

"Do it, Rory," said Ben, walking into the room behind her.

"What's this, a sodding *deputation*?" snarled Rory.

"Yes. Look – I don't know what's going on any more than you do. But if we don't get rid of Poppy soon – the whole house'll fall apart. Kaz has gone – Chrissie's moved in with Ellis – what d'you want, us all to leave? It used to be great, here. I just trust Amber to sort it. And if that means Poppy's got to be out of the way – well, you're the man to do it. Now get up, get showered, and get charming." Then he pulled the duvet off him with a swift tug.

Amber glanced away, grinning, then she walked out.

Then she went out to the phone box at the end of the little parade of shops halfway up the hill, the one she sometimes used to phone her mother, and made the hardest call of all.

Chapter
Fifty-three

And then it was just a question of waiting. Waiting for Rory to get Poppy out of the house, waiting for the antique dealers to come round. Marty and Amber sat side by side on Kaz's bed, looking out of the big front window. "I s'pose I'd better go and have a shower and stuff," said Amber. "So I look a little respectable before the dealers get here."

"You look great," Marty answered.

"I haven't washed!"

"You *smell* great." He put out a hand and stroked her hair. "What's up?" he asked, softly. "You were on turbo charge earlier – have you worn yourself out?"

"I've spoken to my mum," croaked Amber. "I phoned and broke it to her that Poppy's had another . . . *setback*, as she likes to call them."

"How did she take it?"

"Oh – as I expected. *Devastated*. Just this side of hysterical, wanting to know all the details, crying over everything I told her. . ."

"Which was?"

"I said she'd fallen out with the people in the house –
Mum of course blamed *them* – and said the attic was
beginning to scare her, affect her. . . Mum asked why hadn't
I swapped rooms. . ."

"Oh, *Amber*. Tell me she at least asked how you *were*,
how you were coping with it all."

"No. Not once. And you know what gets to me so much?
Every time Poppy *crashes*, Mum acts as though it's the first
time, as though it's a new and terrible tragedy . . . she just
can't rise above it to see the pattern and maybe start getting
it *fixed*."

There was a silence, then Marty asked, "How much
detail did you go into . . . about this place being haunted?"

Amber turned to look at him, face to face. "You know
something?" she said. "You're fantastic. You are such a great
bloke. You just . . . you accepted it all, didn't you? 'Cos I said
it was true, you accepted it."

Marty grinned. "Why wouldn't I?" he said.

His eyes were too much for Amber. She laughed, and
looked down, and said, "I didn't go into the ghost stuff.
Nothing about Poppy actually *liking* the attic, and the tin
chest, and the keys . . . and *liking* this twisted old dead
ghoul who used to terrify little children. . ." Amber suddenly
got to her feet and paced over to the window, wringing her
hands.

"Amber?" said Marty, alarmed. "What's up?"

"All this time," she said, wildly, "all this time I've been

thinking how creepy it was, the way Poppy liked Ivy . . .
wearing her clothes, rocking in her chair . . . sleeping in her
bed . . . *Ivy liked Poppy just as much*! As soon as Poppy
moved in . . . Ivy got stronger. It was like she . . . she woke
up, and started drawing energy off her. Because they're the
same. Deep down, they're the *same*."

Marty walked over and put his arms round her. "Maybe
they are," he said. "Poppy's certainly an evil little cow. And
you won't change that, Amber. No matter how much you
want to. Now go and get showered, yeah? Those dealers'll
be here before long. . . *Shhhh!*"

They both looked towards the door. They could hear
Rory's voice, saying, ". . .and it does wonderful pasta . . .
trust me, you'll love the place." They heard Poppy's excited
giggling. Together, hidden by the dark red velvet curtain,
they peered out of the window. Poppy was hanging on to
Rory's arm as they both went down the path, gazing up at
him greedily.

"He's taking her out to lunch," whispered Marty. "Game
on."

Chapter Fifty-four

Amber raced upstairs to get into the shower, and get changed. If Ivy Skinner had any sense of an impending threat hanging over her house, she made no sign of it. At least none that Amber, squirting body wash and shampoo, lathering hard, turning up the water pressure, would let herself be aware of.

Wet haired, she returned to Marty, who was looking out of the front window. "The dealers are here," he said. "At least – two of them. Not too pleased to be walking up the path together."

Amber opened the front door. "Someone's got the times muddled!" snarled the younger of the two, a burly, brown-haired man wearing an ugly green jacket.

"It was deliberate," said Amber. "We need this stuff shifted out today – but we also want to get the best price for it."

"Well you might have said over the phone!" he grumbled. "You might have told us you was conducting your own little auction!"

"Sorry!" cooed Amber. "If it bothers you . . . well, I suppose you've had a wasted journey. But honestly I think you'll think the stuff is worth it."

"Let's get going, then," said the other dealer, who was grey-haired and wiry.

"There's one more of you," said Amber coolly, "but he can catch up once he's arrived. Let's make a start, shall we?"

As she led them into Kaz's room part of her was standing back from herself, marvelling. A few months ago, she'd never have had the confidence to take charge like this. Marty was admiring her, too. He grinned at her as she led the men into Kaz's room, and made no attempt to butt in or help. She so clearly didn't need any help.

"There's that big mahogany table," said Amber, pointing. Then she put her hand on the old wing chair whose cushion had concealed the witch's parcels of needles and teeth. "And this chair."

"What about that oak plant stand?" asked the grey-haired man, scanning the room with sharp eyes.

"Yes," said Amber, although she hadn't noticed it before. "All the Victorian and Edwardian stuff in here."

There was a knock at the door. Marty went to let the third dealer in; the first two dealers drew out ring-bound notepads, and jotted a few figures down. Amber showed the third dealer the items for sale. She wanted to keep the group together; she knew Ivy wouldn't be passive for long. Soon, they all headed towards the stairs. Amber paused to grab a cleaning cloth and spray-cleaner she'd left on the bottom step, explaining everything was a bit dusty and she hadn't had time to give anything a wipe yet.

The air on the stairs was clotting, thickening. The mirror lowered at them, heavy and sinister, showing distorted reflections as they climbed. "I'm not sure about this," muttered one of the men. "Why d'you want to get rid of it all so quickly?"

"We told you!" boomed Marty, voice warm and assertive. "The builders are coming in soon – they're gonna start taking walls down – this old stuff'll get ruined."

"Wonderful mirror, isn't it?" cried Amber, focusing on the burly, bad-tempered dealer. She reckoned he was the one most likely to hold out against Ivy's miasma.

Because Ivy was there with them. She was coming in and out of the mirror. Amber felt her rage like a toxic flood overwhelming her. The urge to appease, to retreat, was almost irresistible.

She resisted it.

In the top corner of the mirror, the dust had moved. There was a straight line, and a squiggle like a snake.

I.S.

Ivy Skinner.

Amber stepped up, took aim with her cleaner spray, then rubbed furiously, obliterating it. "God, it's all so dirty!" she carolled. "It's a magnificent piece, though, isn't it?"

"Magnificent," the burly man agreed, almost despite himself. "Will it come away, though? There's decades of paint there, sealing it in. . ."

Marty produced a screwdriver, and started scraping paint from one of the huge sunken screws that attached it to the wall. "Sure it will," he said, confidently. "Look at that. I could unscrew it now."

Glancing at him, Amber could tell he was feeling it too, Ivy's hatred. Sweat stood out on his forehead, but he kept on scraping, unscrewing. "OK," said the grey-haired dealer, nervously. "OK, let's get on." Gloom, *dread*, was all around them, like a fog. The dealer who'd arrived last started inching his way back down the stairs. "I've . . . I've just had a call," he said, although his mobile had been silent. "I've got to go. I'll call you . . . all right?" And he slammed out of the front door.

"Fine," said Amber. "One less in the bidding, right? Come on – there's a wonderful piece in here." She pushed open Ben's room, showed them the oak chest of drawers. Then she took them to her room. Ivy had been at work, strewing her jewellery across the top again, pulling jeans and jackets from the wardrobe and dropping them on the floor. "Sorry," Amber giggled, "I'm such a slob." She scooped up an armful of clothes and tossed them casually on the bed.

The grey-haired dealer was no longer properly examining the furniture she was showing them. He looked like he was just trying to hold himself together. But the burly dealer was examining the mirror-stand with interest, pulling out the drawer to check it was sound.

"That should get a good price, shouldn't it?" asked Marty, genially.

"Hmmm," replied the burly dealer. "It's been mended."

Ivy wasn't in the room with them, Amber knew. She was waiting, on the attic stairs. "Come on," Amber said, "come and see the bed."

As she went up the narrow stairs, her heart hammered. The air curdled round her, pressing down on her. She climbed on, feeling the same heady mixture of terror and exhilaration she'd felt the few times in the past that she'd faced down Poppy. In the skinny corridor, the smell of corrupted violets smothered her. She raised the cleaner spray, sprayed it straight ahead of her, imagining it blasting into Ivy's white face, and marched on.

"What about these two rooms?" asked the burly dealer. "Anything in them?"

"Nothing," said Amber firmly. "It's all in the end room."

At Poppy's door, the grey-haired dealer stopped, held on to the wall for support. "You know what," he muttered, "I'm not feeling at all well." One of the framed photographs jumped out, fell to the floor, glass shattering. "Sorry," muttered the dealer. "Sorry, I must've knocked it . . . I need some air. Can you. . ." He clutched at Marty's arm. "Can you give me a hand downstairs, mate?"

"*Don't you dare,*" hissed Amber, then she took the dealer's arm, all concerned, and cooed, "There's a window in here. And a chair, a lovely rocking chair. Just sit down for a minute."

She didn't care if she was being cruel to the dealer; she didn't care if she was sacrificing him. She propelled him into the room and on to the rocking chair, and Marty went to stand beside him and put his hand on his shoulder. Then she took hold of the window pole, and opened the window as wide as it would go. A cold, earthy November wind blew in, stirring the wide strip of lace Poppy had laid on the chest of drawers.

"Now that bed," said the burly dealer, "is something else. *Amazing* condition."

"Isn't it?" enthused Amber. She could sense Ivy screeching silently round the room, distraught, furious. "And look at the rocking chair . . . and the chest of drawers. . ."

The burly dealer consulted his notebook, then said, "Well, I know what I want. I'll take all of it if Sonny Jim here's not interested. Job lot."

"Brilliant!" exclaimed Marty. "So – let's go back downstairs and discuss prices."

The grey-haired dealer got to his feet, eager to be out of the attic. "Oh, there's stuff I want too," he muttered.

"Good," said Amber. The smell of violets in the room was intensifying. She sprayed cleaner on the end of the bed rail, and polished it briskly.

"And you say you want it shifting today?" said the burly dealer.

"Now, if possible."

"Well – I got the van outside."

"I can help you carry it," said Marty. "We'll get this bed down if we turn it on its side."

"And Ben's here," added Amber. "He can help too."

The burly dealer stooped down. Ivy's tin box had caught his eye. "I was in New York last year," he said. "Went to Ellis Island – you know where all the immigrants were processed through, and given medical checks? They had a whole pile of boxes, just like these. Really brought it home to you, it did. I'll take that off your hands, too."

Just for a moment, Amber saw Ivy's face like a shadow, stooping over the box. Contorted with rage, and agony, then fading, fading. . .

The burly dealer saw nothing.

"Excellent," said Amber. "There's some bits inside it, jewellery and stuff, you might want. But most of it just needs *binning*."

"OK, let's go," said the dealer, cheerfully. He picked the box up, tucked it under his arm, and headed out of the door.

Chapter
Fifty-five

"How long have we got, d'you think?" muttered Amber, filling the kettle at the sink as the two dealers, seated at the kitchen table, haggled over what they thought the big mirror was worth. "Before Poppy gets back?"

"Why are you worried?" said Marty. "You've stuck it to Ivy."

"Yeah, but. . ." Amber exhaled sharply, like a runner. "I don't want to have to deal with both of them."

The grey-haired dealer rallied once he got a mug of hot, sweet tea inside him, and he bartered with the burly dealer over each piece, each agreeing who had what and what was a fair price. It was all settled fairly quickly. Amber then phoned the landlord for his OK; he was pleased by the prices they'd settled on, and told Amber to pay ninety per cent of it, as agreed, into his bank account with the next month's rent.

Then he paused, told her to take off an extra twenty pounds and keep it. She'd done a good job, he said. It was a relief, frankly, getting the house cleared after all the years he'd just never got round to it. . .

"Well," said the burly dealer. "Let's get on with it, then. As I say, my van's outside."

"And mine," said the grey-haired dealer, downing the last of his tea. "Let's start with that bed, shall we?" The four of them trooped upstairs, Amber knocking for Ben as she passed, and on into the far attic.

It seemed to Amber that the room vibrated with Ivy's bitter fury, but the burly dealer was oblivious. He didn't sense her, or feel her, or smell her. She made not one jot of difference to what he was doing. And that, thought Amber, is how I'm going to be with Poppy from now on.

To the grey-haired dealer's intense relief, it only took three of them – Ben, Marty and the burly dealer – to manhandle the bed through the attic door and manoeuvre it down the stairs. He shot down the stairs ahead of them. Amber stayed behind to clear Poppy's clothes out of the chest of drawers.

The small room shimmered with Ivy's malevolence. As Amber pulled open the drawers and started removing the piles of clothes, Ivy's face flashed round her, like a series of old photographs, faint, half-exposed. Amber, weak with fear, carried on, methodically layering them into Poppy's suitcase, ready for her to leave.

The old ebony hand-mirror slid off the chest of drawers, lay shattered on the ground. The rocking chair moved back and forth, back and forth.

Amber carried on with what she was doing.

"You don't scare me, Ivy," she said, quietly. "Well –

actually you do, but the point is – I can ignore the fear now. You've no power any more, not over me. Poppy hasn't, and you haven't."

There was a sudden blast of rot and violets, a stab of fingernails at her scalp. Amber shot to her feet, grabbed the cleaning spray, and pressed the trigger long and hard, so that the room filled with droplets of bleach and detergent. "Come on – come out!" she cried. "What you gonna do? *Move* something a few inches?"

Silence. Silence, and a sense of dreadful, impending horror.

Amber made herself ignore it. "I'm going," she said, "I'm not staying in this house. So maybe you'll think you've won – I don't really care what you think. I'm going because having you here is like living over bad drains, that's all."

Ben, Marty and the burly dealer came back through the door, to collect the chair and the chest of drawers. As he went to pick up the chair, Ben batted at his face, as though a cobweb had trailed across it, then he carried on stolidly towards the door. Marty and the dealer took the chest between them.

Amber stood alone in the doorway. "Time to rest, Ivy," she said, quietly. "Time to let go."

But somehow she knew there'd be no leaving for Ivy, no departure for heaven or hell. Just a slow, relentless, bitter dwindling.

She shut the attic door, and went on down the stairs.

Chapter Fifty-six

With help from Ben and Marty, the dealers unscrewed the mirror from the wall, collected the big mahogany table and the smaller pieces from downstairs, and loaded everything into their vans. Then they paid in cash, and left. Amber and Marty sat opposite each other at the kitchen table, Amber counting the money into piles. Most for the landlord, then the rest – Amber insisted – divided between the three of them, apart from twenty pounds set aside for Rory to cover lunch. As Marty said, Rory would have earned it.

They sat on, waiting for Rory and Poppy to come back, no idea what had happened, if they'd be together, what state they'd be in. . . Amber checked her watch. "Should I phone him?" she asked.

"Give him another thirty minutes," said Marty. "If Poppy gets wind of a plot. . ."

They fell silent again. Amber felt exhausted, but knew she couldn't rest, not yet.

"What will you do tonight?" Marty asked. "You know you can come back with me, don't you. . .?" He picked up her hand and squeezed it, and she squeezed it back, grateful and glad.

"Yes," she said. "Thank you. But I've got to see what happens with Poppy, first."

"You're hoping your mum will turn up."

"I'm *relying* on it. She can't phone me, I never gave her my mobile number. But if she set out as soon as I phoned her . . . well, she should be here pretty soon, too."

"To take Poppy back with her."

"That's the plan."

"And if she doesn't come?"

"I don't know. I don't want to even think about that. I can't believe she won't come, if she thinks Poppy's in trouble."

They sat on. Ten minutes later, they heard footsteps outside. They looked at each other, then together got up and went to the door.

Poppy was either drunk, or sleepwalking. Rory, face haggard, was almost carrying her up the front path.

"What's happened?" gasped Amber. She went to Poppy's other side, helped support her up the path. "Did she have too much to drink?"

"We had a bottle of wine between us, that's all," gritted out Rory. They half-steered, half-carried Poppy into Kaz's room, and laid her on the bed.

"So what *happened* to her?" repeated Amber.

"God knows." Rory groaned. "It was going fine. Well – not fine. I was having to pretend to enjoy her company, laugh at her stupid non-jokes, look at her like I thought she was cute. . ."

"Get to the point," snapped Marty.

"Yeah, well – we had lunch. Then I said – let's take a walk to the sea. So we walked to the sea. We sat down on the beach, and I put my arm round her . . . I let her *kiss me*. You owe me big time, I can tell you."

"Oh, shut up," said Amber. "What happened? Why is she like this?"

"I don't know! She suddenly started crying . . . and I mean really *sobbing* . . . rocking herself back and forth, back and forth . . . it was bloody disturbing, I can tell you."

Amber looked at Marty. "It was when we were clearing out the furniture," she muttered. "It was when Ivy was going mad."

"And then . . . she just seemed to go into this state. Like she was concussed or something. I couldn't make her answer me . . . I couldn't make her *blink*. I sat with her like that for a while, but I started to get really freaked. . . I mean, I kept checking she had a *pulse*. So in the end I pulled her to her feet and got her on the bus and got her here. Thank Christ. So now it's over to you, babe."

Amber pulled the cover up over Poppy, right up to her chin. Some impulse in her wanted to pull the sheet further, cover her as though she was a corpse, but she resisted it. "OK," she said, "now we go into the kitchen. And wait."

Rory drifted off to his room, muttering that he was shattered. Ben, oblivious, took a shower and went out. And Marty and Amber sat opposite each other at the kitchen table and drank tea. "What d'you think she's doing?" whispered Amber.

"Ivy?"

"Yes."

"You're worried she'll get to Poppy, aren't you," said Marty. "You're worried they'll . . . I dunno. *Join forces* again."

Amber shuddered.

"D'you want to go and check on her?" he asked. "See if she's woken up yet? I'll come with you."

Together they crossed the hall and looked round the door to Kaz's room. Poppy didn't look as though she'd stirred; Amber felt repulsed at the thought of going any closer.

There was no sense of Ivy in the room, or in the hall. The great pale oblong where the mirror used to hang was like a gravestone at the top of the stairs.

"I wish Mum would hurry up," Amber muttered, and went back into the kitchen.

An hour and three quarters later, Mrs Thornley turned up, in a cab. She didn't kiss Amber, or acknowledge Marty when he was introduced, she just asked where Poppy was. Her whole face radiated *you've failed, you've let me down.*

She wouldn't even look at Amber as she showed her into Kaz's room.

Poppy stirred when she heard her mother's voice cooing and calling to her, and soon she was sitting up with a cup of sweet tea, provided by Marty, and listening to her mother tell her that she'd booked a bed and breakfast for that night, they were going there now, and that first thing in the morning, the two of them would get the train home, where she'd be safe.

Amber stood and absorbed her mother's rejection of her, absorbed the fact that she was asking no questions of her, just fleeing back home where she and Poppy would be safe. Marty, standing close behind Amber, pushed his shoulder into hers, like a caress. Then Poppy sagged back on the pillows, sighing.

"Oh, look at her!" Mrs Thornley wailed. "Oh, this has set her back – *way* back. Oh, Amber – how could you let her get in this state?"

The silence in the room was like an explosion. These were the first words she'd spoken directly to Amber. Who answered, in a voice so low she hardly recognized it as her own, "I'm not her keeper, Mum. I told you what happened, on the phone."

"Yes, but –" Mrs Thornley batted this away. "If you'd given her a bit more support, if you'd stood up for her against these *other* people. . ."

Amber took in a deep breath, and said, "You'd better go."

"What do you mean *I'd better go?*"

"Just that," said Amber.

"I'll give you a lift," said Marty. He had his old Beetle outside. "Where's the B and B?"

Goodbye. It was suddenly so easy to say it. It was so easy to see her mother and Poppy to the door and into Marty's car, not knowing if she'd see either of them again.

Chapter
Fifty-seven

As soon as Marty's car disappeared at the end of the road, Amber pulled the front door shut behind her and went down to number eleven, to see Miss Bartlett. They sat down in her kitchen and Amber explained, briefly and unemotionally, about the furniture being sold and her mother coming to collect Poppy. "And you, dear," said Miss Bartlett, eyes huge. "What about you? You won't stay there on your own, will you? Not tonight . . . Ivy may take terrible revenge. . ."

"No, I'm not staying. But . . . it's over, Miss Bartlett. I think . . . Ivy went with the furniture, somehow. Or her *will* did. It was like – the furniture was her anchor, her connection to the house. And I think it broke her, standing up to her like that, facing her down. And, well. . ." Miss Bartlett leaned a little closer, and put her hand on Amber's arm ". . .Poppy's gone, hasn't she?"

"You brave child," whispered Miss Bartlett, eyes shining. "You really think the house will be OK now?"

"Yes. I'm convinced of it. There's no need for you to

watch any more. Any debt you had, to the past – you've paid it off."

Miss Bartlett sat back sighing, her lips trembling.

"You must sell up," Amber went on, "and get yourself a home in that complex you were telling me about, the one with the warden. Let *him* watch from now on. Make new friends. Walk in the gardens, walk by the sea."

"Oh, I'd like that. I'd *love* that."

"So do it. I'll come and see you there."

There was a silence. Then the old lady said, quietly, "I can't believe she's gone."

"Miss Bartlett, she was never really *there*. She was just . . . a miasma, an old feeling. Poppy was the really scary one. She was the one with the real power, at least as far as I'm concerned. And now she's gone, too."

When he got back to the house, Marty was amazed to find Amber up in her bedroom, efficiently packing her things. "You OK?" he asked.

"Yes," she answered, then she walked over and they held each other, and she said, "Thanks for giving them a lift."

"You're amazing, Amber. You're so calm."

"Why wouldn't I be?"

"Well – it's pretty primal, isn't it? Having your mum walk out on you like that. I was hoping I could come back with a nice message, something to make it all right, but. . ."

"She didn't say anything. She wouldn't. And it's all right."

"It is?"

"She thinks *I* rejected *her* – and Poppy. If I'd played by her rules, she wouldn't have gone like that – if I'd cried, and been upset about Poppy, and, and . . . you know what? I'm sick of talking about it. I just want to get packed up, and go."

"Go?" Marty grinned. "Go where?"

She grinned back. "I was kind of hoping a friend might ask me to stay."

Part 3

Chapter
Fifty-eight

Ten days later, Kaz met Amber in a small, old-fashioned café in the middle of town. Amber had written to Kaz saying she hoped she was well, and explaining about impersonating her when she'd phoned the landlord to ask if she could sell the old furniture. Without going into any details about Ivy Skinner, she told Kaz that she, too, had moved out of 17 Merral Road. She'd signed off with the hope that Kaz would get in contact sometime and, just over a week later, Kaz did.

"I've been in touch with college," Kaz explained, mouth full of scone and still not quite looking at Amber directly, "and I'm going back. They were pretty understanding, really. I've got a couple of essays to catch up on over Christmas – apart from that, it's fine. I'll borrow the notes and. . ." She trailed off. Then she muttered, "I'm sorry I left without saying anything to you. I just . . . I freaked. I thought I was going mad. I was hearing things, seeing things . . . all that stuff with Poppy, and . . . you know. . ."

"Yes. You thought there was a ghost in the house. There was."

Kaz stared.

"Neither of us imagined anything," Amber went on, matter-of-factly. "She's called Ivy Skinner and she's a sick, twisted, bitter old bitch who's been hanging around since 1939 when she died and who was given a new lease of life by my sister moving in. Because, I think, they share the same endearing qualities. Ben, Chrissie and Rory have never so much as caught a whiff of her but you and I did because we're . . . I dunno. More vulnerable. More intelligent. More psychic. You decide."

Scared, enthralled, awed, Kaz questioned her, teased the whole story out of her, from Miss Bartlett's stories to the day the furniture was sold.

"Just as well you wrote to tell me about that," Kaz said. "The landlord phoned me up the other day, and thanked me for paying the money into his account!"

"Right! Well, I thought I'd better warn you."

"And he *also* asked if he could terminate my renting contract early because he was going to convert the place into three flats."

"Yeah, Ben told me. That'll really scupper Ivy, won't it."

"Yeah. Although I wouldn't want to be the person in the top flat. . . So you've seen Ben?"

"We all met up the other night. He and Rory are living at Merral Road, same rent, till the builders move in or they find another place, whichever comes first. . . Chrissie's moved in with Ellis."

338

"Well, it was on the cards. Are the boys gonna get another place?"

"Definitely. Ben's already on to it. You should get in touch with him, Kaz. He'd love you to move back in with them. Rory too."

"Yeah. Dunno, though. Dunno if I can stomach more of Rory. What about you?"

Amber smiled, but didn't answer, and Kaz let out a nervous laugh and said, "*God*, I still can't believe it. That Ivy was actually *in your room*, moving stuff. . ."

"Trashing it."

"You *sure* it wasn't Poppy?"

"Poppy didn't have the key."

Kaz shook her head, took another sip of lukewarm tea. "So Poppy . . . Poppy was always kind of in *league* with her?"

"Oh, the best of buddies. Ivy must've thought it was Christmas when my darling little half-sister appeared in her attic. Then . . . the night Poppy slept in my room . . . Ivy got to her. *Accessed* her, somehow. And it went on, it grew."

Kaz exhaled a long, amazed breath. "You know, it actually makes me feel better," she breathed. "Christ, I ought to feel shit-scared, I've been living with an evil ghost, but I feel great."

" 'Cos it wasn't you, imagining things."

"Right. It wasn't me, cracking up." There was a pause, then Kaz went on: "So those . . . *things* . . . the things we found in the cushion . . . where do they fit in?"

Amber shrugged. "I've thought about that. More than I want to, I can tell you. My guess is, she did it in front of her nephews and nieces. Using their teeth. She'd tell them she was a witch — Cornwall's always had a big tradition of witches. She'd tell them she owned their souls, or something. That'd make them behave, wouldn't it. God, you should've seen that photo I found. They looked sick with fear of her. Poor little sods."

Kaz's face had closed down. "Did you ever hear them crying?" she muttered.

"What? No. No, nothing."

"I did. Just once. The night before I left — it was what made me leave. This desolate, hopeless crying. I couldn't bear it."

"Well, let's hope they're at rest now that evil old hag has gone. Shall we get some more tea?"

Neither of the girls wanted to leave the table, or each other. They talked on as the light dimmed and the elderly waitress switched on little lamps around the room.

"Abuse takes all kinds of shapes," Amber said, in a low voice. "All sorts of cruelty goes on. It doesn't have to leave a mark on the skin. The fact that Ivy controlled those children by turning herself into some kind of witch figure . . . who would know, if they behaved themselves. Who would *care*."

"Control by fear," murmured Kaz.

"Yes. Those kids, living with that . . . that *absolute horror* of being tied to someone who harms you. They'd have to convince themselves she wasn't too bad, wouldn't they . . . just to survive. Like kidnap victims form relationships with their captors, just to survive."

"Like you did, with Poppy."

There was a throbbing pause. "Yes," said Amber, at last. "I used to tell myself I loved her . . . I *hated* her. But it was all muffled up by guilt. I couldn't admit it to myself because if you're stuck with someone you have to pretend they're OK, don't you?"

"Yes. And now you're free of her. How is she – do you know?"

Amber shook her head. "I phoned home once – Mum put the phone down on me."

"Jesus. Well – she'll be better away from Ivy, won't she."

"Yes . . . but she's still *Poppy*. I'm hoping she's . . . I'm hoping she's had a breakdown, a real breakdown, and Mum's been forced to get help. Tony – Poppy's dad – he said he'd pay for therapy and stuff. Then maybe there's hope for her."

"You don't sound so sure."

"I'm not. But . . . I've done what I can. I really feel that."

Kaz smiled, agreeing. "You won't call home again, will you?" she asked.

"No. They can contact me at The Albatross, if they want to."

The fresh pot of tea arrived and, as she was pouring it out, Kaz suddenly smiled, wide, and looked Amber straight in the eye. "You know, when you first came, I felt sorry for you. You were so timid, and anxious – you acted like you didn't have a clue. Now look at you. You're the strong one. I did a runner and you stayed. You had the courage to face down that . . . *eeeeuurgh*, that *thing,* and . . . God, Amber, it must have been so hard, what you did – breaking off with your family like that."

"It was horrible. It's still like a grief inside me, but . . . I couldn't go back to pretending and lying. I can live now."

"And where," asked Kaz, "*where* are you living?"

Amber grinned.

The Albatross was going from strength to strength. Bert was revelling in his new role as head chef, leaving the basic running of the place to Amber and Marty. Three weeks before Christmas Bert announced that, despite being out of season, they were serving around fifteen per cent more customers and profits had gone up by maybe eighteen per cent, and he gave both of them a fifty quid, cash in hand bonus. "If this keeps up," he added, reluctantly, "I s'pose we're looking at a rise."

They arrived hand in hand at the café one day to find that Bert had taken down two big paintings to reveal a wide door flush with the wall. "What's that lead into?" said Amber.

"A huge storage cupboard," said Marty, "for all the summer tables."

Bert pulled the door open and disappeared into the cupboard. "What the hell's he up to?" muttered Marty. He too headed into the cupboard, and Amber followed.

Inside were stacked eight long, pub-style tables with benches attached, and eight umbrellas advertising lager. Bert was at the back of the cupboard, tapping at the wooden wall. "I can put a good large window in here," he said. "The joists and cross-supports are thick and solid." He turned round, beamed at them. "Kids – The Albatross is about to expand! I'll take off that door, enlarge the entrance a bit, bung in a window – and hey presto, we got an L-shaped café. And room for four more tables."

"What about all this summer stuff?" demanded Marty.

"There's part of an old boat shed I can rent, dead cheap, further along the beach. It'll be a pain to shift them in and out, I'll need to get a lorry along the beach, but it's only twice a year, isn't it? It'll be worth it. We've got people queuing for tables every day now."

"Bert, you're *brilliant*," said Amber.

"You think?"

"Yes. This is a great space. You might even get five tables in. But it mustn't be a kind of overspill area, you need to make it just as good as the main bit. . ."

"I will. Pictures up, good tables – and I'll put another little stove in the corner. It'll cost, but I can afford it. It'll pay me back."

"It's going to be class!" exclaimed Marty.

"It is," agreed Amber. "And while you're doing all that, you must do something about the toilets."

There was a pause, as both men looked at each other, perplexed. "What's wrong with the toilets?" said Bert gruffly.

"Bert – they're awful. For a start, they're *outside*. Who wants to get frozen and/or drenched when you go for a pee?" She strode towards the door of the café, drawing them along behind her by the force of her enthusiasm, and went outside. Two wooden cubicles, with old-fashioned doors that didn't reach the floor or ceiling, stood at right angles to the café. "I'm not knocking those cubicles down," said Bert. "That's good solid work. And they're plumbed right into the municipal sewers."

"I'm not suggesting you knock them down. Take their roofs off and build over them."

"*What?*"

"Build a covered entrance to the café, right over the cubicles. Do it with a big glass door, and you could leave the café door open, and let more light in." She yanked open the nearest toilet door. "There's room here for a little basin on the wall, Bert."

"What's wrong with the outdoor sink?"

"It's *outdoors*? The towel's always salty and wet!"

"I'm not wasting that sink!"

Amber smiled. Marty's hand was moving on her back, moving down. She squirmed with pleasure, moved away. He followed her. "People can use it for swilling off their flip-flops. Keep sand out of the café."

"Humph."

"Bert – *focus*! You need to make these toilets self-contained. A washbasin, a mirror and a blow-dryer in each –"

"And posh soap," added Marty, coming up behind her again.

"– then you put signs on the doors – Men and Women."

"Men and Women," Marty repeated, into her ear.

"I'm not about all that fuss," grumbled Bert. "I'm about cooking."

"It's not fuss. It's basic twenty-first century comfort."

"My regulars don't complain."

"Yes they do! Only last week I had to get a towel for Mr Miller to dry his hair off, when he'd gone for a pee in a storm! Hey – when you've built this vestibule, you could put up a big coat stand opposite the toilets. So people's wet coats can stay out here and not drape all over the floor dripping."

There was a long pause. Bert's face was working silently. Then Marty said, "If you're putting in a new stove just the other side of the wall, could you run a little radiator off it? Heat the whole thing up a bit? Nothing worse than freezing your bare arse off, is there?"

"Great idea!" cried Amber. "It's just the basics, Bert! You've got to get the basics right!"

"*You* two!" Bert exploded, but he was suddenly grinning. "When you going to open your own place, eh, like you're always going on about, and leave me in peace?"

"Not yet," said Marty. "We're sorting out somewhere decent to live first. And then we're going travelling. And *then* we're gonna open a place that'll put you out of business."

"Hah!" scoffed Bert, fondly. "That'll be the day. Right. Here's what I do. Sam Snead'll do the new window and the stove – I'll get him to quote for your stuff too."

"It'll be worth it," said Amber, "even if you have to take out a bank loan."

"Maybe. And if we go ahead – d'you want to oversee it, Amber?"

"*Me!*"

"Yes. You seem to know what's needed for toilets and blow-dryers and stuff. There'll be a bonus in it for you if you get it right."

Amber grinned. "Oh, I'll get it right," she said.

The basins had shiny chrome taps and a matching chrome blow-dryer and soap dispenser, which Amber undertook to keep refilled. Marty teased Amber mercilessly about her desire to fill the cubicles with shells, seahorses and starfish, and put a mermaid and merman on the doors in lieu of Men and Women signs. But Amber knew she had to keep it simple, in the spirit of The Albatross. Then a woman from a local gift shop came in with two mirrors with driftwood frames. She offered them free as long as they had small "available at" advertisements underneath them. Amber gratefully agreed, and hung them over the basins. Then she found two flat, beautiful pieces of driftwood on the beach, and with a red-hot skewer burnt an identical W into both. The one for Men she simply nailed on the door upside down. It was plain, stylish, perfect.

Bert was a bit gruff in his thanks, but he gave her seventy quid cash, as a bonus, and almost immediately started an artistic pile of driftwood growing in the corner by the new glass door, just like the one inside the café.

Marty, kissing her in bed that night, told her this was the surest sign of his approval you could get.